This time, she w

"Hello, Delia."

Her fingernails crushed the Styrofoam cup. She forced herself to relax. Inside her, a gleeful voice was shouting, *It's Marsh! It's Marsh!* and someone was jumping up and down like a child at Christmas.

Marsh couldn't believe how beautiful she looked. He hadn't seen her for three years, but it felt as though they had parted only yesterday.

Marsh met Delia's gaze and was startled to realize she was looking right at him. Almost the instant the thought occurred to him, she lowered her eyes.

Hiding again, Delia? What made you nervous? Are you still as attracted to me as I am to you? Or is it something else? Do you know what I've discovered? Have you always known? Is that what's kept you away from me all these years?

But this time they were both free. This time, she wouldn't get away.

Romances by Joan Johnston

JOAN JOHNSTON

I Promise

AVON

An Imprint of HarperCollinsPublishers

This is a work of fiction. Names, characters, places, and incidents are products of the author's imagination or are used fictitiously and are not to be construed as real. Any resemblance to actual events, locales, organizations, or persons, living or dead, is entirely coincidental.

AVON BOOKS
An Imprint of HarperCollins*Publishers*
195 Broadway
New York, NY 10007

First Avon Books mass market printing: June 1996

Avon Trademark Reg. U.S. Pat. Off. and in Other Countries, Marca Registrada, Hecho en U.S.A.
HarperCollins® is a registered trademark of HarperCollins Publishers.

Printed in the U.S.A.

20 19 18 17 16 15 14 13

This book is dedicated to
my editor, Carrie Feron,
for giving me the opportunity
to send my muse in a new direction

❧ Acknowledgments ❧

I want to acknowledge the assistance of several individuals who gave willingly of their time and knowledge in researching this book: Loring N. Spolter, Esq., trial attorney in Ft. Lauderdale, Florida, previously Assistant District Attorney in Brooklyn, New York; Edward Bowman, Principal Court Clerk, Brooklyn Supreme Court; Andrew W. Stone, Principal Office Assistant, Brooklyn Supreme Court; my good friends Billie Bailey of San Antonio, Texas, and Jack and Carolyn Lampe of Uvalde, Texas; Dr. Susan Dombrowsky, Miami Shores, Florida; Miguel R. Hernandez, Deputy Sheriff, Uvalde County Sheriff's Department; Amaro Cardona, Uvalde-Real County Juvenile Probation Department; and Ray Romo, Administrative Sergeant, Uvalde Police Department.

For their help as able critics I am indebted to Lynda Wojcik, Gloria Dale Skinner, and Sherryl Woods. For their support and encouragement I would like to thank Carla Neggers,

Mary Lynn Baxter, Pam Mantovani, and Sally Schoeneweiss.

Loads of appreciation to my son, Blake, for his advice on Power Rangers and for managing alone during the hours I spent attached to my computer, and to my daughter, Heather, for proving single working mothers can raise great kids.

I Promise

*Don't fork a saddle
if you're scared
of gettin' throwed.*

❧ *Chapter One* ❧

They called her The Hanging Judge. That might have been fine in her native Texas, which had a history of hanging judges dating all the way back to the infamous Judge Roy Bean. But Delia Carson was an oddity in Brooklyn.

Delia thought the New York press, which had given her the label, was overreacting. She had pronounced the death sentence only three times since it had been restored in New York. It wasn't her fault that happened to be twice more than any other judge. She made certain justice was served in every sentence she handed down. If she tended to be tough on criminals, it was only because they deserved it.

She was getting tired of justifying her decisions, especially to people like District Attorney Sam Dietrich. Sam should have known better than to submit a plea bargain that

3

would virtually let a murderer go free. She had thrown it out faster than chain lightning with a link snapped.

Delia had only a year's experience as a judge in the Brooklyn Supreme Court—a trial court despite its high-sounding name—but she had made her position clear in her campaign. Tougher dealing with criminals. The maximum sentence where possible. No leniency.

One of Sam's assistant DAs had requested an interview with her in chambers to discuss her decision. Delia had no intention of changing her mind, but she wanted Sam to know exactly where she stood, so she had agreed to see his envoy.

When her phone buzzed, she figured the ADA had finally arrived. "Is that Frank Weaver?" she asked her secretary through the intercom.

"You have a long-distance call from your sister on line two. She says—"

"I'm expecting Mr. Weaver any minute, Janet. Tell my sister I'll call her back."

"But she says—"

Delia cut off her secretary. "Let me know when Mr. Weaver gets here."

"But—"

"Not now, Janet. Tell my sister I'll call her back." Delia punched the button turning off the intercom. She loved her sister, but dealing with Rachel always reminded her of things she would rather forget. Delia knew she was only postponing the inevitable, but she needed her mind clear to deal with the ADA.

The intercom buzzed again. "Mr. Weaver is here," Janet said.

Delia squared the shoulders of her black robe, brushed at her bangs, and smoothed her straight, shoulder-length black hair away from her face. "Send him in."

She watched as Frank Weaver opened the door and entered the room without meeting her eye. Never a good sign.

"Good morning, Mr. Weaver."

"Morning, Judge Carson." He cleared his throat and focused his gaze on the oil painting of Texas bluebonnets that filled the wall across from him. Delia could see the attraction. The painting featured a dirt road winding through a field of bluebonnets graced with a single, majestic live oak. There was nothing visible in the distance. It was a road leading nowhere, or taking you exactly where you wanted to go—depending on how you felt at the moment. She had experienced both reactions.

She gestured to the two maroon brass-studded leather armchairs in front of her desk. "Have a seat."

Frank perched on the edge of the chair closest to the door, set his briefcase on his lap, and opened it to remove a sheaf of papers, all without looking at her. "Judge Carson, the district attorney asked me—"

"I won't waste your time, Mr. Weaver. The Lincoln deal won't fly with me. You might as well open the jail door and wave Leroy Lincoln out to kill another kid. I won't have it.

Tell the district attorney to go back and try again."

The ADA rubbed a hand across his chin. "With all due respect, Judge Carson, if the district attorney and the public defender agree on the deal, I don't understand your problem."

"My problem, Mr. Weaver," Delia Carson said in clipped tones that compressed her Texas drawl, "is putting a dangerous criminal back on the streets where he can hurt innocent people."

Delia tossed her copy of the agreement across her desk. "We've been through this too many times over the past year. I don't care if the docket gets backed up the rest of my term trying criminal cases the DA thinks ought to be settled. If Sam Dietrich wants things concluded out of court, tell him to negotiate a sentence that will let me sleep nights."

"Look, Delia—"

"Don't start, Frank," Delia warned, rising irritably from her wooden swivel chair. She thrust an agitated hand through her hair. "And it's Judge Carson in chambers when I'm wearing this robe, even if we are alone."

Frank stuck his papers back in his briefcase, closed it, and stood, waiting to be dismissed. He was looking at her now. She was afraid he saw too much.

She turned away from him and took a few steps to the seventh-story window that overlooked Court Street in the center of downtown Brooklyn.

The Brooklyn Supreme Court Building where Delia worked, a monument in marble and mahogany, had been built in 1958 with as much artistry and as little public acclaim as Studebaker's Golden Hawk Coupe. Below her a statue of Christopher Columbus stood amid ice-laden, newly laid cobblestones in front of the courthouse. Come spring, the brown patches would be grass, but it looked stark and barren now.

Delia missed the mild south Texas winters. She missed . . . Delia caught herself before she could remember too much. It was never safe to remember.

A few hardy souls bundled up against the January cold in trench coats and wool scarves scurried like industrious ants across the plaza to the Municipal Building around the corner. ADAs heading back to the Muni Building from the Criminal Courts Building could be seen detouring through the Brooklyn Law School. It had the cleaner toilets.

Right now in south Texas, Delia thought, the earth would be warm. The live oaks that never lost their leaves would be rustling in the ever-present wind. The picture of one tree, one great old live oak with two people standing beneath it, appeared before her. Her heart began to race, and she forced away the troubling image.

Delia turned to face Frank Weaver, leaning her palms on the inside window ledge, feeling the morning sun—the only sunlight she got all day—heat up her black judicial robe through the wooden venetian blinds.

She let her gaze travel the length of the rumpled-looking man before her. She and Frank had worked together when she had first started in the DA's office eleven years ago. The two of them had been on investigative duty together for six months, working twenty-four-hour shifts every third or fourth day, spending nights sleeping on futons in the Muni Building—when they got to sleep. Usually they were woken and called out for a ride to the police station, or occasionally the scene of the crime when there had been a felony with a victim or a child molestation.

She had been the "young" DA and Frank had been "senior." She had followed him around learning how to make sure the police collected sufficient legal evidence for an indictment by the grand jury.

She had watched Frank and realized he cut corners. He was neither scrupulous nor ambitious. She was both. She had left Frank behind in the ten years she had steadily risen to prominence in the Brooklyn DA's office.

Delia had learned in the year since she had become a supreme court judge that it was necessary to keep herself distanced from her former colleagues if she was going to do her job right. Sometimes, like now, it was awkward. Perhaps a little less formality was what she needed in this situation.

Delia sighed. "What is it you want, Frank?"

"The DA wants you to lighten up. You've been putting him through hoops with these plea bargains, and he wants it stopped. I know I'm probably not the right person to be confronting you about this," Frank said, "but Sam knew we worked together, and ..." Frank paused. A dark flush stained his throat above his permanent-pressed polyester-cotton blend collar and the loosened knot of his paisley tie.

"He figured we probably had an affair that would give you an extra edge in negotiating," Delia finished for him. That had happened too frequently with a male-female investigative duty matchup for it not to have been true of her, as well. Delia had a reputation for being standoffish with men that should have precluded the assumption. Except Frank had an even worse reputation for being an alley cat with women.

"You told him, I hope, that he was off the mark," Delia said.

The flush deepened. "He didn't believe me," Frank muttered.

Delia caught a glimpse of tired brown eyes before Frank turned to stare at another wall filled with a framed history of her accomplishments—graduation from the University of Texas at Austin School of Law, membership in the Texas bar, membership in the New York bar, authorization to practice as an attorney before the United States Supreme Court, certification as a judge in the Brooklyn Supreme Court. There were no photos of family, of a husband or children.

It revealed a full life and an empty one.

Frank sieved a hand through thick black hair that had fallen rakishly onto his forehead and turned back to face her. He was undeniably a handsome man. She might have been tempted by him once upon a time—if she had liked him better as a person. And if she hadn't felt the way she did about older, wiser men who took advantage of younger, innocent women.

"Tell the DA I understand very well how the system works," Delia said. "That two trials for every five hundred dispositions is the norm. But I refuse to turn a travesty into a sham. I have the right to insist that some minimum sentence be served. If that interferes with the DA's plans to get cases through the court mill, too bad. Take that message back to Sam for me."

"In case you haven't noticed, you already have more than your quota of trials scheduled this year. Settle this one, Delia," Frank urged.

"No."

Frank turned without another word and started for the door.

"And Frank," Delia said, halting him in mid-stride. He looked back, and she said, "Tell Sam the next time he wants a dirty job done, to come do it himself."

A grin flashed on Frank's face, chasing away the look of fatigue. "You going to sell tickets? I'd like to be there to watch."

Delia shook her head and laughed. "Sam Dietrich is a reasonable man. I'm sure we'll be able to work something out."

Frank paused with his hand on the doorknob and gave her a searching look. "Watch your back, Delia."

Before she could ask Frank what he meant, he was gone.

Delia started to sit down, glanced at the Seth Thomas clock on the credenza across the room, and realized her fifteen-minute court recess was over.

At that precise moment, when it was too late to do anything about it, it dawned on her that maybe her sister had not been calling simply to chat. Maybe something had happened. Maybe she should have taken Rachel's call. Another glance at the clock left her feeling anxious and torn. She insisted on promptness in her court. Her call to Rachel would have to wait.

Delia walked across the hall to her courtroom and entered with all the pomp and circumstance given to jurists with the power of life and death over convicted criminals.

The courtroom was spacious and had high windows that let in light but kept the outside world from seeing in, or unfortunately, as far as Delia was concerned, anyone inside from seeing out. At least the paneled walls, the Doric columns and gabled arch that framed the doorway, the benches, and the jury's railed pews were all made of rich, warm wood. The pale blue-green carpet muffled the sound and kept it quiet. This was her world, where she spent long, exhausting days, and she loved it.

The court officer, Jerry Speers, called the next case. Another assistant DA, a young woman, was waiting with another assistant public defender, also a woman, to present yet another plea bargain.

Delia listened patiently while the ADA explained the plea bargain arrangement for a two-time offender, a petty thief who had graduated to robbery to support his drug habit. Sam Dietrich had granted the defendant very little mercy in this case. The young man was going to do some hard time in prison up-state. Delia wondered why Sam hadn't done better bargaining on the Leroy Lincoln case.

She was listening to the defendant detail the crime for which he had pleaded guilty when her secretary handed a note to the court officer and whispered in his ear.

Janet's eyes looked worried behind her tor-toiseshell frames. She pulled her reading glasses off her face and let them hang on a gold chain. Janet was slender and proud of looking ten years younger than her age. Every Monday morning she had some funny tale to tell about her weekend dates with younger men. But there was nothing frivolous about Ja-net Gleason when it came to work. If she had brought a note to Delia in court, something was seriously wrong.

The court officer rose immediately and handed Delia the slip of paper. That was odd because, ordinarily, Jerry would have waited until the defendant had finished speaking.

Delia's stomach knotted.

She didn't open the note right away, simply held it in her hand as the defendant's speech drew to a close. She didn't want to be dis-tracted by this news—whatever it was. Delia fingered the pink telephone message as she finished the business at hand, accepting the plea bargain and setting a date for sentencing. Not until the case was concluded did she open the folded pink slip.

Her face remained impassive as she read the

words. A muscle in her jaw spasmed when she clenched her teeth, but otherwise no one would ever have suspected the import—the stunning impact on her—of the few words she had read.

Delia knew now why Janet hadn't left the courtroom, why she was being watched so closely by her secretary.

"Court will recess for the day," Delia said in a quiet voice.

Jerry Speers gave her a queer look but said, "All rise," and got the courtroom on its feet so she could make her escape.

Delia heard the quick tattoo of Janet's pumps on the marble floor behind her in counterpoint to her high heels as she headed back across the hall to her office. She stopped as she reached her door to head off her secretary. "I want to be alone for a little while, Janet. Please make sure I'm not disturbed."

"Yes, Judge Carson," Janet replied. "If there's anything I can—"

Delia closed her door on Janet's offer of help and locked it, then slumped back against the glass and wood barrier and let out a breath of air she hadn't known she'd been holding.

Hattie Carson was dead.

It was only then she realized her hands were trembling. Leftover anger? She hadn't believed her animosity could still be so strong after twenty years. Fear? Fear could be endless, as she was in a position to know. Or was it relief? Maybe now she would be able to let go of the past.

Delia rubbed her throbbing temples with

her thumbs. She would have to go back to Texas, to the Circle Crown. She had no choice. Only she and Rachel were left now. Her younger sister would never be able to handle this by herself. Someone would have to take care of everything, make the funeral arrangements.

Delia was surprised by the lump of feeling in her throat.

I don't care. I won't cry for her. I hate her.

Her nose stung, and her eyes burned. She gave a ragged cry of exasperation.

"I hate you, Mother. I hate you."

That was followed by a wail of grief that echoed off her high-ceilinged chambers. Delia grabbed her mouth with both hands to muffle the sob that erupted and realized with dismay that her legs would no longer support her. She hurried to the closest chair and collapsed into it. Tears squeezed from her closed eyelids. She clenched her teeth to still her quivering chin and tried swallowing over the awful thickness in her throat.

"Noooo." The hoarse, growling sound came from deep in her throat. "Noooo."

Tension knotted her arms and shoulders as she fought the powerful emotions shuddering through her. Her heart thudded loudly. She took a hitching breath that caught in her constricted chest. It shouldn't hurt like this. She didn't want to grieve the woman who had borne her . . . and betrayed her.

Delia had no idea how much time had passed when the phone sounded shrilly on her desk. She wouldn't have answered it, except she knew Janet wouldn't have put the call through unless it was important. Delia tried to reach the phone from where she was but couldn't get to it. Two swift kicks got rid of her heels before she made her way stocking-footed across the Navajo rug, dropped into the swivel chair with one leg folded under her, and picked up the receiver.

"Judge Carson." Her voice sounded surprisingly calm to her ears.

"Delia? It's me."

She could tell her sister had been crying. "Hello, Rachel."

"Delia . . ."

"I know," Delia said, her voice suddenly choked. "I'll be catching the first plane to San Antonio. I'll take care of everything, the arrangements, I mean."

"As far as I know, everything's been taken care of for the moment."

Delia frowned. "Even the funeral arrangements?"

"What? Why would we need—Good Lord!" Rachel exclaimed. "You mean Cliff didn't call you back? I was on the phone to the hospital, and I asked him to call you again and—He said as soon as he finished—" She cut herself off with an irritated, aggravated sound in her throat. "Mom's not dead, Delia!"

Delia felt the hair prickle on her arms. "Not dead?"

"The Fire Rescue folks managed to resuscitate her a few minutes after the housekeeper called to tell me she was dead. That was after

I spoke with your secretary the first time. Cliff was supposed to call you back.

"Mom's in Memorial Hospital in intensive care. They want to do bypass surgery as soon as she's stabilized. That's why I called, to see if you can be with her. I can't get away right now."

Delia was still trying to wrap her mind around the fact her mother was alive. "Don't worry, Rachel. I'll be there."

"I'd go myself except there's a political fund-raising banquet tonight in Dallas and Cliff . . . My husband needs me."

Delia made a moue of disgust. The day U.S. Congressman Clifford McKinley from the great Lone Star State of Texas needed anyone but himself was the day she would eat her snakeskin cowboy boots. But Rachel loved the man, and he had given her sister an adorable son, so he couldn't be all bad. "Put your mind at rest," she said. "Get there when you can."

"Thanks, Delia. I'll be on the first flight out of Dallas tomorrow morning."

"Do you want me to pick you up in San Antonio?"

"I'll rent a car and drive the rest of the way to the Circle Crown myself."

"Are you bringing Scott?" Delia asked.

"I think a six-year-old would be in the way."

"I'd love to see him," Delia coaxed. "Mother's housekeeper could take care of him while we're at the hospital."

"I . . . I can't," Rachel said. "Cliff doesn't like it when—"

"Forget what Cliff would like," Delia interrupted brusquely. "What would you like?" Delia felt Rachel's uncertainty on the other end of the line.

"I'll ask Cliff if Scott can come," Rachel said at last.

"I'll see the two of you tomorrow," Delia replied firmly.

"I'm sorry to leave all of this in your lap," Rachel said. "Especially since . . ."

"Don't worry about it," Delia said. "I can handle it."

"Can you, Delia? Really?"

Delia heard the concern in her sister's voice. They had seen each other rarely over the past twenty years, the visits occurring either at Rachel and Cliff's home in Dallas, their place in Alexandria, Virginia, or her stomping grounds in New York. The moments of connection had been few and far between—Rachel's wedding, Scott's christening, Christmas every few years, and most recently the day Delia had been sworn in by the mayor as a judge.

But your sister was your sister forever, no matter how much or how little you saw of her. She and Rachel had shared a great deal. There were memories that tied them even tighter than blood.

"I should have gone home to the Circle Crown a long time ago," Delia admitted. "It's time things were settled between Mother and me."

She had been given a second chance to re-

solve matters between them. She was going to
take advantage of it. Before it *was* too late.

"Delia . . . Marsh is home."

Delia's heart gave an extra thump. "What's
he doing in Texas?"

"He moved back to his dad's ranch about
four months ago with his sixteen-year-old
daughter," Rachel said. "His ex-wife was
killed in a car wreck six months ago, and the
girl had nowhere to go. Marsh has taken a
leave of absence from *The Chronicle* to get his
daughter through high school. I thought you
should know."

Delia gave a long, silent sigh. She had tried
so desperately to escape the past, but here it
was again, back to haunt her. She had unfinished business with Marshall North. The Pulitzer prize–winning reporter was one of the
two figures under that majestic live oak she
had been remembering just this morning. She
was the other.

They had grown up as neighbors and become far more than that. He had rescued her
from disaster, and she had repaid him by running away and never coming back. It was the
sort of thing Hattie Carson might have done.
It was the sort of thing her colleagues in
Brooklyn would never have believed of her. In
some ways Delia was more her mother's
daughter than she wanted to admit.

"Delia? Are you still there?"

"I'm here."

"It's been a long time since you've been
home, Delia. You won't recognize Uvalde.
There's a McDonald's, and a Taco Bell, and a

new high school. Remember that huge old live oak they took all the trouble to pave around when they built the H.E.B. grocery on Highway 90? It just withered up and died. Not enough water, I guess."

"That's too bad." When the roads in Uvalde were first paved in the 1920s, the mayor had refused to cut down any trees. In the neighborhoods, live oaks grew in the middle of the street and people drove around them. That was the kind of town Uvalde was.

"The ranch hasn't changed at all. Except maybe to age along with all of us. Your room is exactly as you left it. Or it was the last time I was home. I think Mom always hoped you'd come back. At least you'll get to see her again before . . . before . . ." Rachel sobbed.

"Don't cry, Rachel," Delia crooned. The words were hauntingly familiar. She'd had cause to say them before.

Delia felt the tears burning her eyes and nose. Twenty years wasn't long enough. The memories were indelibly etched in her mind and soul. If it were up to her, she would never go back. There were too many ghosts at the Circle Crown.

A knock at Delia's door provided a welcome interruption. "There's someone at the door, Rachel. I have to go."

"Tomorrow," Rachel said.

"Tomorrow." Delia grabbed a Kleenex from the box inside her right-hand desk drawer and dabbed at the tear-smudged makeup at the corners of her eyes while the insistent knocking continued.

"Come in," she said, dropping the Kleenex into the wastebasket. Then she realized she was barefoot and scrambled to get her heels back on.

Whoever was there tried the door and found it locked. "It's locked," a male voice said.

"Just a minute." Delia slipped into the second high heel, crossed quickly to the door, unlocked it, and pulled it open. She stiffened when she saw who was there. She should have recognized his voice, but she hadn't been expecting him. Not so soon.

"May I come in?"

Delia stepped back and let Sam Dietrich in. She endured the DA's scrutiny, hoping her eyes didn't look as red-rimmed as they felt.

"Janet told me about your mother. I'm sorry," he said.

"Condolences are premature," Delia said coolly. "It appears reports of her death were greatly exaggerated."

Sam raised a brow.

"My mother isn't dead after all," she explained. "She was resuscitated by the paramedics."

"Oh."

The district attorney was clearly uncomfortable, but Delia had no desire to help him out. Lately, he had been a constant burr under her saddle. Sam was balding, but doing it gracefully. His sandy hair was trimmed neatly over his ears and above his collar. His pale blue eyes were focused sharply on her from behind trendy, wire-rimmed glasses. A hawkish nose, full lips, and heavy brows gave him a nonspecific ethnic look that was certain to be helpful to Sam's grand political aspirations to become governor.

Sam looked more like a Manhattan corporate attorney than an official of the state in his exquisitely tailored gray wool blend suit and Armani tie. His white-on-white shirt was starched so crisply it could have stood on its own, and his black wing-tipped shoes were polished to a mirror sheen. It was definitely a power suit, and Delia was grateful for the black robe that gave her even greater power.

"I don't have much time, Mr. Dietrich. I have to catch the first flight to San Antonio."

She crossed behind her desk and sat to give herself the position of greater authority. It was unlikely Sam had come on a friendly visit. "What can I do for you?"

Sam turned and checked the hallway before carefully closing her door and locking it.

She raised a questioning brow as expressive as Sam's, but he didn't explain himself, simply turned to her, stuck his hands in his pants pockets, and said, "I got your message."

"I see. And what dirty job have you come to do, Mr. Dietrich?"

The DA's lips flattened. His icy blue eyes narrowed. "I want you to accept the Lincoln plea bargain."

"Five years probation for murder one?" Delia shook her head. "I don't think so, Mr. Dietrich."

"The kid is only eighteen. Two months ago Lincoln would have been a juvenile. He can make a good argument for self-defense," Dietrich said. "The public defender has witnesses who'll testify the victim had a gun on him."

"Then why wasn't Lincoln charged with manslaughter in the first place? The grand jury must have based their decision to go with murder one on something."

Dietrich pulled a linen handkerchief from his pocket and dabbed at the sweat beaded on his upper lip. "Look, Judge Carson, I'm asking you to do this for me."

Delia's brow furrowed. She leaned forward and said, "What's going on here, Sam? If I didn't know better, I'd think the kid paid you off."

The DA's eyes flashed with irritation before he lowered his head to stare at his polished toe tips. When he glanced up at her again, his gaze was completely neutral. "It's nothing as nefarious as that. The truth is, I'm doing a favor for a cop friend of mine who screwed up the evidence on this thing. We couldn't get a conviction now if we tried. Frankly, I need a favor."

Delia shook her head. "I'm sorry, Sam. I don't do that kind of favor. Come back with a different charge if you want a different plea bargain."

"But—"

"Is that all, Mr. Dietrich?" she said, cutting him off.

The DA's eyes narrowed to angry slits, and Delia saw from the way his pants were stretched that his hands had balled into fists in his pockets.

"I won't forget this," he said.

"I won't either," Delia assured him.

She could see Sam wanted to say more, but he resisted the impulse. He turned on his heel and let himself out, leaving the door open behind him.

Janet appeared a moment later in the doorway. "I made reservations for you on the next flight to San Antonio out of La Guardia."

"Thanks, Janet. I appreciate your help. For the record, my mother isn't dead, after all. The paramedics revived her."

"Oh, Judge Carson, that's wonderful!"

Delia bit her tongue to keep from contradicting her secretary.

"I'll let you know as soon as the car arrives," Janet said. "The driver will wait while you pack and then take you on to the airport." Janet backed out and closed the door behind her.

Delia propped her elbows on her desk and dropped her head into her hands. Oh, God, she didn't want to do this! If only there were some way she could avoid going back.

But perhaps it was time—past time—to confront the secrets that had been buried two decades ago. Delia raised her head and threaded her fingers to stop their trembling. Oh, such very messy secrets. She would exhume them and examine them one last time before she buried them again, neatly, once and for all.

Maybe then she could get on with her life.

⊱ *Chapter Two* ⊰

Marshall North's notoriety in Uvalde, Texas, had little to do with being a Pulitzer Prize–winning journalist. Quite simply, the bad boy was back in town.

Marsh had tried to blend into the Texas crowd since his return, which wasn't hard when he mostly wore a chambray shirt and jeans and cowboy boots these days. His hair was a little long beneath a new felt Stetson, and he usually needed a shave, but that shouldn't have caused the kind of stares he'd been getting on the street since he'd returned home.

They were all remembering what had happened twenty years ago. The past had definitely not been forgotten.

It seemed far away right now. He had a new role in life, one that had him as uncertain of where he was going as a pony with his bridle off. He was picking his way, slow and careful, knowing from his years of experience as a foreign correspondent that sometimes it didn't matter how careful you were. Things had a way of happening. And not always for the best.

But South American rebel forces aside, being a parent was about the most uncertain thing Marsh had ever confronted. He and his sixteen-year-old daughter had been two-stepping around each other for the past six months but couldn't seem to get in sync. Either he landed on her toes, or she landed on his. He had no choice but to keep trying, unless he wanted to give up entirely.

Marsh had stopped running from trouble a long time ago. As far as he was concerned there was no way to go but forward. Even if he made mistakes, even if he did things wrong, he was determined to learn how to be a good father to Billie Jo. Certainly a better father than his father had been to him. Which was why he spent most of his time these days as jumpy as a bit-up old bull at fly time.

"Billie Jo, damn it, get up!" Marsh yelled down the hall from the kitchen doorway. "The bus'll be at the end of the drive in ten minutes! Your eggs are getting cold."

A sullen-eyed, slump-shouldered teenage girl appeared at the other end of the hall wearing one of Marsh's best white tailored shirts, arms folded up to the elbows and tails hanging over a pair of ragged, kneeless jeans. The jeans were tucked into a pair of worn black-and-red cowboy boots.

"That's my shirt, Billie Jo," he pointed out. Her chin—the same stubborn chin possessed by generations of Norths—jutted pugnaciously. "Nothing of mine is clean."

"Comb your hair and get in here," Marsh ordered, gripping the doorjamb in lieu of his daughter's slender neck.

Billie Jo shoved a hand through tousled ash-blond curls that were turning dark at the roots and clomped down the hall toward him. "It is combed."

Marsh stood where he was and watched her edge along the water-stained, rose-papered wall as she passed by him. Not that he had raised so much as a pinkie to her in the six months they had been living together, but she must have noticed he was running out of patience. He brushed a knuckle against the curling paper. His grandmother had loved it. He wasn't looking forward to stripping it down and putting up new.

But the house was barely fit for habitation. It had been empty during the two years since his father had died, and it hadn't been in good shape even then. He had hired a man to take care of the livestock since his father's death, but the ranch house had been neglected. A storm must have torn some shingles loose, because the roof leaked when it rained. Too bad about the wallpaper.

Too bad his grandmother wasn't here to help him with Billie Jo, but she had died when he was ten. Grandma Dennison had a way of soothing pain, a way of easing trouble that he wished he had inherited from her.

The best he could do was sympathize with his daughter's need to rebel against authority.

He had been wild as a boy himself, quick to anger and rash to a fault. But he had learned in the years since to control his anger and his impulses. The sooner his daughter learned that he expected her to obey him, the easier it would be for both of them. But there was nothing easy about any of this.

He remembered how euphoric he had been the first time he'd held his daughter in his arms. She was so tiny and helpless, needing him the way no one had ever needed him before. He had felt a swell of emotion inside that made him want to cry. He'd been worried because she hadn't had a lick of hair. His wife had laughed at him and promised it would grow.

By the time Billie Jo had a few curls, he and Ginny were already arguing about his long and frequent absences overseas. Before those curls reached Billie Jo's shoulders, he and Ginny were arguing all the time. They had stayed married for ten long years. It got so he came home only to see Billie Jo, and the arguments with Ginny forced him out of the house sooner than he wanted to leave his daughter.

Which didn't explain why he had seen so little of Billie Jo in the years since his divorce. The reasons for staying away were harder to justify. Fathers were supposed to keep on being fathers. It hadn't taken him long to learn that the pain of parting each time—when Billie Jo clung to him and begged him not to leave— was worse than not seeing her at all. He supposed that was a cop-out. It was also the truth.

There had been no time to prepare himself when Ginny had been killed so suddenly. Either he took Billie Jo or sent her away to some boarding school for girls whose parents didn't want them around. Even though they were no longer close, he couldn't do that to his daughter. He knew too well what it felt like not to be wanted.

For Billie Jo's sake, he had tried staying in Ginny's Boston condominium. But he would rather leave his hide on a fence than stay in a corral—and that high-rise box had felt like a jail cell after roaming free for so many years. Carting Billie Jo around the world with him wasn't practical. So he had opted for the wide open spaces of southwest Texas—specifically the North Ranch. At least there he knew he wouldn't feel so hemmed in.

Billie Jo had balked at leaving all her friends behind, but he had been adamant. They were both going to have to give a little for this to work. She would have to give up Boston. He would have to give up the rest of the world.

She was still angry about the move, and he couldn't really blame her. He was fighting his own share of resentment at having to deal with a hostile stranger who happened to be his daughter. To tell the truth, he was about at the end of his rope.

Before he had moved back into this old ranch house, full of creaky floors and disturbing memories, he would have said he had learned to control his feelings. But it seemed Billie Jo knew all the right buttons to push. She had been on him like a roadrunner on a rattler ever since the two of them had been forced willy-nilly into the father-daughter role. The fight wasn't over by a long shot.

He consoled himself with the thought he only had to get her through another year of high school after this one, which was, thank God, half over. Then he could send her off to college with a clear conscience and go back to the work he loved best.

His editor at *The Chronicle,* Lloyd Harrison, had been furious when Marsh had left the tiny African nation where he was reporting on one of the many uprisings over the past decade and flown home to take custody of his daughter.

"I need you, Marsh," Lloyd had ranted.

"My daughter needs me more," he had replied. Luckily, he had put most of what he'd earned over the past fifteen years in the bank, so money wasn't a problem. When Lloyd continued haranguing him, he had hung up.

Lloyd and *The Chronicle* were simply going to have to wait until Marsh could get his life in order. That meant getting his daughter through high school, the prospect of which seemed more iffy by the minute.

When Marsh arrived in the kitchen he discovered Billie Jo had grabbed a piece of toast from the wholesome plate of breakfast he had prepared for her and was making a beeline for the kitchen door.

"Where do you think you're going, young lady?" he said, stepping in front of the screen door and blocking her way.

"Daddy, I'm going to be late," she protested.

"Haven't you forgotten something?"

She looked up at him, the soul of innocence. "I don't think so." A pause, and then, "I don't need a sweater. It's going to be warm today."

He hadn't even thought about that. Another sign of his shortcomings as a father. She was probably right. It was going to be another warm January day. He stared down at her, watching her chew worriedly on her bottom lip. He felt a jolt of recognition. Ginny used to do the same thing.

Marsh realized he had let himself be distracted from the matter at hand. He pulled a folded paper from the back pocket of his jeans and shook it open in front of his daughter's pretty young face. "What is this?" he demanded.

Billie Jo's cheeks flamed. She shot a guilty look at him, but that didn't last long before her dark brown eyes—her mother's eyes—flashed with anger. "Where did you get that?"

"I found it on your floor when I—"

"You were in my room? My room is *private*. How could you!" Angry tears spurted from her eyes as she retreated to the sink, where she hunched her shoulders against him and stared out onto the backyard.

He felt a little like crying himself. He hadn't meant to confront her like that. He had meant to have a quiet, civil discussion of the matter at the breakfast table. Only, she had never made it to the table.

Silence reigned while she stared out the

window. There wasn't much to see, some
prickly pear cactus and a few scrubby mesquite trees on flat, rocky ground. It was supposed to be grassland, but the drought had
taken its toll. There wasn't much grass out
there, which the feed bill for the few remaining Santa Gertrudis cattle on the North Ranch
attested to. Neither were there any vestiges of
the vegetable garden his grandmother had
maintained. Nature had long since reclaimed
the land.

He conceded that Billie Jo would likely
stand there all day rather than give in. She
looked sweet as mother's milk, but she fought
his attempts to father her like a bronc with its
teeth clenched against the bit.

"You haven't told me about this paper," he
said.

"You went into my room to get it," she muttered, her back still turned to him. "You must
know what it is."

"It looks like a suspension from school."

"Right the first time," she quipped, turning
to face him.

"Damn it, Billie Jo—" He cut himself off.
She was doing it again. Pushing buttons. "I
want an answer."

Her lips flattened mulishly, and she glared
at him, hugging the worn, leather-trimmed
hiker's knapsack he had left behind one trip
because he thought it was worn out, and
which she was using as a bookbag, protectively against her chest.

"This requires a parent's signature," he said.

"It's already been signed, but I never signed it. Who did?"

She dropped her eyes to the floor, tightened her grip on the knapsack, but said nothing.

"Look, Billie Jo, we have to talk about this."

Her lips remained sealed.

"It says here you were suspended for fighting with another girl. What kind of fight? About what?" He hadn't known high school girls resorted to tearing hair. At least, they hadn't in his day. On the other hand, he had seen enough violence by kids in his travels to convince him they could be brutal.

"It also appears you only get a suspension after you've had three warnings. Why didn't you say something to me if you were having trouble in school?"

She shrugged, a small, vulnerable gesture that tore his heart out.

He had blithely, naively, assumed Billie Jo had fit right in at her new school. It was considerably smaller than the school in Boston. She never talked much about activities at school, but she hadn't complained, either. It was upsetting to realize how blind he had been. There were problems he hadn't even suspected.

"What happened to the warning notices?" he asked. "Did you sign them, too?"

She sneaked a chagrined peek at him, looked down again, and nodded her chin slightly.

"Is that a yes?" he demanded.

"Yes!" she shot back. "I got into a fight with Eula Hutchins because she said you . . . she said . . . It doesn't matter what she said. She won't be saying it again.''

Marsh wondered what Eula Hutchins had said about him. He could make a pretty good guess. It wasn't a secret that as a kid he had been accused of rape. Even though he hadn't been found guilty of any crime, there were plenty in Uvalde who believed he was. It was a lot of the reason he had never come back to his father's house after he had left, even when things had been resolved with the law so he could.

It was also why he had never brought Ginny here to meet his father before the old man died. There was too great a chance she would hear the rumors that persisted years after the charges against him had been dropped. He should have told Ginny the truth from the beginning, but he could never find the right moment to speak. The daughter of the American ambassador to West Germany, who had willingly consented to marry a Pulitzer Prize–winning journalist, might have balked at the notion of wedding an accused rapist with a drunk for a father.

Those two secrets had sat between them their entire marriage. It meant he could never fully confide in Ginny, never let down his guard with her, because the truth might come out. In later years, when the marriage was failing, he wouldn't have cared, but by then he had learned to keep everything to himself.

Maybe he should have sat Billie Jo down the day they got to the North Ranch and told her the whole story. Maybe then this wouldn't have happened. But old habits die hard. Being a journalist had taught him to be wary of spilling his guts. He had seen too much, knew too much that could hurt other people, told to him off the record.

He opened his mouth to ask if Eula Hutchins had accused him of being a rapist and snapped it shut again. Things were bad enough between him and his daughter. He wasn't sure she was old enough—worldly enough—to understand even if he explained what had really happened. There was always the chance her fight with Eula had been over something else entirely.

Marsh shoved a frustrated hand through his sun-bleached chestnut hair and realized he needed a trim. Because he was always in some godforsaken place without amenities, he was used to getting along without a haircut and a shave. Which was a good thing, because there had been so much to do around the dilapidated ranch he hadn't found time to get to Red White's Barber Shop in town.

"Where were you going this morning, if you're suspended from school?" he asked.

Billie Jo frowned at him, lipstick-red lips pursing. "To school, of course."

"But you're suspended for three days."

"It's an *internal* suspension."

"What the hell is that?"

"You go to school, but you stay in a room separated from the other kids. If you don't let me leave soon, I'm going to miss the bus."

Marsh pursed his own lips, unsure whether to believe her. She had shown she was capable of deceit by signing all the warnings and the suspension. But what she suggested made sense. He took the suspension notice and leaned it against the refrigerator, got a pen from the collection in the Yellowstone Park coffee mug by the phone, signed his own signature above her forgery, and held the paper out to her.

"Daddy! Oh, no! Look what you've done!"

"I've signed my name, like I was supposed to."

"Now they'll know I signed the other notices myself," Billie Jo wailed.

"Tough."

"How can you—"

Marsh held a thumb over his shoulder aimed at the door. "Get going before you miss the bus."

She scurried for the door, snatching the suspension notice from him as she went.

He caught the screen door on the mud porch before it could slam behind her. "Billie Jo," he called after her. "Don't bother throwing away that notice. I'll be calling the school to let them know I'm aware of the situation."

She gave him an outraged look over her shoulder, mumbled something he was glad he couldn't hear, and ran for the iron gate, where the school bus had screeched to a halt and was honking for her. She tiptoed over the wide-spaced bars of the cattle guard, then stomped her way up the stairs onto the bus, and headed down the aisle. He caught a glimpse of her staring back at him forlornly from a window near the back of the bus.

He was a failure as a father. Just as his own
father had been.

Marsh let the screen door go and crossed
back to the clutter of dishes in the kitchen as
it slammed behind him. He wasn't doing too
well as a substitute mother, either.

There wasn't time to clean up the mess. He
had somewhere he had to be. He grabbed his
Stetson from the deer antler rack by the refrigerator and tugged it down before shoving his
way out the door. It felt good to be wearing a
hat again. He had given up wearing one on
assignment, because the damned things kept
getting lost, stolen, or left behind when he had
to get out in a hurry.

He left the kitchen door unlocked. There
wasn't much to steal, and no burglars around
this far from town to steal it. Besides, people
still left their doors unlocked in the West as an
age-old gesture of range hospitality.

Marsh stepped into his pickup—the same
rusted-out '57 Chevy he had driven as a teenager—and headed down the dirt road leading
to the highway. The truck rattled over the cattle guard, and he turned right onto U.S. 83
headed north to Uvalde.

The town seventy miles southwest of San
Antonio where Marsh had grown up had few
claims to fame. Former Texas Governor Dolph
Briscoe had declared it home and might be
seen during his term as governor emerging
from the local 7-Eleven on a Saturday night
and stepping into his pickup with a six-pack—
of Coke. The governor was a teetotaler.

More importantly, one of Roosevelt's vice

presidents, John Nance Garner, had been born there. His home on Park Street was a carefully tended Historic Landmark. The nineteenth-century opera house on the square had been donated to the town by the Garner family.

Uvalde was the kind of town most Americans yearned to live in, with tidy pecan and live oak-lined streets. Getty Street featured stores that had been owned by the same families for generations. But Uvalde had a modern high school, a junior college with strong programs in shop and auto mechanics and cosmetology, not to mention one of the best rodeo teams around. Very little serious crime occurred, and the few existing pockets of poverty were hard to find.

On the downside, there wasn't much entertainment available for teenagers, or adults either, for that matter. The local pool hall had video games, if the current owner wasn't bankrupt, and the Forum Four on Highway 90 had replaced the old El Lasso theater on Getty.

In the fall, everyone in town attended the high school football game on Friday nights. On Saturdays they enjoyed the Texas two-step and the cotton-eyed Joe at the Hermann Son's Hall in Knippa, while the Dallas Cowboys and Houston Oilers kept everyone glued to the TV on Sunday afternoons.

Marsh could two-step with the best of them, but he wasn't about to brave the stares—or a refusal—if he asked some local lady to dance. While he loved the Dallas Cowboys, he hadn't seen much of them in the places he had been. It might be nice to start watching again, once he got a living room chair to replace the one his dad had sat in.

There was dove, quail, and deer hunting in season. Every pickup in town boasted a rifle rack in the back window, sort of like fans in the big city who put a team sticker on their bumper to remind them of their favorite sport year-round. Marsh had done his share of hunting as a kid, but he had seen enough of death and dying—animal and human—over the past twenty years to last him a lifetime.

Parties in private homes took up the slack. Marsh had been invited to a score of them since he had arrived back in Uvalde. He had refused all invitations, citing the need to spend time with his daughter. But it really had more to do with disliking hypocrisy.

The grown-ups who were inviting him to their homes as the prodigal son were the very same teenagers who had been the first to believe him guilty. He supposed the Pulitzer Prize for investigative reporting washed away a lot of sins.

Marsh pulled into the Memorial Hospital parking lot and keyed off the ignition. The pickup ran another few seconds before it died. It needed a tune-up. He took a deep breath and let it out while he worked up the courage to go inside.

Marsh hated hospitals. In his experience, nothing good ever happened in them—the one exception being the birth of his daughter. His nose curled. He was smelling blood and the stench of gangrene in a filthy field hospital. Hearing the shrieks of pain, the moans of agony as doctors treated patients without anesthesia. It could have been in Africa, or Asia, or South America, or Eastern Europe. Mankind had a way of repeating its mistakes.

This hospital would likely be antiseptically clean, the pain and suffering eased by medicines. It didn't matter. His stomach clenched, anyway. But he had to go in there.

He had called early this morning and learned that Hattie Carson was scheduled for heart bypass surgery at 10:00 A.M. Delia Carson would be there and maybe Rachel, too. He didn't know how he could face them.

He had nearly killed Hattie Carson yesterday.

Or, rather, he was responsible for the heart attack that had nearly killed her. He had known she was going to be upset when he confronted her. He just hadn't realized how frail she was. She had acted as tough as ever.

He had come unannounced, afraid she wouldn't see him if he called ahead of time. It was a reporter's trick that often worked. He saw the surprise on her face when she opened the door. He had stuck his foot inside to keep her from slamming it in his face.

Coming to the front door instead of the back had signaled he wasn't there as a friend. Her scowl made it clear she had gotten the message.

"Hello, Mrs. Carson," he said. "I'd like to talk to you."

"There's nothing we have to say to each other."

When Hattie tried to close the door, he put

his palm against it. There was no contest. He was six-foot-four and weighed 212 pounds. She was five-foot-two, her blond curls bleached white with age, and had the kind of wiry strength common to sixty-year-old ranch women used to hard physical labor. But her 103 pounds wasn't going to keep him out.

She realized it at once and stepped back with a quiet dignity that surprised and humbled him. "Come in," she said, "since there doesn't seem to be anything I can do to keep you out."

He took off his gray felt Stetson and stepped inside. His boots made a hollow sound on the hardwood floor that echoed off the high ceiling.

His eyes scanned the large parlor. He had never seen it before. He had been in through the back door to the kitchen once, and the study, but had never made it to the front of the house. Delia's father had thrown him out when he came to ask permission to take her out. He hadn't been good enough for Carson's daughter. He felt acid in his throat as the humiliating memory rose. He forced the acid, and the memory, back down.

He perused the Victorian sofa, wing-back upholstered chairs, and Tiffany lamps on the end tables, all left over from the nineteenth century. Framed daguerreotypes from the Civil War sat on the mantel above the stone fireplace, a Turkish rug on the hardwood floor. The furnishings were surprisingly shabby. But spotlessly clean.

You had to wonder what Hattie was trying

so desperately to wash away. He thought he knew. He was there to find out for sure.

It wasn't an impulsive visit. He had thought a lot about his life in the six months since Ginny's accident, about all the mistakes he had made with her and Billie Jo . . . and Delia Carson. His return to the home he had fled so many years ago had forced him to relive memories of all that had happened, all he had felt and said and done. He thought of all the things he could have done differently. Of all the things he had lost.

He was older now. He knew more about himself and what was missing in his life. He acknowledged there was a hole inside him where something precious had been ripped out. His heart, to be precise.

Though he had not seen her for twenty years, he had never gotten over Delia Carson. He could live the rest of his life without her if he had to, but he would rather not. He wanted another chance to fix what had gone wrong. Or get her out of his system, once and for all.

It wasn't going to be easy. Not after letting the past lie unresolved for so long. That was why he had come to the Circle Crown. To confront Hattie Carson and ask for the truth.

"What is it you want?" Hattie said.

Marsh turned the brim of his Stetson in his hands. He had faced a gun-toting Bosnian Serb with less nervousness than he felt facing this tiny woman. She had known him as a boy, inexorably altered his life, was maybe even responsible for him becoming the wanderer he was.

Hattie sighed at his continued silence. "Sit down, North," she said, gesturing him toward the sofa.

He took one of the chairs instead, leaving the narrow-seated Victorian sofa to her. He kept his hat in his lap, because it gave him something to do with his hands.

"Out with it," she said, once the two of them were seated.

"I know everything," he said. "Everything he did. And how you ignored it."

Hattie's face turned chalky. Her silvery blue eyes disappeared as eyelids crepey with age slid closed. Her hands—he noticed the joints were swollen with arthritis—threaded together in her lap. When she opened her eyes again, he saw she was angry.

"Why couldn't you have stayed gone? Why do you have to drag all this back up?"

"It was all waiting right here for me when I came back, Mrs. Carson."

She rose in agitation and paced away from him. "You were no good for Delia. You ruined her life."

"If Delia's got problems, I didn't cause them." He rose and crossed to stand in her path. "You've got that shoe on the wrong damn foot."

She whirled to face him, fury making her eyes spark. "Everything was fine until you came along. We were a family. We were happy. It was only after Delia met you that everything went wrong."

"I didn't rape her, Mrs. Carson. I didn't get her pregnant."

Hattie took a couple of hitching breaths. At first he thought she was expressing indignation. It was only after she grabbed at her chest and said "Help me" that he realized she was having some sort of attack.

She collapsed in his arms.

Marsh bawled like a branded calf for help, and the housekeeper, Maria, came running.

"Dios mio!" the old woman cried. "Her pills. Give her one of her pills!"

"What pills?" he bellowed back.

Maria reached into Hattie's jeans pocket to get a bottle of nitroglycerin pills, shook one out, and handed it to him. "Put it under her tongue."

Marsh did as she ordered while she raced to call 911.

The pill didn't work.

Marsh's heart was barging around inside his chest like a moose in a tepee. Which was more than Hattie's heart could manage. It wasn't beating at all.

He pressed his fingers to her carotid artery. No pulse. No sign of her chest moving up and down. He leaned down to see if he could feel breath coming from her nostrils. Nothing.

He had performed CPR twice in his lifetime on war victims in the field when there was no other help available. His success rate wasn't high. He flinched from the thought of pressing his mouth over Hattie Carson's and breathing his air into her lungs. Not when he felt the way he did about her. Not when she felt the way she did about him.

If she dies, the truth dies with her.

"Help her, *señor*," Maria begged. "The ambulance is on the way."

Reluctantly, he tilted Hattie's head back, checked the airway, and lowered his mouth to cover hers.

He performed CPR until he thought he was going to keel over himself, Maria crying over his shoulder the whole time, before the paramedics arrived. They shoved him out of the way, asking questions and issuing orders with the kind of efficiency people learn if they want to have any hope of saving lives.

They had revived Hattie in the ambulance on the way to the hospital. Overnight she had stabilized, and this morning she would have surgery. *Hattie Carson had damn well better make it*, Marsh thought. He wanted her alive so she could spill the secrets that had been kept for too many years. The secrets that would free his life.

Marsh huffed out a breath and stepped down from the pickup.

Delia's probably inside.

His heart did a flip-flop in his chest. An image of Delia as she had looked the first time he met her formed in his mind.

It was a hot summer day in June. A bunch of kids had gotten together to go floating down the Frio River on huge tractor tire inner tubes. He had driven his '57 Chevy pickup— not quite as bad a rattletrap in those days— downriver several miles to where they would take their tubes out of the water and gotten a ride back to the starting point with Joe Taylor. When he stepped out of Joe's pickup, he gave a wolf whistle at the crowd of girls wearing skimpy swimsuit tops, indecently cutoff jeans, and Keds without socks.

He might not have noticed Delia, except at that moment she pulled off a baseball cap and about a yard of silky black hair fell to her waist. The sight of all that hair captivated his imagination. What would it be like to make love to a girl with hair like that? he had wondered. Unfortunately, the owner of all that marvelous hair wasn't much to look at from the back. Skinny as a bed slat. And way too short for someone as tall as he was.

Then she turned around.

Her blue eyes caught on his gray ones and remained. She smiled at him tentatively, shyly.

He couldn't have said what it was about that look, about that smile, that surged like a raging river into the gaping hole inside him and filled it up. It was as though she knew all of his fears and desires and offered solace and satisfaction.

He forced himself to step back mentally from her, to look at her objectively.

She had a small bosom, the bare hint of a waist, and good legs, but not much of them. It was her face that drew his gaze and compelled it to stay.

Her eyes were wide-set, wise beyond her tender years, understanding, compassionate. Her nose was short and straight, her chin a little square. Her mouth was wide, her upper lip slightly bowed. He felt an uncomfortable urge to press his mouth to hers, to put his tongue inside her and taste, to join himself to her in a way most nice girls wouldn't allow.

He wanted her to say something, so he could hear her voice. But she remained silent.

One of the other girls called to her, and she hurried to grab her tractor tube and join the others. She gave him a fleeting look over her shoulder. But it wasn't an invitation to further their acquaintance, as he might have expected. More like a sad farewell.

Looking back, he recognized the melancholy in her eyes. But he hadn't seen it then. He had only been thinking of himself, of how he could get her pants off and get inside her. He had set out to do exactly that.

Marsh sighed. If only he had known then what he knew now. Would things have turned out differently? No sense wasting the energy to speculate. He couldn't go back. He could only go forward. He and Delia had once belonged together. Did they still?

He headed inside the hospital to see the woman he had fallen in love with at twenty. A woman who had urged him—begged him with tear-filled eyes—to lie and confess that he had raped her.

Life ain't in holdin'
a good hand
but in playin' a poor one well.

❧ *Chapter Three* ❧

June 1976

As Delia Carson stood on the bank of the Frio talking to her best friend, Peggy Voorhees, she felt her neck hairs rise. She turned and caught a tall, broad-shouldered young man staring at her. She looked right back from beneath lowered lashes and felt her lips curve into a reassuring smile. He seemed to need it. He appeared to be a couple of years out of high school, but he knew most of the others. She wondered who he was.

She turned away reluctantly, wishing things were different. She was far older in experience than a boy like him could possibly imagine. And she was damaged goods. Not that anyone knew, not even her best friend.

"Last one in is a rotten egg!" Peggy yelled as she dragged her tube into the thigh-deep water and dropped spread-eagled back onto it.

"You cheated!" Delia shouted back as she lugged her tube toward the river's edge.

"Here, let me help you with that."

The young man had come up behind her and taken hold of the huge tractor tire tube.

"I can manage," she said.

"I'll keep it steady while you hop on," he said, taking the tube from her and setting it in the water.

"All right," she agreed, because she didn't see a courteous way to avoid his help. She stood in the shallow water, getting used to the cold, then settled back gingerly onto the tube, shivering as the water soaked her fanny. Her tennis shoes hung over the front edge in the water, and her elbows rested on either side. "You can let go now."

He gave her a little push into the center of the river, and she began drifting downstream.

"Watch out for barbed wire," he warned as she floated away from him. "It's strung across the water along the Johnson property line. Only one strand shows above the water. If you'll wait, I'll—"

"I'll be careful," she shouted back to him as the current carried her away. She and Peggy, along with everyone else, would have to get out of the water and go around the barbed wire before continuing the trip downriver.

Peggy had settled her feet on the stony bottom to stop her forward movement until Delia caught up to her. She lifted her tennis shoes out of the water, and they rafted down the river side by side. "Who was that you were talking to?"

Delia shrugged. "I don't know. I saw him for the first time today."

"He's really cute. Too old for you, though. Your dad would go bonkers if somebody like him showed up at your door."

Delia made a dismissive sound in her throat. "There's no chance this guy is going to show up at my door, so don't get your drawers in a knot. I don't plan to worry about a thing for the next three hours. I'm going to settle back and enjoy the ride."

As she floated lazily down the Frio, lying stretched out in the sunshine across the tractor tube, her fingers trailing in the frigid water, Delia wondered what the future held for her. She knew she couldn't stay here, couldn't continue her outward role as a dutiful daughter. So far, no one had guessed her awful secret. But she was afraid if anybody really looked close, they would see the truth.

"Penny for your thoughts?"

Delia glanced at Peggy. "They aren't worth that much."

Peggy laughed. "You're so funny, Delia! 'They aren't worth that much'—and you the smartest girl in the junior class. That is so funny!"

"I'm a barrel of laughs, all right," Delia agreed. Especially late at night, when her father came to her room.

Because everyone was strung out for half a mile along the river, Delia didn't see the young man again until after the float. Everyone was gathered around a rusted-out pickup, throwing their tractor tubes in the back and tying them down, when she caught him staring at her.

She turned her back on him, knowing Peggy was right, that there was no point in getting to know him. The bed of the pickup was crowded, between teenagers and tubes, and she was one of the last trying to cram on when she noticed him standing beside her.

"Come sit up front," he said, barely touching her elbow.

The touch of his fingers on her flesh was electrifying. Her body drew up tight inside with pleasure. She automatically fought back the feeling, the way she did when such feelings came when her father touched her, because they were wrong. Only this wasn't wrong. Or shouldn't have been. Nevertheless, she flinched away from his fingertips, confused and upset.

The young man gave her a questioning look, and a flush crept up her throat. Thankfully, he didn't ask for an explanation, and the awkward moment passed. He waited for her to join him, and Peggy said, "Go ahead, Delia. There's no more room back here, anyway."

The ancient pickup had a red leather bench seat, but the four-speed gearshift took up the middle of the floor, so she sat by the passenger door with her elbow perched out the open window. Once they were moving, the breeze whipped the hair slipping from beneath her duckbill cap into a frenzy. "Darn this hair," she said, dragging it away from her mouth and eyes. "I hate it!"

"It's beautiful," the boy said.

The compliment surprised her. She stared at the young man openly before she realized what awful truths he might see if he looked back into her eyes. She lowered her lids protectively.

"You can roll up the window," he said, "if the wind's bothering you."

"It's too hot for that." She yanked off the Dallas Cowboys cap and threw it on the seat between them. She gathered her hair, twisted it several times, and tied it in an ugly knot at her nape. She snugged the billed cap back down on top of it and said, "That ought to keep it tamed for a little while."

"If it gets in your way so much, why don't you cut it?"

Because my father likes it this way. She stared out the window. "Maybe I will someday."

"Would you like to go to the movies with me tonight?"

She turned to look at him in stupefaction. "I don't even know your name."

He shot her a charming grin. "I thought everyone knew me." The grin cocked up on one side into something more cynical. "Or about me. I'm Marshall North."

He said it almost defiantly. She raised a skeptical brow. He was right. She did know about him. No kid in town had a worse reputation. The North Ranch bordered the Circle Crown, where she lived, but her parents and Mr. North weren't on speaking terms, which helped explain why she and Marsh had never crossed paths.

"Well? How about it, Miss Odelia Josephine Carson?"

"You know my name!"

His eyes twinkled. "*I* asked."

She laughed. She admired his boldness. Oh, how she wished she could get to know him better. But it was impossible. "I'm sorry," she said. "My father doesn't allow me to go on dates."

"If you're worried about what your folks would say, I could meet you at the theater."

She glanced sideways at him. He was so very good looking, with sun-streaked brown hair, a smile that created a single dimple on his left cheek, and a straight nose with a slight bump on the bridge. His gray eyes were shuttered against her in a way she recognized because she did it so often herself.

She wanted to go out with a boy close to her own age, like other girls. She wanted to pretend she wasn't . . . what she was. And Marsh North was far from perfect himself, which made her deceit seem less profound. "All right," she said. She felt her heart speed up slightly.

"I'll wait out front for you. Seven-thirty?"

She nodded.

And felt guilty. Even though she didn't have any intention of letting North touch her. She was only going to the movies with him. There wasn't anything wrong with that.

She wasn't able to dress up for the date, because that would have given away the game to her father, and she had been forced to bring Peggy in on her secret.

"I won't lie for you unless you tell me who he is," Peggy said.

"It's Marsh North," she admitted.

"Oh, geez, Delia! Marsh North! Oh, geez! He's so—"

"Nice," Delia inserted before Peggy could finish. "He's been nothing but nice to me."

"That's not what Tricia Stewart said about him."

"I don't want to hear any gossip about Marsh. Will you cover for me, or not?" Delia asked.

"Of course I will," Peggy said. "Oh, Delia, this is so exciting. Geez. Marsh North! Just be careful, okay?"

"I'll be fine," Delia said.

"You have to promise to call me later and tell me *everything!*"

At the supper table Delia said casually that she needed her dad to give her and Peggy a ride to the movies. She said Peggy's mom was picking them up, figuring North could take her home in his pickup. She held her breath until her father said, "That sounds fine."

As Delia stood at the curb in front of the El Lasso next to Peggy, waving good-bye as her father drove away, her heart was pounding.

"He's here, Delia," Peggy whispered in her ear.

North was standing behind her and to her right by the Coming Attractions poster, a cigarette dangling from his mouth.

"Thanks, Peggy," she said. "You can go in now."

"Call me later." Peggy gave Marsh one last surreptitious glance before she hurried over to buy her ticket.

Marsh didn't move until Peggy had gone inside. He threw the cigarette down and snuffed it with his boot as he sauntered toward her. He was wearing worn jeans and a clean, long-sleeved plaid Western shirt folded up to reveal muscular forearms. His hair was still damp, as though he wasn't long out of the shower.

"Hi," he said with a lazy smile that belied the tension she saw in his shoulders. "I wasn't sure you'd come."

She gave him a shy smile in return. "I'm here."

He paid for the tickets and took her elbow to usher her inside. To her surprise, she felt the same jolt she had earlier in the day.

"Popcorn? Milk Duds? Coke?" he asked.

She shook her head. "I just had supper. But you have something if you want."

"I'd rather have my hands free for other things . . . like holding yours," he said in a quiet voice. He reached down and slowly, gently twined his callused fingers in hers, giving her a chance to pull away if she wanted.

She stared at their joined hands before lifting her gaze to his face. There was no glib smile waiting there, no coaxing glint in his gray eyes. He was big enough to force himself on her, but he wasn't demanding anything. She tightened her fingers slightly around his as her mouth curved in a warm smile.

He smiled back, letting what he felt—a corresponding warmth—show in his eyes.

They walked hand in hand into the dimly lit theater and chose secluded seats in the back near the side wall. They spoke in whispers, never stopping until the theater darkened and someone nearby shushed them.

The movie playing that evening was *Jaws* and featured a man-eating shark. Her eyes were riveted to the screen from the opening rumble of chords on the movie sound track. She left crescents in North's arm with the fingernails of her free hand when the shark attacked its first victim.

North was a bastion of safety through the next two hours. Her body tightened with unbearable tension, which was released with laughter, only to build again. When the lights came up, it stunned her to realize her legs were still as wobbly as Jell-O from the last dose of adrenaline that had seen her through the destruction of the shark. She needed North's arm to steady her when she rose.

"That was incredible!" she said.

Marsh chuckled. "Once or twice I didn't think you were going to make it."

She had hidden her face several times during the movie against North's sleeve. Fresh heat washed already pinkened cheeks. "Well, I did, thanks to you."

"Would you like to go have some pie and coffee at the Amber Sky?"

The busy café on Highway 90, the main east–west thoroughfare through town, had been run for as long as anybody could remember by Mrs. Black, who made the best chocolate chiffon pie in Texas. A lot of locals ate supper there with their families. "I don't think that would be a good idea. Someone might see us."

The smile left his face. "Oh. I see." He turned his face away while he waited for her to exit up the aisle.

"Marsh . . ." She waited until he looked at her. His expression was closed again. "I had a wonderful time. But my parents think I'm out with Peggy. If we go to the Amber Sky, one of my father's friends might see us and say something to him."

"How about the Sonic?"

The Sonic Drive-In was a hamburger joint frequented by local teens. You could order from one of a dozen microphone boxes under a long red-and-white awning and have a tray of hamburgers and a couple of milk shakes delivered to your car window. Being seen by the wrong kids at the Sonic could be as disastrous to her as being seen by their parents. "I don't think that would be a good idea, either."

"How about if I buy some beer at the 7-Eleven, and we go drink somewhere private?"

She wasn't sure that was such a good idea for entirely different reasons. But so far North had been a perfect gentleman. "All right," she agreed. "But I'd rather have a Coke than a beer, and I need to be home in an hour."

"No beer?"

She wrinkled her nose. "It tastes awful. How can you stand it?"

He shrugged. "I suppose you learn to like it."

"I wouldn't have guessed you were old enough to buy beer," she said, as he handed her into the passenger side of his pickup.

"I won't be for another month. But a friend

of mine works at the 7-Eleven. He'll usually sell me a six-pack of Pearl or some Dos Equis if no one's around."

"You won't get drunk, will you?" she asked as he slid in on the driver's side. "I'd hate for us to get into an accident."

"I tell you what. If it'll make you happy, I won't even have the beer." He put the truck in gear and headed north on Getty Street toward the 7-Eleven near the high school football stadium on the edge of town.

A thoughtful crease grew on her forehead as she waited in the truck while he went inside and bought the Cokes.

"Something wrong?" he asked as he headed the rattling truck north again toward the hill country where they had spent the afternoon tubing.

"Why do people think you're so bad? You've been nothing but nice to me."

"Disappointed?"

She shook her head. "No. I'm glad you asked me to come with you tonight."

"You're not scared I'll get you off somewhere alone and turn on you, like some Jekyll and Hyde character?"

"Would you?"

"Naw. I like you."

She arched a brow. "And if you didn't like me?"

A devilish grin appeared. "You'd be in serious sh—trouble."

He pulled the truck off the paved highway onto a dirt road that ended abruptly. The night was quiet and still, much as it might have been two hundred years ago, before any settlers had come to disturb the wilderness. He pulled the Cokes out of the paper bag, crumpled it, and pitched it on the floor. He pulled the metal tabs from the lids and dropped them inside, then gave a can to her.

She sipped it gratefully, the fizz easing the dryness in her throat. She thought about how exciting it was to be having her first date with a boy. She would have to call Peggy later, but she didn't think she could find words to explain what tonight had been like.

It was too bad she couldn't share this wonderful experience with her mother and father. But her mother agreed with her father that she was too young to date, and her father . . . He would be furious. Any boy she dated would be bad enough, but someone with Marsh North's reputation was sure to be ten times worse. Her sister Rachel could have kept her secret, but she was too young to think a date with a boy was anything worth crowing about. Besides, Rachel had to be in bed by 9:00 P.M.

Marsh got out of the truck, came around to open her door, and held out his hand to her. He set his Coke on the Chevy fender as she stepped down, and eased his arms around her from behind.

She stiffened immediately.

"Don't be afraid. Lean back against me," he murmured in her ear. "Then look up."

She did as he asked and saw an immense black sky filled with a million stars. A full moon was half-hidden by scudding clouds. "Oooh. It's so beautiful."

"Umm," he agreed. He turned her in his arms, took her Coke from her and set it on the rusted fender next to his, then caught her chin with his forefinger and thumb.

She stood there, knees quaking, staring up at him, aware of what was coming. Her heart slammed against her rib cage, then climbed all the way to her throat and caught there.

"I don't know what it is about you . . ." he said as he stared down at her. He fingered her hair, which she had worn down and parted on the side, and she felt it in the depths of her belly.

She looked up into his face, but his back was to the moon and all she saw was shadows. "Marsh, I—"

His fingertip stopped her speech. "Don't say anything. I know this is crazy, but I have to kiss you. I won't take advantage, I promise. Just . . . may I?"

"That wild North boy" *asking* if he could kiss her? Delia knew she had to be dreaming. She would wake up and be in her bed and it wouldn't be Marsh at all. She wished she could see North's features better.

She reached up with her hand to trace the shape of his brows, his nose—where she found the unfamiliar bump on the bridge— and his mouth. Her father had a scar on his cheek where he had been caught by an unraveling strand of barbed wire. The scar wasn't there.

"All right," she said. "You can kiss me."

She stood frozen, waiting, wondering if it

would feel different. If it would feel good . . .
clean . . . right.

The lips that settled on hers were utterly soft
and searching. He missed her mouth slightly
in the darkness, and came back with better
aim, slanting his lips more exactly across hers.
He pressed more firmly this time, and his
tongue danced across the seam of her lips,
teasing, titillating.

It *was* different. Her body felt tingly, achy,
and she was suddenly breathless. She opened
her mouth to him hesitantly, and his tongue
slipped inside, warm and wet.

She made a sound in her throat, half surprise, half pleasure. Her fingers curled around
handfuls of his cotton shirt as she rose on her
toes to make their bodies meet more completely. And felt his arousal.

A moment later she had freed herself from
his grasp and was standing across from him,
eyes wide with fright, panting for breath.

"Delia, I'm sorry," Marsh hurried to say. "I
. . . I know you're not that kind of girl. I can't
help it if I'm attracted to you that way. I want
to touch you. I want—"

"No," she said abruptly, harshly. "Take me
home, Marsh."

She crossed past him toward the truck, expecting him to try to stop her. But he stepped
aside and opened the pickup door and let her
get in without touching her.

She felt sick. Not because of what had happened between them. The kiss had felt good
. . . wonderful. But if she had let it go any further, if she ever let things move toward their

logical conclusion, Marsh would find out the truth. He would know she wasn't a good girl, like he thought, that she was worse than he could ever dream of being. She wouldn't be able to bear the look in his eyes if he ever found out the truth.

They made the trip south out of town on Highway 83 toward the Circle Crown in silence. Twenty minutes later he turned off the highway and drove down the winding road to her house, which led through what was left of a pecan orchard. He stopped the pickup and turned out the headlights before they illuminated the white columns along the front of the two-story mansion.

Delia had no idea why her ancestors had built a Southern mansion more suited to Mississippi or Georgia instead of the more typical Texas dogtrot home. Four two-story white columns held up a railed veranda, and the double-wide doors downstairs led up an impressive staircase inside. A single twisted live oak shadowed the house.

"Will you go out with me again?" Marsh asked.

"I don't think I should."

"How about riding horseback with me tomorrow afternoon?"

She glanced at his face in the glow of the dash lights he had turned up to give them some relief from the darkness. "I want to, but my father..." She swallowed hard. "I'm sorry. I can't."

"If you change your mind, I'll be at the windmill by your north pasture gate, under the live oak, around one. Good night, Delia."

"Good-bye, Marsh."

She closed the pickup door quietly and watched him back a ways down the road before he whipped the truck around, nearly hitting one of the pecan trees that stood sentinel on either side of the drive. He punched the headlights on and headed off of Circle Crown property.

She turned to look at the house. There were no outside lights on, but she could see a yellow glow upstairs in her mother's bedroom, which opened onto the veranda. She knew the kitchen light would be on, too, because everyone in this part of the country entered and left their homes from the back door. The front door served only for funerals and strangers.

She half expected her father to be sitting at the kitchen table waiting for her, and heaved a sigh of relief when he wasn't.

Ray John Carson wasn't really her father, he was her stepfather. He had adopted her and her sister four years after he married their mother. She had loved him dearly at the time.

When Ray John had come into her life, he had been the third man in as many years wanting her to call him "Daddy." Her own father had been gored to death by a rodeo bull when she was five. Her mother had remarried a year later to another cowboy, a drifting man. He was gone within a year, but not before he had stolen her six-year-old heart with his big smile and throaty chuckle. He had left her sister, Rachel, as a parting gift.

Two years later Ray John Smith, another de-

vil-may-care cowboy, had entered their lives.
Delia had been wary of liking him, certain that
he, too, would abandon them. Gradually, Ray
John Carson—her mother had insisted, as she
had with her first two husbands, that it made
more sense for Ray John to change to the ven-
erable Carson name when they married—had
won her over. He always had been a glib
talker.

Delia headed toward the stairs at the front
of the house that led to her bedroom, which
took her past her father's gun room. A single
light was on over the massive pine desk Ray
John used as a work surface when he was
cleaning his guns. The glass door to one of her
father's gun cabinets hung open.

"Daddy?" She stepped tentatively into the
high-ceilinged room. It was a totally masculine
place, with a saddle brown leather couch,
built-in bookshelves along one wall filled with
dark tomes some long-ago Carson had pur-
chased, and which she was certain none of
Hattie's three husbands had ever touched. It
also contained Ray John's pride and joy: several locked wood and glass cabinets full of antique rifles and revolvers her father had
collected since his marriage to her mother.

Wooden shutters kept the ivy-papered room
perpetually dark, and Ray John used an elbow
lamp on the desk to give him enough light to
work. The lamp highlighted the ring of old
skeleton keys that opened the various gun cabinets. That was odd, because usually Ray John
kept the key ring locked inside the rolltop
desk. He kept the desk key in his wallet.

Delia watched for Ray John in the shadows as she made her way on tiptoe up the carpeted stairs. She didn't want to run into her father tonight, didn't want to remind him of her existence, fearful that the sight of her would make him decide to visit her later, when the house was asleep.

Her bedroom was at the opposite end of the upstairs hall from her mother's bedroom. Rachel slept across the hall from Delia, and more than once Delia had cautioned Ray John to be quiet, lest he wake her sister. She knew where the creaks were in the old hardwood, and walked along the edge near the wall to avoid making a sound.

Her bedroom door was closed, the way she had left it, and a glance showed that Rachel's door was closed as well. She glanced back down the hall over her shoulder and saw light spilling into the hall from her parents' bedroom. Her mother was probably reading. She wondered where her father was.

Her bedroom was a place of moonlit shadows when she stepped inside. She leaned back against the door as she closed it behind her and waited for her eyes to adjust to the absence of light. Soon she could make out the familiar shapes in her room. And realized someone was lying on her bed.

"Daddy?" she whispered.

Her heart pounded as the dark figure rose from the bed without saying a word. Had someone broken into the house? Was that why her father's gun room had been left in such disarray?

"Daddy?" she said, her heart thundering so loud and fast she was afraid it was going to burst.

"Shh," her father said. "Don't make a sound."

"Mama's door is open, and her light is on. What are you doing in here?"

"Shut up!" He snarled. He grabbed her arm in a viselike grip, and she felt something small and cold pressed painfully against her temple. It took her a second to realize it was the bore of a gun.

"Where were you tonight?" he demanded.

"I went to the movies."

"Who was with you?"

"Peggy and I—"

"Don't lie to me!"

Her stomach shifted sideways. He knew. Somehow he had discovered she was out with a boy. Someone in the theater must have seen her holding hands with Marsh. Or maybe someone had seen her waiting in the truck while Marsh went inside the 7-Eleven to buy Cokes.

"I was with a boy," she said hurriedly.

"What boy?"

"I won't see him again, Daddy. I promise. I—"

He manhandled her over to the bed. "Sit down."

She perched at the very edge of the bed, poised to run if that became necessary, unsure what he was going to do next.

He turned on the light beside the bed and sat down beside her. "I thought I'd made it clear I don't want you going out with boys."

"You did, Daddy."

"You stay away from them. All of them," he said. "Otherwise, I'm going to have to take matters into my own hands and get rid of the next boy myself. It would be just this easy."

He rolled the chamber, put the revolver to his temple, and pulled the trigger.

Delia gasped.

The gun clicked on an empty chamber. "Bang," Ray John said with a ghoulish grin.

Delia shivered with revulsion.

It was something she had seen him do before when he had his guns out cleaning them. He almost always had a grin on his face, and he made a big production out of pointing the revolver at his head, knowing she was scared to death he would get hurt.

She would beg him to put the gun down. Before he did, he would pull the trigger while she waited with her heart in her throat to see if he really was going to splatter his brains all over the room. He never had. His behavior had always seemed stupid to her, but never sinister, as it did now.

He spun the chamber and put the gun to her temple again.

Fear constricted her chest, because as crazy as Ray John was acting, she wasn't sure whether there might not be a bullet—perhaps more than one—in the gun. She squeezed her eyes shut and made a whimpering sound as he pulled the trigger.

It clicked on an empty chamber.

"Have you got the message, Delia, honey?"

"Y-y-yes, Daddy," she said.

"Now get undressed for me and get in bed."

"But Mama—"

"Your mama's not home. She had to go to San Antonio to pick up some special medicine for that Grand Champion bull of hers. Don't expect she'll be back before midnight."

Delia glanced at the wind-up alarm clock beside her bed. "It's eleven-thirty now!"

"Then you better hurry on up, girl, hadn't you. Ray John's got an itch, and he wants it scratched."

That night, for the first time, Delia dreamed of murdering Ray John Carson. She shot him in the head. His brains splattered all over her pillow.

⨳ *Chapter Four* ⨳

Marsh drove his pickup to the back door of the Texas dogtrot home that had been the North ranch house for generations. In the old days, the one-story house had consisted of a central hallway—a shotgun blast going in the front door would come out the back—with two large rooms on each side.

Years later, someone had added a shaded porch out front with a couple of willow rockers for sitting and watching the sun set. A kitchen had been appended to the back of the house and, more recently, a mud porch behind that. The yellow clapboard house, with its slanted porch, peeling paint, and lopsided shutters, looked every bit of its 150 years.

Marsh had spent a great deal of his youth sleeping on the screened-in mud porch, and he had fond memories of nights lying there on an iron cot listening to the crickets and the lowing cattle and the occasional raccoon that came by to raid the garbage can out back. Sleeping outside hadn't been entirely a matter of choice. In the first years after his grandmother died, it had been safer to keep the back wall of the house between himself and his father.

Their relations hadn't improved much since.

The kitchen door wasn't locked, and Marsh let himself into the darkened house. He went directly to the knotted string that turned on the bare lightbulb above the sink. One of these days he was going to replace the broken bulb cover.

The red-and-white checkerboard linoleum laid over the hardwood floor in the 1940s had worn black in front of the sink and the refrigerator, where he retrieved a bottle of Pearl. He set the cap against the Formica counter and popped it off, then took a long, cold swig.

He found his father in the parlor. An eerie glow from the television provided the only light in the room. Cyrus North was sitting frozen, eyes glazed over, holding a longneck Pearl braced on the arm of a ragged, overstuffed chair. It looked like a scene from "The Twilight Zone."

"I'm home, Dad."

His father didn't answer. Marsh was already headed toward his room when he heard his father's favorite cop series, "Starsky and Hutch," break for a Ford Mustang commercial. His father's head swung around, and he said, "Where the hell have you been?"

"What the hell do you care?"

His father came out of the chair as though to backhand him and seemed to realize belatedly that Marsh was four inches taller than him and wasn't budging an inch. Cyrus halted in his tracks. A scowl appeared on his craggy face as he took a belligerent stance across from his son.

"If I'd ever talked to my father the way you talk to me, he'd have knocked me flat," Cyrus said.

Maybe he was more of a father to you than you've been to me, Marsh thought. But he said, "I do my share of the work around here. I don't have to account to you for where I go."

"If your mother was alive—"

"She isn't," Marsh interrupted. "She's dead. Been dead since I was born." *I'm all you've got left, Dad. Why can't you love me?*

The commercial ended, and as though a bell had sounded for the next round, Cyrus turned abruptly and settled himself back in his chair. Eyes glued to the TV set, he said, "Make sure you mend that fence along the south pasture tomorrow. Got a call from the Circle Crown foreman that a few of my cattle have strayed onto Carson property." His father smirked. "Seems that Santa Gertrudis bull Hattie Carson is so persnickety about was giving out free stud services to North cows."

Marsh made a disgusted sound in his throat as he turned away. His father had been talking for weeks about how easy it would be to shove down some fence and let a few of his cows in season stray over to where Hattie Carson's prize bull could get a sniff at them. Come spring, Cyrus would have himself some pretty good-looking calves. Damned if the old man hadn't done it.

"I'll take care of it, Dad," he said.

His father wasn't listening. He never listened. Mostly he ignored his son, except when he wanted the stock fed, or the barn roof repaired, or some fence mended. Then he wanted it done quick and done right. He had used his belt liberally, along with his fists, to give instruction—until the day fifteen-year-old Marsh had punched him back.

Marsh had been as astonished as his father when the old man hit the ground that day nearly six years ago, but it hadn't been necessary for either of them to repeat the lesson. After that his father had browbeat him with words, but he hadn't laid a hand on him again.

Marsh stepped into his bedroom and closed the door behind him, shutting out the sound of a police siren across the hall.

The room reminded him of his grandmother, the one person in the world who had ever given a damn about him. He missed her. He bought a lavender sachet at the H.E.B. every so often when he was grocery shopping and hid it under his pillow, because that was the scent she had always worn.

Doilies Grandma Dennison had crocheted adorned his bedside table and the chest. She had made the quilt on his old sleigh bed from colorful scraps of material that each had some family history she had explained to him.

"This here red is the dress your mama wore on her first date with your pa to the high school dance. Ooo-eee they were so much in love! That's why your pa gets so testy sometimes that she's not here with us anymore. And this is a piece of your pa's Air Force uniform. In the Big War he was stationed in Burma refuelin' fighter planes.

"This lace-covered satin bit is from my weddin' gown. Don't pay no 'tention to all these wrinkles I got now. Believe you me, I was one bee-u-tee-ful bride! And this flowered calico is a piece of your great-grandma Hailey's Sunday-go-to-meetin' dress."

He listened to the stories sitting cross-legged at her feet, the porch creaking as she kept her rocker moving with a boot-shod toe.

They were wonderful tales. Like, how Great-grandma Hailey had locked Great-grandpa Hailey out of the house one spring until he tilled her garden. "This piece of chambray is from the shirt he had on that day," she confided to him.

"This is part of your great aunt Eulalie's dress she wore on the train to St. Louis to meet her beau. Only, she borrowed it from me without askin', so I guess her claim to this here scrap of cotton is only secondhand.

"And this here patch is from your first pair of long pants. I made 'em myself. Kinda cute, don't ya think, boy?"

He could remember feeling agonizingly embarrassed as a nine-year-old by the scrap of pale blue denim embroidered with a brown teddy bear. Now every time he glimpsed it while making his bed, he got a lump in his throat.

A photograph of his grandmother as a young woman sat on the copper-plated dry sink. It was the only thing he had that gave him even a remote idea what his mother might have looked like. He had overheard his grandmother confiding to a friend that his father had torn up every last picture of Rosemary North in front of Marsh's crib one night in a drunken frenzy.

If it hadn't been for Grandma Dennison telling him again and again that his father was only grieving, that he didn't mean the awful names he called his son, Marsh might have turned out a lot worse than he had.

As it was, he had absorbed enough of his father's invective in the years after his grandmother's death to become the worst discipline problem Uvalde High School had ever known. He had been angry with his father and taken it out on the whole world.

He had spent almost as much time suspended from high school—for smoking in the bathroom, disrespect to teachers, and fighting—as he had in class. He lost his driver's license the third time Sheriff Davis caught him driving drunk. He was nabbed shoplifting at Shepherd's clothing store on Getty Street and spent an uncomfortable hour sitting on an upended wooden crate in the storage room until his father came to get him. Cyrus had paid for the fancy tooled leather belt Marsh had swiped, then taken him home and beaten him with it.

Because of his looks—and because he seemed reckless and a little bit dangerous—a lot of wide-eyed girls had been his for the asking. He had taken his share of them out in his pickup and kissed them and held them and pretended he had more experience than he really did.

Gloria Perkins, the mother of one of his classmates, had seduced him the summer he turned sixteen. After that, he had found girls with reputations like his who would go all the way. He had been lucky none of them ever got pregnant. It sure wasn't because he had been careful, because he hadn't.

A short stint for vandalism in the Texas Youth Commission's Brownwood Correctional Facility—he had spray painted some downright nasty words on the bus of a visiting football team—had made him realize that his father wasn't suffering as much from his antics as he was. After that, he had pretty much straightened up his act, at least enough to finish high school.

Of course, the damage to his reputation was already done. In a small town, once you'd made a name for yourself, it was pretty near impossible to change people's opinion of you. He was known in Uvalde as "that wild North boy" and would be until the day he died.

It had never much mattered to him what people thought. Until now. He had an idea what kind of hassle his reputation was going to cause with Delia Carson's family. She was the pampered princess of the Circle Crown. He was the town's bad boy.

Why had Delia agreed to go out with him in the first place? Maybe there was a little bit of rebel in her, too. All Marsh could think about was seeing her again. He wondered whether she would show up at the live oak to meet him. He hoped she would. It surprised him just how much it mattered.

Delia knew she was asking for trouble. Her father had made it plain what the consequences would be if he caught her with Marsh North. But it had occurred to her as he held a gun to her head and threatened her, that he might kill her someday whether she was guilty or not. She might as well be guilty.

When she arrived at the spot where North was supposed to be waiting for her, she was disappointed to find he wasn't there. She stepped down off her horse in the shade of an ancient, moss-draped live oak and tied the reins out of the way on the saddle horn so her palomino gelding wouldn't step on them as he grazed.

She stuck her hands in the back pockets of her jeans and stood with her hip cocked, staring across the barbed wire fence dividing Carson cultivated pasture and North scrubland, wondering what she should do now.

"Hi."

She whirled so fast she lost her balance and nearly fell before North steadied her. She stepped back as soon as she could free herself from his grasp, but it was too late to avoid the jolt of pleasure where his callused fingertips had touched her.

"Where did you come from?" she asked, as annoyed at being scared half to death as she was glad to find him there.

"I was leaning up against the other side of

the tree. I heard you coming, and I wanted to see if I could surprise you."

"You did," she said. "Where's your horse?"

Marsh pointed, and she made out the rangy buckskin camouflaged behind the tall yellow grass and a thick patch of scrub mesquite on the North side of the fence.

"Do you want to ride some more right now, or would you like to rest a while?" he asked.

"The shade is nice," she said, lifting her hair to let the breeze catch the sweat on her nape. She saw his nostrils flare and felt her body tighten like a drawstring. "Why don't we sit here for a while." Her knees felt weak. If she didn't sit down, she was going to fall.

She made it the few steps to the base of the live oak and settled herself on a thick branch growing about a foot off the ground. To her consternation, Marsh sat so close their thighs nearly touched.

She noticed the ring of sweat around his hatband and the grass stains on the knees of his jeans. She pointed to the leather gloves hanging out of his back pocket and asked, "What was so important it had to get done on a Sunday morning?"

"I had some fence to repair."

She chuckled and relaxed against the rough bark of a slightly higher branch of the tree behind her. "I don't think that's going to make Max very happy."

"Who's Max?"

"My mother's Grand Champion Santa Gertrudis bull. I think he was enjoying the company."

A muscle worked in Marsh's jaw. "My father shouldn't have done it. It was stealing, plain and simple."

Her eyes widened. The town's bad boy was constantly amazing her. She waited for him to continue the conversation, but he didn't say anything, just stared at his boots.

"Do you work for your father?"

He nodded. "There's more than the two of us can handle sometimes. I've been trying to talk him into hiring some help, but he doesn't want strangers around."

"They wouldn't be strangers for long once they started working for you."

"That's what I told him, but there's no making him see reason. Sometimes I get so mad I feel like quitting."

"Why don't you?" Delia asked.

From the startled look on Marsh's face, the idea had never occurred to him. "What else would I do?"

She shrugged. "I don't know. What would you like to do?"

"I never really thought about being anything but a rancher. How about you? What are you planning to do when you graduate from high school?"

"I'm going to college." She took a deep breath and added, "Then I'm going to law school."

Marsh whistled. His face cracked into an amused grin. "Those are pretty big plans for such a little lady."

Delia bristled. "These days a woman can be anything she wants. I want to be a lawyer."

"Why?"

"I . . ." She narrowed her eyes at him. "You'll laugh."

"I promise not to laugh," Marsh said, crossing his heart with a forefinger. "Tell me."

She wasn't sure he wouldn't laugh, but she had been wanting to talk to someone about her plans for the future, and it wasn't anything she could comfortably discuss around her father. And these days, her father seldom left her alone with her mother.

She took a deep breath and said, "I want to be a lawyer so I can help kids in trouble."

Marsh's brow furrowed. "Like juvenile delinquents?"

"Not exactly. Kids who have problems."

"What did you have in mind?" Marsh asked.

"Kids who . . ." She shrugged, unwilling even to hint at her own problems. "I don't know. Just helping in whatever way I can."

"Sounds dumb to me," he said.

She socked his shoulder with her fist. "I knew you would laugh!"

"Hey!" he said, catching her wrist. "Not one chuckle escaped my lips."

Their eyes met and held. His thumb caressed her knuckles. Her pulse leaped.

"Delia . . ." His voice was raw and needy.

She leaned toward him and he leaned toward her and their mouths met, softness on softness. Her body quivered. She swallowed, and their lips parted. But their faces remained so close she would have had to look cross-eyed to see him.

Delia wanted more but knew she should quit now before things went too far. Her hand had somehow found its way to Marsh's forearm. It was rock hard with tension. But she didn't move away. She didn't move at all.

Her eyes slipped closed as Marsh lowered his mouth to hers once more. His kiss was hungry this time, his lips and teeth and tongue devouring her mouth, though no other part of him touched her. Her hand on his arm remained the only other contact between them.

Feelings rose inside her, emotions so powerful and compelling they frightened her. She jerked her mouth free and sat staring at Marsh, panting, wide-eyed. But she didn't stand up. She didn't run away. Neither did he.

"Delia."

The sound of his voice rasped over her, making her shiver. She had just met him. She didn't know him. Yet she wanted to belong to him. It was crazy. She was crazy.

"Marsh." Just his name. Said with yearning.

She wasn't sure who moved first, but a moment later he held her clasped tight and her arms were around his waist and their mouths had merged.

Her breasts were crushed against the hard wall of his chest, and her hips slid into the cradle of his widespread legs. His hands curved around her buttocks and pulled her tight against him so she could feel his arousal.

Alarm bells went off in her head.

She wrenched her mouth from his and

struggled to free herself. "Let me go, Marsh," she cried. "Let me go!"

He let her go and took a step back, but there was nothing understanding about the look on his face. He was madder than a rained-on rooster.

"What the hell is going on, Delia?" he demanded. "Don't try to say you didn't want to be kissed, because I was hearing yes all the way!"

"I know, but . . ."

"But nothing!"

Tears welled in her eyes, but his face didn't soften with sympathy. His jaw stayed locked, and his fists remained clenched.

"What kind of game are you playing? Did you make a bet with somebody? Is that it? You'll get me all hot and bothered and see how far you can make me go?"

"No!" she retorted. "It's nothing at all like that!"

"Then what the hell is going on?"

Delia nearly blurted the truth. She caught herself in time. Marsh wouldn't want anything to do with her if he knew what went on in her house. "I'm not playing games, Marsh," she said in a subdued voice. "I . . . I simply never realized how fast . . . I never wanted . . . like I want you."

"What's stopping you?"

"I . . . I just can't."

"Saving yourself for your husband?" he sneered.

She flushed to the roots of her hair.

He shoved a hand through his hair and paced away from her before turning back to demand, "Why did you go out with me in the first place? Why did you come here today?"

"I like you. I had a wonderful time with you last night. I thought we could be friends."

His lips curled up on one side, and he shook his head. "I'm not someone most people would choose for a friend."

"I'm not most people."

He stared at her suspiciously for a moment longer. "You really want a friend?"

"Yes, I do."

"All right." He held out his hand for her to shake. "You got one."

She smiled and tentatively laid her hand in his. Sparks flew. Her gaze shot to his, and she discovered he was equally affected by the simple clasp of hands. She looked down at their joined hands and back up at him. Slowly, carefully, she eased her hand from his and threaded her fingers together to avoid reaching out to him again.

"Can I be perfectly honest with you?" she said.

"I wish you would."

"The truth is . . . I like it when you touch me. I mean, when you kiss me and hold me. Isn't there some way we could do that without . . . without the other?"

"You mean, just neck and pet and not go all the way."

That was plain speaking. She felt her cheeks heat. "Yes, that's it exactly."

He stood with his hip cocked, his hands stuck in his back pockets in an imitation of her earlier stance. "I guess so. It's hard . . . Sometimes, if things go too far, it's hard to stop."

"But you would stop if I asked, wouldn't you?"

"I'll do anything you want, if you'll keep on seeing me."

Her smile broadened. "Then we're agreed?"

"Agreed. Shake on it?"

He held out his hand, and she put hers in it. He pumped it up and down twice. There was an awkward moment before they let go of each other, followed by a longing to connect again. Delia resisted it. She needed more time to get used to him, for the electricity to wear off between them, for them to become more comfortable with each other.

"I think we should take that horseback ride now," she said.

"You're probably right," he said. "Would you rather ride on Circle Crown or North property?"

"It might be better if we rode on your land."

"All right. I'll open the gate, and you can come on over."

They rode for the better part of the afternoon, and Marsh showed her the borders of his father's property. He didn't take her anywhere near his house, because his father was there.

"My dad could turn out to be as big a nuisance as your father if he saw us together," Marsh told her.

"In what way?" she asked.

"He's . . . I'd rather not talk about him."

"All right," Delia said. "No more talk about fathers."

"You've got a deal," Marsh replied.

Delia managed any number of clandestine meetings with Marsh over the summer. They talked a blue streak when they were together about anything and everything. Except their fathers. By mutual agreement, their fathers were off-limits as a topic of conversation.

And they kissed and touched, learning each other's bodies, learning what felt good and what felt better. She knew it was hard for Marsh, but he always stopped before the critical moment.

"Lord have mercy, Delia, that was close," Marsh said one afternoon as they lay panting in the grass beneath the live oak that had become their trysting place.

Delia's head was on Marsh's shoulder, and her hand lay across his naked belly. Her sleeveless pink blouse was unbuttoned, and her bra was scrunched up around her throat. Her nipples were damp from his mouth. The sensible white cotton panties she wore had been shoved down by Marsh's hand inside them, so only flesh showed in the V created by her unzipped jeans.

They were too exhausted to rearrange their clothing, their bodies still shivering from orgasmic tremors. A wet spot stained the front of Marsh's jeans.

"I want to be inside you so bad . . ." Marsh

groaned against her throat. "I can't stand it, Delia. I . . . I love you. I want us to belong to each other."

Delia stiffened, and Marsh put a hand beneath her chin to force her face up to his. She resisted.

"Look at me."

She glanced up at him, then hid beneath lowered lashes.

"I want you to marry me when you graduate from high school next year. I want us to spend our lives together. I promise you won't regret it. I promise I'll take care of you."

Delia felt her nose sting. Her eyes burned with unshed tears. "Oh, Marsh, don't! I've told you what I want to do with my life."

"That was before we fell in love."

"What makes you think I love you?" she demanded, her blue eyes flashing up at him.

"I know everything about you, Delia."

She stared at him aghast. Then realized he didn't know everything—at least, not the most revolting thing. She rolled away from him and onto her knees, tripped on her jeans as she stood and pulled them up, then stuck her hand back down inside to straighten out her underwear as she rearranged her clothing.

She turned to confront him. "You don't know what I feel inside, Marsh North, what I need most. Otherwise, you'd know I have no intention of staying in this podunk town one instant after I graduate. I'm going away and make something of myself."

He had come off the ground the same time

she had and was buttoning up his jeans with one hand while he reached down to snag his shirt from a low limb of the tree with the other. "What does that make me? Nothing?"

She froze and shot a stricken look at him. "Oh, Marsh, no, I didn't mean that you—"

"What did you mean, Delia?"

She came to him and laid her cheek against his bare chest and circled his waist with her arms. She heard his shirt drop and felt his arms close around her. "Knowing you . . . falling in love with you . . . has been the best thing that's ever happened to me," she said.

"Then why do you want to leave?"

Delia let herself look fully into his eyes for the space of a heartbeat. She saw the hope there, the yearning, and it tore her apart to think of leaving him behind. "I have to, that's all."

"Say you'll come back to me," Marsh urged. "Say you'll be my wife."

Surely her stepfather wouldn't dare touch her if she were Marsh's wife. *Marsh's wife.* It had a lovely sound. She did love him, so very much. "I promise I'll think about it."

Her promise appeased Marsh, and he lowered her back down to the ground for another bout of deliciously dangerous—because it had to remain unconsummated—lovemaking. The subject of the future was put aside. Delia refused to think about it, because she had her whole senior year of high school to make up her mind. For now, she loved Marsh, and he loved her. She glowed with happiness.

Marsh's offer of marriage gave her the courage to do something she had wanted to do for a long time. At supper that night she whispered to her father that she needed to talk to him privately.

"Sure, baby," Ray John said. "After your mom leaves for San Antonio, I'll come to your room."

She wished she had the nerve to tell her father to meet her somewhere else, but the moment passed, and she resigned herself to meeting Ray John—one last time—in her bedroom.

She didn't undress for bed that night. She sat waiting for Ray John to come, her heart in her throat, her body as tight as new-strung barbed wire.

"Your mama's gotta finish her phone call before she leaves, but I thought we could get started on our talk right now," Ray John said as he closed her bedroom door behind him and locked it. "Why aren't you in bed waitin' for me?"

She was sitting cross-legged on her bed, fully dressed, with every light in the room on. She looked him in the eye and said, "I can't do this anymore, Daddy."

He walked around the room systematically shutting off lights. "Now, doll baby, if you've got a problem, Daddy'll fix it." When only the dainty ballerina lamp beside her bed was still on, he sat down next to her and put a hand on her knee. "What do you mean, you can't do this anymore?"

"I mean I want you to stop coming to my room," she said.

His hand started up the inside of her leg. When she tried to scoot backward out of his way, his hand tightened painfully on her thigh.

"See here, missy," he said in a hard voice. "That's enough of that."

"I won't do it, Daddy," she said, her heart racing, her whole body tensed to fight or to flee. "If you try to force me, I'll scream."

"Your mama will come runnin' if you do."

"I don't care if she does," Delia blurted. "I don't care if she knows!"

"She won't believe a word you say," Ray John said in a silky voice. "'Specially with me just sittin' here, and you all dressed. She'll think you made it up."

Delia was having trouble catching her breath, she was so scared. "I'll . . . I'll tell someone at school. They'll believe me." It was a bluff. She was terrified he would call it.

"Well, now, honey, if that's the way you really feel, I s'pose I gotta leave you alone. But I've got these itches, and somebody's gonna have to scratch 'em." He rose from her bed and headed for the door. "Guess I'll just have to go across the hall and see your sister."

"Wait!" Delia was off the bed in an instant and grabbed hold of Ray John's arm to keep him from opening the door. "Daddy, you can't! Rachel's barely twelve!"

"Same age as you were, sweetie. Course, she ain't comin' along as fast as you did. But she'll grow."

Delia felt sick. Stomach acid crawled back up her throat. For a moment she almost let him go. Her chin dropped in defeat.

"Don't leave, Daddy. Stay here with me."

"Why, Delia, honey, have you gone and changed your mind on me?"

"Yes, Daddy."

"You know what I like."

Hattie called up the stairs, "So long, Ray John. I'm leaving now."

Ray John unlocked Delia's door, leaned out, and called down, "Hurry back, darlin'. I'll be missin' you every minute."

He closed Delia's door and leaned back against it while she undressed down to her white cotton bra and panties. She left them on, because he liked to take them off himself. She folded the bedcovers down, then slid under them and lay on the left side of the double bed, flat on her back. The last thing she did was turn down the covers on the other side of the bed to a welcoming angle for him.

Delia turned the light off and heard two thumps as each of Ray John's boots hit the rag rug beside her bed, then the rustle of denim and cotton as Ray John stripped himself naked. He slipped under the covers, and she could smell the sweat he hadn't washed off after a day of work on the ranch. He usually showered afterward, before he got in bed with her mother. Delia's breath caught as he laid his hand on her belly.

"Delia, honey," he said as his hand slid

down between her legs, "you are the absolute best daughter a man could have."

Delia could not honestly return the compliment.

❧ *Chapter Five* ❧

Marsh stood at the Carson's kitchen door trying to summon up the guts to knock on it. He rubbed his sweaty palms along the sides of his jeans, formed a fist, and pounded the screen door twice. His heart was caterwhomping in his chest.

It was barely dawn. Most ranchers hereabouts had already done an hour or two of work and were heading for the Kincaid Hotel in town to have a cup of coffee and trade the latest market information on beef and mohair, the other cash crop in Uvalde. Marsh hoped to catch Ray John Carson before he left home. His hands were damp again by the time the Carsons' housekeeper answered his knock.

"Buenos dias, señor."

He tried to speak, couldn't, cleared his throat and said, "I'm Marshall North. I'd like to see Mr. Carson."

"Come inside, señor. I will get him for you."

The housekeeper left him standing inside the door. As he looked around, he got a harsh reminder of how far above his reach Delia Carson was. Most of the North ranch house would have fit in the Carson kitchen. It was filled with shiny appliances, including one of those new-fangled microwave ovens that cooked without heat. The brick-tiled floor didn't have a single chip that he could see. And the kitchen table was nothing like the gouged red Formica surface he and his father ate off of. He ran his callused fingertips over the polished oak, jerking his hand away when the maid reappeared. "*Señor* Carson will see you."

Marsh stood dumbstruck when she turned and left again, until he realized he was supposed to follow her.

She led him down the hall to a high-ceilinged room filled with guns in glass cases. The wooden shutters were closed, not that there was much daylight yet, even if they'd been open. An intensely bright lamp on the desk provided a circle of light on the cluttered surface.

Delia's father sat facing a desk where a revolver was spread out in pieces on a cloth in front of him. He appeared to be cleaning it. Delia's younger sister, Rachel, sat perched on a ladderback chair beside him. She was wearing short shorts and tennis shoes. The ribbon on her blond ponytail matched her sleeveless powder blue shirt.

"What can I do for you?" Ray John asked without looking up from what he was doing.

Marsh glanced at Rachel, who gave him a

curious look back. "I wanted to speak with you. Alone."

"I'm giving Rachel a lesson here. You want to talk? Talk."

Marsh felt a furious sense of futility. When he and Delia had met the previous day, he had told her what he wanted to do. She had warned him not to try.

"He won't listen, Marsh," she had said. "He doesn't want me dating and that's that. You'd be wasting your time trying to get permission to see me."

It seemed she had been right. Carson wasn't even going to do him the courtesy of speaking with him privately. He felt like turning right around and marching back the way he had come. Except, he wanted something he could only get from the other man. He reined his temper and said, "I want your permission to date Delia."

"Check to see the bore is clean," Ray John said to Rachel, completely ignoring Marsh's statement as though it hadn't been spoken.

Marsh wasn't sure what to do except keep talking. "I would treat her with respect, and I would abide by whatever rules you want to set down."

"Everything fits back together exactly the way it came apart," Ray John said, putting the gun together with a rapidity that amazed Marsh. When Ray John was done, he held the 1876 model Colt Peacemaker in his hand and admired it. "A Colt .45 is a thing of utter beauty."

Ray John put the gun to Rachel's temple. "And certain death."

"Hey!" Marsh yelped in protest. His heart climbed to his throat. He hadn't seen Ray John put any bullets in the gun, yet a glance at the desk revealed several—four—bullets scattered on the cloth. Had Ray John loaded the gun when he wasn't looking?

Rachel's eyes were closed, and her hands tightly gripped the edge of the desk. She sat absolutely still.

Ray John looked at Marsh intently, pulled the brass trigger, and said, "Bang."

Marsh felt a shudder go through him as Rachel's body jerked. "Hey!" he said again. "What's the big idea? You could have killed her!"

"You think there are bullets in here? Weren't you watching?" Ray John put the gun to his own head and, as Marsh watched in horror, pulled the trigger again. "Bang," he said.

Marsh gasped.

Ray John laughed. "If you could only see the look on your face!"

"You're sick," Marsh blurted.

Ray John's smile disappeared, and Marsh could have kicked himself for insulting the man—even if he was sick. He was on thin enough ice as it was. He wanted Ray John's permission to see Delia. He was tired of sneaking around, tired of hiding. This had seemed the best way to solve the problem. But he could see now that coming here had been a mistake.

"What you were doing looked dangerous," Marsh said, the only concession toward apology he was willing to make.

Ray John's hand settled on Rachel's nape, and his eyes narrowed on Marsh. "It's only a game we play. Right, Rachel?"

"Yes, Daddy," Rachel said. "Can I go now? I have to get ready for Vacation Bible School."

Ray John gave her a kiss on the cheek and a pat on the rump as she ran from the room. Marsh caught the disapproving look Rachel gave him on her way by.

Ray John reverently placed the Peacemaker back in its place in one of the cabinets, locked it in, then carried the ring of skeleton keys to his desk and set it down. He folded up the cloth, then pulled the rolltop down and locked it, putting that key in his wallet.

"Now, then, what was it you wanted? Oh, yes. Permission to date my daughter." He turned to face Marsh, his hands gripping the back of the desk chair. "The answer is no."

"But—"

"If you so much as come near Delia, I will personally take one of these guns and shoot you dead."

Marsh paled. "You can't threaten me like that."

Ray John smiled unpleasantly. "I already have. You and yours are trash, North. Believe me, I'll convince Sheriff Davis it was necessary to shoot you. Stay away from my daughter, or so help me, I'll kill you."

At that moment Delia arrived, breathless, at the door to the gun room. "Rachel said—

Marsh! What are you doing here?" It was almost a wail.

"I came to ask your father—"

"Has this saddle bum been botherin' you, Delia?" Ray John asked.

Marsh met her stricken glance. *Tell him what we mean to each other. Fight for us*, he pleaded with his eyes.

"No, Daddy," she said at last.

Ray John held out his arms. "Come here, Delia, honey."

In front of Marsh's disbelieving eyes, Delia crossed past him as though she didn't know him. She kept going until she reached her father. Ray John put an arm around her shoulder and turned her to face Marsh.

"You haven't been seein' this boy behind my back, have you now, darlin'?"

Marsh watched Ray John's fingers tighten like claws on Delia's shoulder. He silently urged her to look at him, but she kept her gaze lowered.

"No, Daddy. You know I wouldn't do that."

"Take yourself outta here, boy, and don't ever let me catch you sniffin' 'round my girl again."

Marsh didn't say another word, simply turned and left the house. His chest felt as though someone had tightened a steel band around it. He got into his truck and gunned the engine viciously, a mechanical cry of rage as he raced away.

He felt hurt and confused. Angry and frustrated. No wonder Delia hadn't wanted him to confront her father. The man was certifiably crazy. Marsh had only made the situation worse: Ray John had forbidden him to see Delia. Her father was certain to keep a closer watch on her now. It would be harder than ever to find a safe time and place to meet.

Marsh wanted to tell someone what he had witnessed that morning. He wanted to rescue Delia and her sister from their insane father's clutches. But he could just see Sheriff Davis's look of disbelief if he went to him with his story. Ray John would surely twist Marsh's early morning visit to his advantage. Who could blame a father who refused to let the town's bad boy date his daughter? The sheriff would end up laughing in Marsh's face.

He shouldn't have accepted Ray John's no. He should have argued with the man. He would have, if Delia had given him any encouragement. But she had let him stand there like some stranger she hardly knew. She had said nothing, done nothing. He could understand why she had remained silent. But it didn't bode well for their future together.

They were supposed to meet at the live oak at noon. He intended to be there to ask Delia where they were supposed to go from here.

Delia couldn't believe what Marsh had done. How could he have come to her house and confronted her father like that? What had he been thinking? She had told him it would be no use. It had taken a great deal of persuasion after Marsh left to convince Ray John that Marsh meant nothing to her, that he was merely someone she had met when she was tubing with the other kids. She wasn't entirely sure he believed her.

They were still discussing the matter when her mother appeared at the door. Delia wished she could believe an ally had arrived, but she knew better.

Hattie Carson might have held the reins of the Circle Crown with an iron hand that wouldn't let go even for Ray John Carson, but where Delia and Rachel were concerned, her mother catered to Ray John's every wish or whim.

He thought the girls should learn how to handle a gun? Fine. He didn't want Delia to date? Fine. He wanted Rachel to come right home after school? Fine. He wanted Rachel in bed by 9:00 P.M.? Fine. Delia needed a lock on her door? Fine.

Delia would never understand how a woman who ran a ranching empire the size of the Circle Crown practically single-handed could let herself be manipulated by some slick-as-goose-grease cowboy. But she did. At least where her daughters were concerned. The unpleasant conclusion Delia had drawn was that the ranch meant more to Hattie than her own flesh and blood.

"What's all the commotion about?" Hattie asked as she stepped into Ray John's gun room. "Rachel said we had a visitor."

"That good-for-nothing North boy was here," Ray John said, "wantin' my permission to date Delia."

Hattie's eyes widened in alarm. "You refused, of course."

"You damn bet I did!"

Delia dared a glance into her mother's silvery blue eyes. "Marsh seems like a nice person," she said.

"He's about the worst juvenile delinquent this town has ever known," Hattie corrected. "Stay away from him, Delia. A boy like that will only cause you trouble."

"But, Mama—"

"Not another word about it, Delia. Your father has spoken."

"And that's it?" Delia demanded, her eyes flashing up to meet her mother's startled gaze. "Daddy speaks, and we all obey?"

"Delia!" her mother exclaimed. "What on earth has come over you?"

"I should be able to see whoever I want. I'm not a child anymore, Mama. I'm nearly grown."

"You're not too big for me to tan your hide," Ray John threatened.

Delia gasped. "You wouldn't dare!"

"Both of you stop it," Hattie ordered. "Your father only has your best interests at heart, Delia. The two of you say you're sorry and make up."

"I'm sorry, Delia, honey." Ray John slipped his arm around her waist and pinched her hard on her backside where her mother couldn't see.

Delia winced, but she had caught his warning. She would pay for her defiance.

Oh, how she wanted to blurt out everything to her mother, to tear the mask from Ray John's smiling face and reveal the fiend he was. But it was clear from this small venture into rebellion that her father was right about one thing. When it came to disagreements between her husband and her daughter, her mother was always going to take Ray John's side.

"I'm sorry, Daddy," Delia mumbled.

"There, isn't that better?" Hattie said, putting her arm around Delia from the other side so the three of them were linked. "It took me a while to find the right man, but I'm a fortunate woman to have such a loving husband and wonderful father for you two girls."

Delia felt a sinking feeling in the pit of her stomach, but with Ray John's eyes boring into her she said nothing to contradict her mother.

Fifteen minutes later at the breakfast table, Delia watched her father's eyes narrow as she explained how she and Peggy were going riding and taking along a picnic lunch. He looked suspicious, but he only said, "You girls stay in the south pasture. I don't want you anywhere near the North fence line. Do you understand?"

"All right, Daddy," she promised, knowing full well she intended to disobey him.

She met Peggy as planned at eleven-thirty and warned, "My dad expects me to be riding in the south pasture. I'll meet you by the south gate in a couple of hours, okay?"

"My mom's starting to get suspicious."

"You don't think she'll call my parents, do you?" Delia asked with alarm.

"Naw. But I'll be glad when school starts in

a few weeks. There'll be a lot more good excuses for us to get together then."

Delia kicked her gelding into a lope. "Be back in two hours," she called over her shoulder.

"Delia! Wait, I—"

Delia kept going. Her horse was lathered by the time she reached the live oak. Marsh was leaning against the tree waiting for her. He came forward to catch her as she took her left foot from the stirrup, lifted her right leg up over the horse's neck, and slid down into his arms.

They hugged tightly, as though they had been separated longer than the twenty-four hours since they had last held each other, as though they hadn't seen each other six hours ago.

"I thought you'd never get here, Delia. I was afraid you weren't coming, that your father would keep you at home." Marsh clung to Delia, overwhelmed by the fear that their time together was coming to an end, that this was only a respite and that disaster loomed.

She pressed her face against his shoulder. "He suspects something. I know he does. What are we going to do?"

"I was going to ask you the same question."

"Daddy will be watching me like a hawk from now on. It's going to be harder than ever to get away." She leaned back and gave him a despairing look from beneath lowered lids. "I warned you not to come to the house. Why did you do it, Marsh?"

He levered her an arm's length away. "Because I'm tired of sneaking around. Because I want us to be together without having to meet like this."

"We have no choice!"

"Are you ashamed of me, Delia?"

She shot him a look of disbelief. "How can you even think such a thing!"

Marsh let her go and shoved a restless hand through his hair. "I don't know what to think. I only know I want to be able to take you places, enjoy a movie holding hands, have pie and coffee at the Amber Sky. Is that asking so much?"

"No. I suppose not. Except my father won't allow it."

"There has to be a way to get around your father."

Delia folded her arms defensively across her chest. "There isn't. Why do you think I want to go away to college?"

He grasped her shoulders. "I feel like I'm already losing you."

"We have another year, Marsh."

"Another year of pretending we're strangers when we meet in public? Another year of slinking around meeting you in secret?" His hands tightened on her flesh, but he could already feel her slipping from his grasp.

"Would you rather we stopped seeing each other?"

He ground his teeth. "That's not a choice. I need you too much." The words were torn from him, from somewhere deep inside him.

"I need you, too. Please don't be angry with me. I don't dare defy my father. You've seen

him. He gets so mean when he's angry.
He . . ."

Her tears surprised him. And made his
throat ache.

His arms slid around her, and he pressed his
cheek to hers. "Don't cry, Delia. Please, don't
cry. We'll figure out a way to be together.
Whatever it takes, whatever we have to do,
that's what we'll do."

"I . . . I love you, Marsh."

He felt her clutch at his neck. She burrowed
her face against his chest as though to get inside his skin. He wondered if she felt the same
sense of desperation he did.

They heard the sound of hoofbeats at the
same time. It took only a second for them to
identify the rider.

"It's my father!" Delia cried. "Oh, God,
Marsh! You can't let him find you here with
me. Hide! Quick!"

"I'm not leaving you alone to face him,"
Marsh said.

"Damn it, Marsh, do what I ask," Delia said,
enraged and terrified. "I can handle him if
you're not here. Just go, please!"

"I'll hide in the brush on the other side of
the fence," he said. "I'll be watching, Delia. If
he tries to hurt you—"

"He won't. Just go!" She gave him a push
and watched him urge his horse through the
pasture gate and into the tall yellow grass
where he had hidden it the first time she had
met him there. A moment later, no sign of either him or his horse remained. But she knew
he was there. She could feel his eyes on her.

She turned to face her father, forcing back the terror she felt at his sudden appearance. Had he followed her? Had he already seen her with Marsh? What could she say to explain her presence here when he had told her to stay away?

"Hi, Daddy," she said as he stepped down off his horse. The animal had been ridden hard. Its legs and neck were shiny with sweat, and a salty lather covered its chest.

"I went lookin' for you and your friend in the south pasture. Peggy was there, but you weren't. What are you doin' here, Delia? Did you come here to meet that boy?"

"No, Daddy, I—"

He grabbed her arm and yanked her toward him. "I told you I don't want you seein' him."

"I wasn't," she cried. "I—"

"Don't lie to me!" he snarled. "I know what you're up to, miss hot pants. Don't think I don't! You've had a taste of it, and now you want to try a different flavor. I got news for you, doll baby. Ain't no man puttin' himself inside what's mine! Is that clear?"

Delia felt physically ill. Her face bleached as the blood left it in a rush. "Daddy, I—" Her throat closed, making speech impossible.

"Get on your goddamn horse and get home!"

Ray John gave her a shove toward her horse. She stumbled and nearly fell. When she caught her balance, she saw that Marsh had risen from his hiding place. His face was grim, his hands fisted, his body taut. She shot him a horrified look and mouthed a desperate "No!"

He ducked back down as her father turned to face her again.

"Starting right now," Ray John said, "you're grounded. You're not to leave the house till school starts. You can forget about seein' that North kid again. As far as you're concerned, he no longer exists.

"You're not goin' anywhere I can't keep an eye on you. Get my drift?"

She got it, all right. She was trapped. Trapped forever.

She ran to her horse and clambered on. While her father mounted she glanced quickly toward the spot where Marsh was hiding and saw a flash of color.

He had heard every word her father said. He must have figured out the truth by now. The blood that had left her face came back in a rush, until she felt as though her whole body was on fire. She wanted to crawl into a hole and die.

Ray John slapped his reins on her gelding's rump and the animal bolted. She leaned into the gallop, running away from Marsh as fast as she could, knowing she was leaving behind any hope she had ever had of a life beyond her father's reach.

∞ *Chapter Six* ∞

Delia lay huddled under the covers in her bed crying. She should be having her period. For the second time in two months, it hadn't come. The first time she had ignored the problem, hoping it would resolve itself. This time she couldn't. She didn't know what to do. She didn't know where to turn.

She hadn't seen Marsh since the incident three weeks ago with her father. Marsh had tried to contact her through Peggy, but she had refused to see him. She couldn't bear to see him. Not after what he had heard.

Now, when she had thought things couldn't get worse, something worse had happened.

She was pregnant.

It wasn't only the missed periods. She had been sick in the mornings, and her breasts were painfully tender. She was not so ignorant that she didn't recognize the signs. Her senior year of high school started in two days. She would be delivering a baby, instead of a valedictory address, at graduation.

She needed to tell someone.

She couldn't tell anyone.

Oh, God, what was she going to do?

Wretched sobs racked her body, and she muffled them against her pillow. She didn't hear her door open. She didn't know anyone was in the room until she felt a hand on her shoulder.

She jerked herself upright and found herself reflected in Rachel's worried hazel eyes.

Rachel sat in her nightgown on the edge of the bed, one leg tucked under her. The first rays of morning light touched her tangled hair and turned it golden. "Delia? Are you all right?"

A tear crawled its way down Delia's cheek. She brushed it angrily away, and clutched her pillow tight against her chest. "Do I look all right?"

Rachel stared down at the hands knotted tightly in her lap. "Did Daddy hurt you, too?"

Delia's heart stopped. For a whole second. "What?"

Rachel glanced up, and Delia saw the age-less look of despair in her sister's eyes.

"I cried, too, Delia. It hurts awfully, doesn't it?"

"Rachel . . . Did Daddy . . . ?" She didn't need to ask. She knew. And felt a terrible, ungovernable rage. Ray John had said if she let him keep using her, he would leave Rachel alone. But he hadn't.

Rachel's revelation also explained why Ray John hadn't come to Delia's room once in the past three weeks. Delia had thought it was because he was angry with her. He must have been going to her sister's bed instead. Oh, poor Rachel!

"He loves us, Delia. He doesn't mean to hurt us," Rachel said in a small voice.

Delia recognized the words. They were what Ray John had told her in the beginning, too. She knew them now for the lies they were.

"He doesn't love us," Delia countered. "He doesn't love anyone but himself."

"I . . . I hate him, Delia," Rachel whispered. "I wish he were dead."

Delia watched the tears spurt from her sister's eyes at this horrendous confession. "Oh, Rachel."

The two sisters clung to one another.

"We have to tell Mama," Delia said. "We have to go to her and tell her what he's done to both of us."

"We can't!" Rachel said. "Daddy said—"

"I know all the things he's said to keep us from telling on him," Delia said. "But Mama has to believe both of us together. She won't have any choice."

"I can't tell Mama. I can't," Rachel wailed.

"Shh," Delia crooned. "Don't cry." She brushed the blond curls back from Rachel's face and kissed the tears from her cheeks. "I'll do it for both of us. Mark my words. If Mama gets mad at anyone, it'll be Ray John, not us. We haven't done anything wrong."

Rachel looked at her with hope . . . and fear. "Are you sure, Delia?"

"It wasn't your fault, Rachel. And it wasn't mine."

Delia felt very powerful suddenly. She would never be a victim again. Ray John had crossed the line when he defiled her sister. Delia was going to make sure he paid for his sins. It was a good thing, she realized, that she would be speaking to her mother alone. Rachel didn't need to hear the full extent of their father's heinous deeds. She didn't need to know he had impregnated his elder daughter.

Delia thought of having to leave home to go have her baby somewhere else. Somewhere nobody knew her. She felt an ache of loneliness. And a deepening hatred for Ray John Carson.

"I'll go see her now," Delia said. "You go to your room and lock the door and don't let anyone but me or Mama in."

"What if Daddy comes? Sometimes he does, when he gets back from the Kincaid. What if he orders me to unlock the door?"

"Tell him he isn't allowed in your bedroom anymore."

"I can't do that," Rachel said, aghast.

"You can. And you will."

Delia escorted her sister across the hall and gave her a hug. "I'm sorry, Rachel," she murmured. "I'm so very sorry."

"For what, Delia?"

"I should have found a way to stop Daddy earlier. Before—" Delia's face scrunched up as she fought tears. She pounded her fist against the doorjamb. "If only I had gone to Mama sooner!"

"Stop, Delia. Please, don't blame yourself." Rachel's lips quirked in a wobbly smile as she laid a comforting hand on Delia's shoulder. "It wasn't our fault. Remember?"

Delia felt her lips wobble in an answering smile. "Right."

Delia made sure Rachel locked the door behind her, then sought out her mother. Hattie usually spent time early in the morning in her office downstairs, which had served as a sewing room for past generations of Circle Crown ladies. Ray John had already left for the Kincaid Hotel to have coffee and hear the morning stock reports. She and her mother had perhaps an hour alone before he could be expected to return.

It had been easy for Delia to say she would confront her mother with the truth. The reality of it was somewhat daunting. She stood for several moments in the open doorway, watching her mother sign checks to pay the expenses of running the ranch.

"Mama?"

Her mother glanced over her shoulder. "What is it, Delia? I'm very busy."

Delia took a deep breath and stepped into the room. "Mama, there's something I have to tell you."

Marsh had been wrestling with his feelings ever since he had been forced to acknowledge the true relationship between Delia and her father. He could think of no other explanation for what he had heard her father say. It made him sick to think of what might be going on between them right now. He hadn't seen Delia for three whole weeks.

Marsh yanked on the strand of barbed wire and tacked it tight to the mesquite post. He wasn't taking any chances on North cows straying onto Carson land again. Ray John had promised a personal visit next time. Marsh wasn't sure what he would do if he met Ray John face-to-face. If he had been carrying a gun with him three weeks ago, the man would already be dead.

Barring murder, Marsh's first instinct had been to go straight to Sheriff Davis. But that would have meant exposing Delia's dreadful secret to the whole world. And he had no proof of anything.

He felt confused. Angry at Delia and sorry for her at the same time. Appalled. Revolted. Disgusted. He had heard such things happened, but not in the town where he lived, not to someone he knew. He wondered how far it had gone. He wondered if Delia had done it with her father.

And hated himself for what he was thinking.

Of course she hadn't. She wouldn't even do it with him.

But maybe that was why she wouldn't do it with him. Because then he would know she wasn't a virgin. He imagined her with her father. And felt the bile rise in his throat.

He pulled off his gloves and tucked them in his back pocket, then dropped his Stetson on the fence post and tunneled all ten fingers through his sweat-damp hair, leaving it standing on end.

He turned to look across the fence. He

should just go knock on her back door and ask to speak with her.

What would he say? What could he say?

I understand. He didn't.

I was shocked by what I heard. She had to know that already.

What the hell is going on between you and your father? He didn't really want to know. He was afraid he already did.

He shoved his hair flat with his fingers, slapped his hat back on, and tugged it down to shade his eyes from the midday sun. He put the tools he had been using back in his saddlebags, mounted his horse, and headed for the live oak where he had spent so many hours with Delia.

She wouldn't be there. She hadn't come in three weeks of waiting. But he couldn't keep himself from going.

Today she might come.

One thing had become clear to him amid all the confusion. He still loved her. He still needed her. He still wanted her. More than that, he wanted to rescue her. Except he had no idea how to do it.

For the first time in a long time he wished he was on better terms with his father. He wished he could talk to him, get his advice, maybe even his help. But Cyrus was drunk most of the time. Marsh wouldn't trust his father to keep what he knew to himself, let alone offer any useful suggestions.

Marsh thought how much worse it must be for Delia. The person responsible for keeping her safe from harm was the very person as-

saulting her. He wondered if her mother
knew. Surely not. No woman could possibly
condone such behavior by her husband. Why
didn't Delia tell her mother, so she could put
a stop to it?

Marsh was formulating answers to that
question in his head when he realized Delia's
palomino stood grazing under the live oak.
His eyes scanned the horizon for any sign of
her and finally located her lying curled up in
the grass.

He spurred his horse to a gallop and raced
the rest of the way to the fence. He leaped off
the animal and edged his way between the
strands of barbed wire rather than fussing
with the gate. He jerked his shirt free when it
caught on a barb, not caring that it ripped, not
even feeling the bloody gouge the barb tore in
his flesh.

All he saw was Delia, lying on the ground
as though she were dead. He ran the short distance from the fence to the tree, and dropped
to his knees beside her, completely out of
breath.

"Delia!"

As he rolled her over, she opened her eyes.
They were red-rimmed and brimming with
fresh tears. She wiped her runny nose on her
sleeve as she sat up.

"Marsh?"

He saw the uncertainty in her eyes. "Come
here," he said.   •

She launched herself into his arms, sobbing
incoherently. He could understand very little
of what she said, but one word stuck out.

Arrested.

"Your mother's having your father arrested?" he asked. "It's what she should do, Delia. There's no reason to cry anymore. It's all over now."

"Not Daddy!" she cried. "You! She's having *you* arrested."

"What?"

"For rape."

"What?"

He rose abruptly, pulling free of her grasp, and stood staring down at her with his mouth gaping. "You told your mother I raped you?"

She scrambled to her feet. "No, no. You don't understand."

"I sure as hell don't!" She laid a hand on his arm, and he jerked himself loose. "If somebody's been fucking you, Delia, it hasn't been me!"

She stared at him, her eyes wide and wounded. "I told her the truth. I told her Daddy got me pregnant. She wouldn't believe me."

"Pregnant? You're *pregnant*?" He realized he was shouting.

She started crying again and slumped to the ground in a heap. "What am I going to do? What am I going to do?"

His mind was too busy whirling with his own problems to handle hers.

Sheriff Davis was going to arrest him for raping Delia. No one would believe he wasn't guilty.

He looked down at Delia, at the pitiful picture she made, and was struck by two other horrible truths.

The woman he loved was pregnant. Her father was the father of her child.

He dropped back onto his knees beside Delia and laid a comforting hand on her shoulder. Her flesh was tensed as hard, and felt as cold, as marble.

"I want to die," she choked out. "I want to die."

He lifted her into his lap and pressed her face against his chest. "It isn't your fault," he muttered.

"How do you know?" she challenged. "Maybe I liked it. Maybe I wanted him to do those things to me."

"Is that what your mother said?" Marsh asked.

She grasped handfuls of his shirt and sobbed against it. "Yes. Oh, God, yes. She said I must have tempted him. She called me terrible names. She said . . ."

She was crying so hard she could barely catch her breath. He made soothing sounds and held her tight against him. He had never felt so helpless in his life. There was nothing he could do to save either of them.

Except hold her. And tell her he still loved her.

Only, when he tried to get the words out, they stuck in his throat.

"I'm sorry, Marsh. I'm so sorry," she moaned.

He couldn't offer solace. There was none to give.

"Can you ever forgive me?"

"You didn't do anything wrong, Delia."

"I let him . . . I let him . . ."

"Shhh," he said. He felt a tickle in his throat, an unfamiliar feeling of tightness. He squeezed his eyes shut, very much afraid he was going to cry. It had been so long, the feelings were foreign.

He fought the tears, battled the ache in his throat, and lost. He tightened his arms around Delia, so she couldn't look up and catch him crying like some dumb kid.

Something else rose to replace the pity he felt. A deep hatred for the man who had done this to Delia. Someone ought to rid the world of Ray John Carson.

He didn't know how long he sat there holding her, but when he looked down, she had fallen asleep in his arms. He brushed away several strands of hair stuck to her damp cheek. His heart welled with feeling for her.

What was going to happen to them?

By now Sheriff Davis would have come to his house looking for him. His father would have told the sheriff he had gone to mend fence. He wondered if the sheriff would come after him, or whether he would wait at the house for his return. Likely the latter, since they wouldn't know Delia had come to warn him. Well, he wasn't going home anytime soon. He had a few things to do before he let himself get put in jail.

"Delia." His throat hurt, and his voice grated like a rusty gate. "Wake up."

Her eyes opened slowly, and he saw the panic before she realized who was holding her close.

"You have to go home now."

She clutched his shirt, and he saw the desperation mount in her eyes. "I can't go back there, Marsh. Can't I stay with you?"

He shook his head.

When she ripped herself from his embrace it felt as though his skin were coming off along with her. "I thought you cared. I thought I could count on you. It was all lies, wasn't it? You're no better than Ray John!"

"Wait one damn minute before you start comparing me to your father," he roared, coming to his feet after her.

"You're both liars," she accused.

"I'm not the one who was having a love affair with my father on the sly," he snapped back.

She looked as though he had slapped her. He might as well have. He couldn't have hurt her worse if he had physically hit her. "I'm sorry, Delia. I don't know what came over me. I—"

She turned and ran, grabbing the reins and throwing herself into the saddle before he realized what she was going to do. Her horse whinnied with fright and shied as she kicked it in the direction of the barbed wire fence.

"Where the hell are you going?" he yelled.

It looked like she intended to jump the fence. It was dangerous and foolhardy, and she was going to get herself killed. Then he remembered what she had said.

I want to die.

"Delia!" he shouted. "Don't!"

She ignored him, aiming her mount at the

barbed wire fence and slapping its rump viciously with the reins. But there wasn't room for the animal to get up enough momentum to clear the fence, and at the last possible instant the gelding sat back on its haunches.

Delia was poised high over its neck, ready for the jump, and she went flying. Her scream of terror was cut off abruptly as her body slammed against the trunk of a mesquite on the other side of the fence.

Marsh was already running when he heard her hit the ground. He set his hands on the top strand of barbed wire and vaulted it, sprinting toward her as he landed on the other side.

A stream of blood trailed from her nose. Her eyes were closed, and her skin was bleached white.

"Delia!" he cried, dropping beside her. "Damn you! Don't you dare die on me!" He felt her throat and found a thready pulse.

He was afraid her back was broken. Or her neck.

He was afraid to move her, afraid he might hurt her worse than she already was.

"Don't die," he begged. "I'll be back with help. Just don't die."

He ran to where he had left his horse grazing and leaped into the saddle and spurred the animal toward home. Sheriff Davis would be there. He could call for help.

He saw the white county sheriff's car parked in back of his house and started yelling long before he reached the door. The sheriff opened the door to the mud porch and looked out. Marsh saw his father standing behind the man.

Marsh came out of the saddle on the run. "It's Delia!" he cried. "She's been hurt. Call an ambulance."

He tried brushing past the sheriff to get to the phone inside the house, but the burly man caught hold of his arm and wouldn't let him by.

"Hold on there, boy. You're under arrest."

"Forget about that right now. I'm telling you Delia's hurt! She needs an ambulance!"

He tried pulling free again, but this time the sheriff whirled him around and shoved him flat against the outside of the house, dragging his arm behind him and clamping a metal cuff around it.

"No! Let me go!"

"Resistin' arrest ain't too smart a move, boy," Sheriff Davis said, as he captured Marsh's other hand in the other half of the cuff.

Marsh was desperate. "Listen to me! Dad, please, make him listen to me!"

He met his father's eyes and saw him look away.

Tears of frustration formed in his eyes. "Please, Sheriff Davis. Delia fell off her horse. She's out by the big live oak near the Carsons' north pasture gate, unconscious. She needs help."

What he was saying seemed to register. "Why the hell didn't you say so, boy?"

Marsh stood there helplessly cuffed while

Sheriff Davis went to his patrol car and radioed for help.

"You shouldn't have done it," his father said.

"I didn't hurt her. She fell off her horse," Marsh replied.

"The other thing, I meant."

Marsh shook his head. There was no sense denying it. His father was already convinced he was guilty. His only hope was that Delia would tell the truth. Surely she wouldn't let him be convicted of a crime he hadn't committed. Only, how could she do that without naming the father of her child? And he knew there was no way she was going to point a finger at her father. Marsh felt a chill run down his spine.

"Paramedics are on the way," Sheriff Davis said. "Oughtta be here any minute."

It took twelve agonizing minutes, and Marsh worried every second of the time whether Delia would regain consciousness and think he had deserted her.

"You'll have to come along to show us where to go," the Fire Rescue driver told Marsh.

The ride across the rutted pasture in the front seat of the ambulance was rough. His hands were still cuffed behind him, so he was bounced mercilessly against the door. "There," he said at last, pointing with his chin. "At the base of that mesquite."

"I see her!" The driver bolted from the vehicle and raced toward the prone figure on the ground, forgetting about Marsh, who twisted himself around to reach the door handle and then followed after him and another paramedic who had been riding in back. The sheriff got out of his car and quickly caught up to them.

When they reached Delia, Marsh saw her jeans were drenched with blood.

The driver turned and demanded, "What the hell did you do to her?"

His face turned ashen. "The baby," Marsh whispered. "She's losing the baby."

The sheriff grabbed his arm. "You got the Carson girl pregnant? Boy, days gone by you'd be garglin' rope by now."

"Marsh," Delia rasped.

"Delia!"

The sheriff grabbed his arm. "Stay away from her, boy. She doesn't want to see you at a time like this."

"Marsh."

"She's calling me. You have to let me talk to her," Marsh pleaded.

Delia's eyes opened, and Marsh saw they were filled with pain.

"You want to speak to this boy?" the sheriff asked her.

"Yes."

The sheriff let Marsh go, and he bent down on one knee beside Delia while the paramedic slipped an IV into her arm.

"I didn't want to leave you, but I had to go for help," he said.

"The baby."

He shook his head.

She closed her eyes, and tears seeped from

them. He wondered if she was mourning. Or if they were tears of relief.

"You don't have to worry about this boy botherin' you anymore," Sheriff Davis said. "He'll be makin' license plates in Huntsville for a long, long time."

"I didn't rape her," Marsh said. "Tell them, Delia."

"Speak up, girl," the sheriff said.

"Marsh . . ."

He watched her swallow convulsively, saw the look of pleading in her eyes. He knew what she wanted him to do. Even why she wanted him to do it. The thing was, he loved her enough to take the blame. It was a small enough sacrifice. Another blot on his already-spotted reputation to save her from having to reveal the truth.

He fought back the feeling of panic at the thought of being put behind bars. He knew what it felt like to be locked in at night, to lose your freedom for days and weeks and months on end.

But surely it wouldn't come to that. It was enough for him to be accused. That would divert the attention of those looking to discover the baby's father long enough to keep Delia's awful secret. She would never testify against him in court, and without her testimony that he'd had sex with her, he couldn't be convicted of anything.

"All right, Delia," he whispered close to her ear. "I'll make them think the baby's mine."

"No! Don't!" she cried.

"Hey, what's goin' on?" the sheriff said,

grabbing Marsh and pulling him away from
Delia. "You've done enough to that poor girl.
Leave her alone."

The sheriff pulled him roughly toward his
patrol car. "You'd better say your prayers,
boy. This town's gonna hang you sure."

But not that day. In fact, Marsh was out of
jail in less than four hours. An advantage, he
supposed, of being arrested early in the day.
Cyrus surprised him by paying his bail.
Maybe the old man cared a little for him after
all, he thought. He thanked him on the drive
home.

"Couldn't afford to leave you in jail," his
father replied. "Need you to get the chores
done around the place."

Marsh swallowed that bitter pill along with
the others he had been served over his lifetime. Whatever his father's reason, he was
grateful he hadn't been left to languish in jail.

That evening, when Marsh went to the hospital to see Delia, he learned Sheriff Davis had
been right about one thing. The town had already convicted him. He got some downright
nasty looks from people in the waiting room
who recognized him.

The nurse wouldn't let him see Delia because her mother was with her.

"When do you think I could see her?" he
asked.

"Tomorrow morning."

"I'll be back tomorrow," he said.

"Mr. North," the nurse called after him.

He turned to look at her.

"I think what you did was despicable. If it

was up to me, they would never have let you out of jail."

It doesn't matter what anybody thinks. I know I'm innocent. And so does Delia.

Only it did matter. Because he had to live here. He was a rancher, and he couldn't pick up his land and move it somewhere else. But there was no way Delia could tell the complete truth, not without making it impossible for her ever to live here with him.

He had almost reached the second set of automatic glass hospital doors when they opened and Ray John Carson stepped inside.

Marsh threw himself at the man headlong. "You bastard! You sonofabitch!"

His attack caught the other man by surprise, and he went down under Marsh's weight. Marsh clamped his hands around Ray John's throat and squeezed. Ray John's eyes were bulging by the time rough hands pulled Marsh away.

"Are you plumb crazy?" Ray John gasped, his hands gripping his mangled throat. "You could have killed me."

"I wish I had!" Marsh raged. "I wish you were dead. I'd like to kill you myself."

"What did I—?"

Marsh kept his eyes locked with Ray John's and saw when the other man realized he knew the truth. Fear flashed. And defiant anger.

"Call the sheriff," someone shouted. "Tell him the North boy is making trouble again."

"No," Ray John said. "Let him go. This is purely personal. The kid and I can settle this between us."

Marsh sneered. Naturally Ray John didn't want the cops involved. The truth might come out. He yanked himself free of the arms holding him captive and backed his way toward the door. "We'll meet again," he said.

"I'll look forward to it," Ray John replied.

Marsh left before he did something else stupid. Like bash the oily smile off Ray John Carson's face.

∽ *Chapter Seven* ∾

Delia sat bolt upright in bed. The sound of a gunshot reverberated in her head. Sweat bathed her body. Her heart pounded in her chest. She had done it. She had finally killed Ray John Carson. She darted a glance at the pillow beside her. Even in the faint light of dawn she could see it was pristine white.

She dropped her head in her hands and groaned. It was the dream again. The same awful, wonderful, vengeful dream that had come every night in the week since her father had insisted—over her mother's vehement refusal—that she be allowed to come home to the Circle Crown after her brief stay in the hospital.

She had called Peggy the first chance she got and discovered that Marsh was out of jail, if not out of trouble. She hadn't seen him, and wasn't sure she wanted to see him. Not after everything that had happened.

She had lost the baby.

Delia felt empty inside. Bereft. Even though

she hadn't wanted the baby. Even though she had wished it away a thousand times before it was gone. She didn't understand her grief, she only knew it weighed on her.

Like her refusal to see Marsh at the hospital. She couldn't face him yet. It was her fault he was in so much trouble. She knew Marsh had seen the panic in her eyes the day of the accident and responded to it. In her weakened state, she hadn't been able to make the sheriff understand that Marsh hadn't done anything wrong. She loved Marsh more than ever for what he had done. But she couldn't face him again until she had gone to Sheriff Davis and made things right. She planned to do it before Marsh had to go before a judge again.

Which meant today. Or tomorrow.

A bloodcurdling scream resounded up the stairs, raising the hair on Delia's arms and nape.

She scrambled from her bed. That was no dream!

The screaming continued. Chilling. Macabre.

It stopped abruptly.

Delia flung her door open, expecting to see Rachel in the doorway across the hall. Rachel's door stood open. Her bed was empty.

"Rachel?" Delia shouted as she raced toward the stairs. "Rachel!" She met her mother at the top of the stairs.

"Was that Rachel screaming?" Hattie asked, as they ran down together.

"She wasn't in her room." Delia caught the newel post and swung herself around toward the source of the sound. She stopped short in the doorway to her father's gun room.

His blood and brains spattered the papered wall.

Rachel stood at his side, her eyes shining white around enlarged black pupils, one hand fisted on the walnut butt of Ray John's favorite Colt .45. Her mouth hung open as though to scream.

No sound was coming out.

Daddy is dead. Rachel shot Daddy.

A tremor of joy and horror rolled through Delia. Followed by guilt and shame. Her younger sister had done what she had not had the courage to do herself.

Delia felt her mother brush past her.

"God. Oh, God." Hattie grabbed Rachel's arm and yanked her around so she faced away from the carnage, then tore the gun from Rachel's iron grip and threw it onto the desk. "What have you done?" she demanded furiously. "You fool! You damned little fool!"

She shook Rachel violently, until her head snapped back and forth.

"Stop it!" Delia cried, rushing to her sister's side. She pulled at her mother's arm, trying to break her grasp on Rachel. She finally managed to separate the two and wrapped her arms protectively around her sister.

Her mother stood facing her, silvery blue eyes narrowed and cold as ice, her body quivering.

"It isn't her fault!" Delia snarled. "I told you what he was doing to her. To both of us. But you wouldn't believe me. Now look what's happened!"

"I didn't kill him," Rachel said.

"Of course you didn't," Hattie said. She turned reluctantly to look at the remains of Ray John Carson and quickly looked away. "It was an accident. Ray John was cleaning his gun and accidentally shot himself." She frowned and said, "Or it might have been suicide. I had asked for a divorce, and Ray John was upset about it."

Delia stared at her mother openmouthed. "Did you?"

"Did I what?"

"Ask Daddy for a divorce?"

"It doesn't much matter now, does it?" Hattie said.

Delia had never seen her mother cry, had never even seen tears in her eyes before. But one spilled onto her mother's cheek and slid down her face.

Delia's throat ached. She wished she could cry. But she felt no sorrow, only horror. And relief.

Hattie swiped at her eyes with her fingertips and wiped the resultant tears on her jeans. A moment later she was back in command of herself and the situation.

"I'll call Sheriff Davis," Hattie said. "Delia, you take Rachel upstairs and put her back to bed. Stay with her. Don't leave her alone."

Hattie stopped them before they could leave the room. She put her hand under Rachel's chin and lifted it to look into her eyes. "I'm going to tell the sheriff you came down here after you heard the gunshot and found your father dead. You saw the gun on the desk and picked it up."

"On the floor," Rachel corrected.

"All right, on the floor. That is all you will tell the sheriff, do you understand?"

"Yes, Mama."

Sheriff Davis arrived with his county patrol car lights flashing and siren blaring. He was followed by Fire Rescue and more police and a crowd of gawkers who had heard the call on their police scanners or through the CB radio network.

Delia sat beside Rachel on her bed and kept her arms around her sister the whole time Sheriff Davis questioned her. She felt Rachel trembling with fear, but she didn't incriminate herself in any way. The sheriff had no inkling she had murdered their father.

Her mother escorted the sheriff from the room, and Delia sat holding her sister, needing as much comfort as she had to offer.

"I didn't do it, Delia," Rachel whispered. "I swear I didn't."

Delia felt a clutch somewhere in the region of her heart. Poor Rachel. She couldn't face what she had done. And who could blame her. Surely the sheriff would conclude Ray John's death had been a terrible accident. Rachel would be safe then.

Oh, God! How could she tell the sheriff now that Marsh had not raped her, that her father had been the culprit? No one would believe her father's death was accidental if they knew the truth about what he had done to his daughters.

"We're free, Delia," Rachel whispered. "Daddy can't ever hurt us again."

Delia looked into her sister's hazel eyes. Innocence had long since fled them. But she didn't see guilt, either. She put her arms around her sister and laid her forehead against Rachel's.

"Yes," she murmured. "Free."

Then why did she feel so trapped?

Marsh had been sitting in the same chair in the same room at the county sheriff's office in Uvalde for sixteen hours. He thought this sort of interrogation only happened in the movies. He hadn't asked for a lawyer because he didn't think he needed one. Now he was beginning to wonder.

He glanced up at Sheriff Davis, who was leaning against the wall with his hands folded over his belly. "I told you before," Marsh said. "I went driving by myself last night in my pickup. I was in my bed sleeping this morning until I went out to feed the stock."

"Nobody saw you?"

"My father was asleep when I got home last night." Out cold in front of the TV. "He wasn't awake when I got up this morning." He hadn't sobered up yet.

Marsh's story hadn't changed. He didn't know why Davis kept asking him the same questions.

"You don't know anyone—besides yourself—who might want Ray John Carson dead?" Sheriff Davis asked.

"No one." Except Delia. He missed her. He needed to talk with her, see her. He was convinced her mother had kept him from seeing her at the hospital. He was anxious for her to get well enough to meet him at the live oak. He knew she would come when she could. He went there every day to wait for her. Except today. He had been in the sheriff's office all day.

He wondered how Delia felt about her father's death. Had it been an accident? Or had she taken revenge for what he had done to her? He wouldn't blame her if she had. He didn't think many people would. His own feelings were no secret. He was glad the bastard was dead.

"There's someone to see you, sheriff."

Sheriff Davis turned to the deputy who had appeared in the doorway to the interrogation room. "Who is it?"

"I think you better see for yourself," the deputy said.

Sheriff Davis turned to Marsh. "You sit there and think about telling me the truth." Then he left.

Marsh rose from his seat at a wooden table that held an ashtray full of Sheriff Davis's Marlboro butts and a Texas Longhorns mug half-filled with cold, milky coffee. He paced the width of the room—four steps across the beige linoleum—then turned and paced the length—five more. He stared at the two-way window, wondering if Sheriff Davis was behind it talking to someone, if they were watching him. He turned his back on it, but there was nothing to look at on the walls except a large black-and-white clock like the ones in schoolrooms that visually ticked off the minutes until you could leave.

He wondered how much trouble he was really in. The rape charge had been bad enough. He had held some hope—fading as his arraignment hearing loomed—that those charges might get dropped.

It surprised him that the sheriff had been so persistent in questioning him about Ray John Carson's death. He had no alibi, but there was no hard evidence to link him to the scene, either. There was no way they could pin Ray John's death on him. Could they?

Marsh was leaning against the wall with his legs splayed far in front of him when Sheriff Davis opened the door.

"You can go now."

Marsh stared at him. "What?"

"You can go." The sheriff swung his hand toward the hallway. "Get on out of here."

Marsh scrambled to get his feet under him. "You're done questioning me?"

"You're in the clear. Ray John Carson committed suicide."

"How do you know?"

"That's official police business, not yours. Now beat it."

Marsh didn't have to be told twice. He grabbed his Stetson from the table and stuck it far back on his head. Whoever the sheriff had spoken with must have given him further information about Ray John's death, something that had apparently cleared Marsh.

He glanced at the sheriff. The man was frowning, deep in thought. "Who was it came to see you?" Marsh asked.

"None of your damn business, boy. Now get on out of here before I arrest you for loiterin'."

Marsh was almost out the door when the sheriff put a flat palm against his chest to stop him. "By the way, the rape charges against you have been dropped."

A silly grin appeared on Marsh's face. *Delia had come to the rescue, after all.* She must have told Sheriff Davis the truth. That also explained why Ray John had committed suicide. Delia must have told Ray John she planned to go to the sheriff. Ray John had killed himself to avoid facing the consequences of his acts.

Marsh spun around, freeing himself from the sheriff's restraint, and backed his way out the door. He touched a finger to the brim of his Stetson. "I *won't* be seeing you!"

On his way out, Marsh looked for Delia, but saw no sign of her. He hunted for the young deputy who had come to get Sheriff Davis, to ask him how long Delia had been gone and which direction she had taken. But the deputy wasn't around, either.

Marsh let himself out the front door of the sheriff's office and realized just how long he had been held for questioning.

It was dark out. A few lightning bugs glowed here and there. It dawned on him he had no way to get home. The sheriff had brought him to town in his county car. He would have to call his father to pick him up. Assuming Cyrus was sober.

He hated like hell to have to call his father. Cyrus hadn't even bothered to come to the sheriff's office. The most his father had done was call to make sure he wasn't under arrest. Marsh had told him, "No, Dad, they're just questioning me."

"Then get home as soon as Davis is finished with you. There's a calf chute that needs to be fixed before branding."

Sometimes Marsh felt like picking up and leaving. Cyrus sure wouldn't miss him. Except he would have to hire somebody to do all the work Marsh had been handling. There was nothing keeping him here—except Delia. And in a year she was going away and leaving him behind, perhaps forever.

You could go with her.

He felt tethered to the land by past generations of Norths, who were counting on him to make the most of what was there. He was trying. But it was hard to do it all by himself. He had learned enough about the ranch in the past couple of years to know some vast changes would have to be made for it ever to become a profitable enterprise.

Maybe the best way to save the land was to go away and make his fortune and then come back and fix things up the way they ought to be. Only, what skill did he have that would earn him a living, let alone make him a fortune?

He could work as a rigger in the oil fields.

There was good money in that. Even better money if he worked in the Middle East. He could do that the years Delia was in college and come back with a nice nest egg. They would have the rest of her senior year in high school to be together before he left, time enough for him to hire and train somebody to help out on the ranch while he was gone.

With Ray John dead and gone, Delia could have no objection to returning here to live. They could be married when she finished college. She could commute to law school in San Antonio during the week. Maybe everything would turn out all right, after all.

In the end, he hitchhiked home. Cyrus was sitting in his chair, asleep. The broadcast day was over. The TV was hissing snow.

He punched the TV off, and the sudden lack of sound woke his father.

"Wh-a-t? What're you doing?" Cyrus demanded in a sleep-slurred voice. "Why the hell'd you turn off the TV?"

"It's time for bed, Dad." Marsh pulled his father up out of the chair and slid an arm around him to support his uncoordinated efforts to stand.

Cyrus stared at Marsh in an alcoholic stupor. "Wouldn't be...like this...if you hadn't killed your mother. Loved her. Hate you for it."

"I know, Dad," Marsh said wearily as he walked his father to his bedroom.

The bed was unmade, the sheets dirty. Marsh missed the days when his grandmother had taken such good care of them. He didn't have time to do everything, and the house had suffered as a result. He would do some laundry tomorrow—Hell, it already was tomorrow—and remake his father's bed with clean sheets.

"Miss her so much," Cyrus sobbed. "Wanta die sometimes."

"I know, Dad," Marsh said. "I know exactly how you feel."

He could almost feel sorry for his dad. Except he couldn't forgive him for his meanness or for being a lush. He didn't think if he lost Delia forever he would spend the rest of his life pining for her like this. Sure, he would grieve. But he would go on with his life. He would never do what his father had done.

Marsh laid his father across the bed so he could pull his boots off, then unbuckled his belt and unzipped his jeans and pulled them off too. He unsnapped his Western shirt and tugged that off, leaving Cyrus in T-shirt, boxer shorts, and socks. He lifted his father's feet onto the bed and pulled the sheet up around him.

He looked down at his father, feeling guilty because he was ashamed of him and angry at him for pissing away his life. If he ever had a kid, he wasn't going to be like his dad. He was going to remember what it felt like to need your father's respect and to want to respect your father. He was going to hug his kid. And ask him about his hopes and dreams. And love him.

Except, even that wasn't enough. He would make damn sure his kid *knew* he was loved.

"Good night, Dad."

He turned out the lamp and closed the door behind him. He went to his room and lay down on his grandmother's quilt and stared up into the darkness.

The next thing he knew, it was dawn.

He awoke with the thought that there was nothing keeping him from seeing Delia. Her father, who had forbidden him contact with her, was dead. He could likely show up at her back door and be allowed to talk with her. Her mother might even give him permission to date her.

He suited word to deed. After a hasty shower and shave he dressed quickly, then realized he didn't want to show up at Delia's door looking like a range bum. So he took off his shirt and pressed it and shined his boots, and took another swipe through his hair with the comb. It needed a cut, but he wasn't willing to postpone his visit long enough to wait for Red White's Barber Shop to open.

He arrived on Delia's doorstep at an indecently early hour for company. Except, ranchers kept such indecently early hours, he knew she would be up. He saw a light on in the kitchen, and several more upstairs. He knocked on the kitchen door and waited impatiently, anxiously, for it to be opened.

He expected to see the housekeeper. Mrs. Carson answered the door instead.

"G-good morning," he stuttered.

"I've been expecting you," she said. "Come in."

Mrs. Carson expecting him? Mrs. Carson inviting him in? This was definitely "The Twilight Zone." He looked for Delia over the small woman's shoulder, but didn't see her.

Mrs. Carson stood back and held the screen door for him. "Are you coming inside?"

He took two steps inside the door, but that was as far as he got, before she let the screen door slam and turned to face him.

"Delia's gone," she said. "She disappeared sometime during the night. She left a note saying she was going away, and that she wouldn't be back. Until you showed up here, I thought she might have gone with you.

"If you're here, she really meant what she said in her note." Her eyes were bleak. "She's gone. And she's not coming back."

Marsh's heart began to race. "Can I see the note?"

Mrs. Carson's lips flattened and the skin around her mouth turned white. "No."

"How do I know you're telling the truth?" he demanded. "How do I know she's not upstairs right now?"

She fixed him with an icy stare. "Get out. Now. Or I'll call the sheriff."

Marsh didn't need a second warning. He slammed his way out the door and ran for his pickup.

Delia was gone. Delia had run away. Without telling him. Without a word.

She wouldn't do that. She loved him. She couldn't leave without telling him, without giving him a chance to talk her out of it.

He knew then where she was. She had gone to the live oak. She was waiting there for him.

She planned to run away all right, but she was going to do it with him.

He drove his pickup like a crazy man back down the road from Delia's mansion to the highway, raising a tail of dust. He skidded from the dirt road onto U.S. 83 and gunned the engine. He hit the accelerator and watched the needle climb to eighty. That was more than he knew was safe with his rebuilt engine, but he didn't care if the damned thing blew.

Then he saw the flashing lights behind him. He was tempted to try and outrun the county patrol car, but it would be faster to stop and let the cop write him a ticket. He hit the brakes, and the Chevy fishtailed as it screeched to a halt.

He was out of the truck and headed back toward the white patrol car before the county cop had gotten halfway to him.

"Stop right there." It was the young deputy who had taken turns with Sheriff Davis questioning him, Koehl, according to his nameplate, the one who knew the identity of the person who had come to talk to the sheriff. He wanted to ask Koehl about that, but not right now. Right now he needed to get to Delia.

"Look, I was speeding. Give me the ticket and let me go," Marsh said irritably.

"You're a lucky man, North. Don't know a man could beat a rape charge slick as you did. Not when he's sure as sin guilty."

"I didn't rape anyone."

Before Marsh could say more, the deputy grabbed him and shoved him up against the side of his truck. "Spread 'em," Koehl said as he kicked Marsh's legs out away from his body. The deputy frisked him and said, "You can turn around now."

Marsh glared at him. "Are you going to give me a ticket, or what?"

"You got a driver's license, North?"

Marsh reached into his back pocket and pulled out his wallet. He took out the license and handed it over.

"This is expired," the deputy said with a smirk.

"What?" Marsh stared with disbelief at the date Koehl pointed out. His birthday wasn't something that he celebrated. It was an easy thing to miss.

"You turned twenty-one more than a month ago. Should have had this renewed."

"I will," Marsh said. "Now write me the ticket—"

"Driving without a license is a serious offense, North. I'm going to have to take you in."

Marsh shook his head. He knew why he was being hassled. The town had convicted him without a trial. He could expect this sort of harassment from now on. And he would handle it, somehow.

But the deputy couldn't take him to jail now. Not when Delia was waiting for him. Not when she might leave if he didn't get there soon.

"No," he said. "I'm not going with you. Just give me the ticket—"

"You resisting arrest, North?" the deputy asked.

"Goddamnit, you can't do this!" Marsh railed. When he saw the deputy reach for his cuffs, he knew what was coming. Another day in jail, and maybe no bail this time if his father got mad enough. Delia would leave town without him. He would never find her.

"Look, you can't do this. Just give me the ticket—"

As the unsuspecting deputy reached for him, Marsh gave him a roundhouse punch to the temple. Koehl went down like a heart-shot deer.

Marsh stared with dismay at the unconscious deputy, realizing too late what he had done. *Resisting arrest. Assaulting a police officer.* He was in serious trouble. It was a good thing Delia wanted to get the hell out of here. After this, it would be better if he put some space between himself and this town.

He didn't have much time before the deputy regained consciousness. He picked the man up and set him in his patrol car, where he wouldn't accidentally get hit by a passing pickup, then got into his Chevy and raced for home and the live oak.

He drove his truck across the pasture, arriving at their meeting spot not too many minutes after he had left the deputy.

She wasn't there.

Maybe she had never come. Maybe she had never really loved him the way he had loved her. Maybe . . .

He saw the envelope on the ground at the base of the tree. It had his name on the outside. He had never seen her writing. It was neat and precise. He tore open the envelope and stared at the piece of school notebook paper that was left in his hands. He could see the writing through the folded paper.

He slumped to the ground with his back against the tree. He didn't want to read it. He didn't want to know for sure that she had left him.

The memory of Deputy Koehl lying unconscious nudged him. He didn't have time to brood.

He unfolded the paper and began reading.

Dear Marsh,

By the time you read this I will be a long way from here. You know by now that Daddy is dead. So you know why I can't tell the sheriff the truth about you not being the one to get me pregnant. I planned to, Marsh, really. I just couldn't. Otherwise, the sheriff might suspect Daddy's death wasn't an accident, after all.

Marsh stopped reading. If Delia hadn't gone to the sheriff and cleared him, who had? Her letter seemed to indicate her father's death had been no accident. Had she murdered him? Was that why she had run away? Then who had convinced the sheriff that Ray John had committed suicide? And how? He glanced down again.

You know what I want to do with my life. My plans haven't changed. Except that I'll be finishing high school somewhere else. I've told Mother what I'm doing, and I don't think she'll try to stop me. I can't forgive her for not believing me when I told her what Daddy was doing. I can't forgive her for getting you in so much trouble. And for other things.

What other things? Marsh wondered.

I know I'm taking the coward's way out. The charges against you are sure to be dropped if I'm not there to testify. But that isn't the same as having your name cleared. I hope you can forgive me.

They would think the very worst of him with her gone. They would think she was running to get away from him.

I'm going to miss you dreadfully, but I know you don't want to leave Uvalde, and I can't stay here any longer. I was afraid you might convince me to stay if I saw you, so I'm running away without saying good-bye, without kissing you and hugging you the way I wish I could.

I can't ask you to wait for me, because I'm never coming back. Please don't try to find me. It would only make it harder, because I'm not coming back, no matter what, and I would only cry more if I saw you.

I will love you forever,
Delia

Marsh crumpled the paper in his fist. *Love.* What the hell did she know about love? If you loved someone you didn't run away from them. If you loved someone you didn't leave them to worry whether you were safe and happy.

Marsh heard sirens in the distance. More than one. Deputy Koehl had woken, then, and called on his radio for reinforcements. He didn't have much time to make up his mind what he was going to do.

The Texas oil fields beckoned. No, that wasn't far enough. The Middle East. He would hop an oil tanker in Houston and go where he couldn't be found by the law. Or by Delia, if she changed her mind and came home. That would serve her right, pay her back good for leaving him hurting like this.

Marsh gritted his teeth to stop his chin from quivering. He would be damned if he would cry over her. And he wasn't going to spend his life pining for her, either. He wasn't going to end up a pitiful wreck of a man like his father.

He didn't care if he never saw her again. He didn't care if she stayed away the rest of her life. He wouldn't be here to know.

He felt a pang of remorse for leaving his father in the lurch. But it wasn't much of a pang. Maybe if he was gone, his father would have to get off his butt and take care of the place himself. He doubted Cyrus would miss him much—and he sure wouldn't miss his father.

Maybe, someday, if he made his fortune, he

would hire a lawyer to clear his name so he could come home.

He hoped his father didn't throw away his grandmother's quilt. It was the only thing he was leaving behind that he cared anything about.

The sirens howled louder. He had to leave.

Marsh pounded his fist on a branch of the live oak as a sob escaped his aching throat.

Damn you, Delia. I loved you. I thought you loved me. How could you leave me like this?

Then he ran.

Even the biggest ball of twine
unravels if you're willin'
to take the trouble.

✑ *Chapter Eight* ✑

January 1996

Delia paced the confines of her mother's private hospital room, still dressed in the black Donna Karan suit, pearls, and Bruno Magli heels she had worn under her robe at the courthouse yesterday in anticipation of attending a reception at the Metropolitan Museum that evening. Instead, her neck had a crick in it from an uncomfortable night spent slouched in a plastic chair waiting for her mother to awaken.

In a very short while they would be speaking to each other for the first time in twenty years. A rueful smile curved Delia's lips. She was definitely overdressed for the occasion. Growing up she had lived in cowboy boots and jeans. Western attire certainly would have been more comfortable, but the designer outfit helped remind her how far she had come from the past.

Delia had been counting the minutes, wait-

ing for it to be 7:30 A.M., which meant 8:30 A.M.
in New York. She wanted to check in with her
secretary. Janet always arrived at the office exactly one half hour before the workday began.
Delia looked at her watch. It was 8:34 in New
York. Janet would be in, have her coat hung
up, her tennis shoes off, and her heels on. Delia took one last look at her mother and quietly
left the room.

She had located the phone bank near the
waiting room when she entered the hospital
and headed for it now. Her body ached, and
she would have traded her favorite snakeskin
cowboy boots for a hot shower. The hospital
corridors were still quiet, with only an occasional nurse or orderly passing by.

She punched in the number for her office,
then her credit card number, and heard the
phone ring once before Janet picked it up,
"Judge Carson's office."

"It's me, Janet."

"Good morning, Judge Carson. How's your
mother doing?"

"She's stable. Surgery is scheduled this
morning. Once that's over, I'll know more
about how long I'll be gone from the office.
What do you have for me?"

Janet went through the messages Delia had
received the previous afternoon. Delia gave in-
structions how to deal with the various matters and said, "I'll be checking in periodically.
If anything comes up, and you can't reach me
here, you can leave a message on the answering machine at my mother's ranch." She gave
Janet the number for the Circle Crown.

"Here's one more message I missed," Janet said. "Wouldn't you know, I set it aside so I'd be sure to remember it. A reporter from the *Times* called and wanted to talk to you."

"Did he say what it was about?" Delia asked.

"I'm afraid not. I told him you were out of town, and he said he'd call again."

Delia thought of all the things a reporter from the *Times* could want with her, none of it good. Her stomach knotted. She forced herself to relax. She didn't need to borrow trouble. "Don't tell him where I am, Janet."

"No problem," Janet said. "You need anything?"

"I'm fine. Thanks, Janet. I'll be in touch."

Delia hung up the phone and stood for a moment staring at it. She ought to call her sister, just to check in, but it was early. She'd call her later, if Rachel wasn't already here by then.

It was like entering a cave when she returned to her mother's room. Venetian blinds kept out the sunlight, and the beige walls reflected the green glow from the computerized machines attached to her mother by wires and tubes. A monitor near the bed beeped in constant rhythm with her mother's heart.

Delia walked to her mother's side, reached out as though to touch her gnarled, age-freckled hand, then drew back before making contact. Hattie Carson, who had always seemed so formidable, so indomitable to her, looked old and helpless lying there.

Delia crossed to the window and used her

fingers to separate the blinds to reveal the last rays of a pastel dawn. The sky seemed bigger in Texas. She had always taken the great open spaces for granted before she moved away to New York. Maybe that was the result of having been raised in a state where everything—from the vast borders to the heroes of the Alamo—was larger than life.

"Delia?"

Delia crossed back to the bed, her gaze focused on her mother's silvery blue eyes. "Hello, Mother."

The heart monitor beeped faster.

"Relax, Mother," Delia cautioned, glancing anxiously at the green computer dial that showed her mother's heart rate climbing at an alarming pace.

"Delia," her mother rasped, the sound more urgent this time. Her hand reached out to Delia, but she was too weak to get it more than a few inches off the bed.

Delia hesitated a moment longer before putting her hand where her mother could reach it. Hattie's eyes sank closed as she gripped Delia's fingers in a surprisingly strong grasp. Delia resisted the urge to pull free. She stood there, watching her mother swallow convulsively, waiting for her to speak.

"You came."

Delia felt a fierce surge of leftover resentment and forced it back. "I'm here, Mother," she said in a neutral voice. "Rest now. I'll go call the nurse and tell her you're awake."

Her mother refused to let go of her hand. "Delia." Her eyes were open again, rheumy

with age, pleading, begging . . . For what? Forgiveness? *Fat chance of that*, Delia thought.

"Rest, Mother. Don't excite yourself."

"We have to talk." Hattie's plea was weak,
whispery.

Delia kept her voice even and unemotional,
though she felt both distressed and perturbed
by her mother's persistence. "Not now,
Mother."

"Yes, now. I might die."

It was a threat, pure and simple. *Listen to me
now or lose your chance forever.*

Delia felt the spur rake deep, opening a
wound she had thought long healed. But she
refused to fight back. "No, Mother." *Not now.
Not yet.*

"Yes," Hattie said, her fingernails digging
into Delia's flesh. "I . . . should have done . . .
more."

Delia waited, but that was all Hattie said.
Delia knew her mother was too proud to hum-
ble herself, that she was probably seeing the
extent of Hattie's willingness to admit she had
been wrong.

It wasn't enough. Not nearly enough. It
hurt. Oh, God, it hurt.

"Delia . . . I . . ." Her mother was visibly
struggling to speak.

"What is it, Mother?" Delia asked, needing
to get away, needing to shed her mother's
clawlike grasp.

"I'm so sorry."

Delia tore herself free and stood there, legs
trembling, eyes pooling with tears, throat aching. She opened her mouth to deny forgive-

ness, but no sound came out. She searched inside for anger and found pain instead. Years of raw feelings came tumbling out before she could stop them.

"No. Oh, no. It isn't going to be that easy, Mother. I'm not going to forgive you so you can go into that operating room and die in peace. I came to you a vulnerable sixteen-year-old girl, violated, pregnant with your husband's—my stepfather's—child, and begged you for help. Do you remember what you did? What you said?"

The heart monitor was beeping wildly, but Delia couldn't hear it for the thunderous pounding of blood in her ears. Her blue eyes, several shades darker than her mother's, burned with anger. Her hands curled into white-knuckled fists. "I haven't forgotten a moment of what happened, Mother. So you are not forgiven. I will never forgive you."

A nurse thrust her way through the doorway. "What's going on! The monitor went crazy and—"

Delia brushed past her. "I'm leaving."

"Delia!" her mother gasped.

Delia didn't stop. She couldn't. She felt sick inside. She couldn't breathe. She came flying out of her mother's hospital room, a tortured animal searching for a place to hide and lick its wounds, and ran headlong into Rachel.

"Delia! What's wrong? Is Mama all right?"

"The old witch is fine! She's not about to give the devil his due." Delia took several gasping breaths and raised a trembling hand to her brow. "I don't believe I said that."

"I do," Rachel said with a wry smile.

Delia gave her sister a ferocious hug. "I'm so glad you're here, Rachel."

"I'm sorry I couldn't get here sooner," Rachel said against her ear.

"Let me look at you." Delia set her sister at arm's length and took another step back to give her a once-over. "You look fabulous, as usual."

Rachel laughed as she brushed at her perfectly coifed French twist. The bright red sleeve of her St. John knit slipped down to expose a bruise above her diamond-studded Cartier wristwatch before she hastily dropped her arm. "Hardly fabulous," she said, self-consciously adjusting both sleeves at the wrist.

Rachel reached out to finger the sleeve of Delia's suit. "Is this what the well-dressed judge is wearing these days? *Très chic,*" she said with a teasing smile.

Delia laughed. "I was planning to go out after work, and I didn't have time to change before I left New York."

"On a date?" Rachel inquired.

"You know better than that."

The two sisters sobered and exchanged a long look. Rachel had gotten married at the end of her first year of college when Cliff, a senior, had swept her off her feet. Delia had never married. She had come close once, a few years back, but it hadn't worked out. Delia told herself she was too busy for a relationship, but sometimes the loneliness crept up on her. She envied her sister. A husband and a son sounded . . . nice.

"Where's Scott?" Delia asked.

"Cliff didn't think the trip would be good for him."

Delia said a word she normally didn't utter. "Why do you let him make all the decisions? Don't you have any say in these things?"

Delia saw the unhappiness in Rachel's eyes and reached out to touch her arm. "I'm sorry. How long can you stay?"

"For the day."

"Oh, Rachel, no." Delia's face mirrored her disappointment. Her grasp tightened at the spot of the bruise on Rachel's arm.

Rachel winced and pulled free. "Don't give me a hard time about this, Delia," Rachel said. "You have no idea what it's like dealing with Cliff. Once he makes up his mind, there's no changing it."

"We haven't had a chance to talk face-to-face for what feels like aeons. And Scott must have grown inches since I saw him last."

"You could come visit more often," Rachel said.

"My work—"

"Is your life," Rachel finished for her. "But it doesn't have to be so much of your life, does it, Delia? You could give the rest of us a little bit of it, couldn't you?"

Delia was surprised at her sister's plea and more aware than ever of how unfairly she had cut Rachel out of her life to avoid having to deal with the shadows of the past.

A nurse came by with a hospital cart, and Delia stepped out of her way. A hospital corridor was no place to be having this discussion. "We can talk about this later," Delia said.

"Not too much later," Rachel replied. "My plane leaves from San Antonio at five this afternoon, and I'll need at least an hour and a half to drive back to the airport."

Delia clamped her teeth on another epithet. "Why did you bother coming at all if you were going to turn right around and leave again?"

"Because I wanted to see Mom. Because I need to be here. You should understand that," Rachel retorted.

The two sisters glared at each other.

Delia huffed out a breath of air, and with it, a great deal of her anger. "We might as well take advantage of the time we have. How about something hot with lots of caffeine?"

Rachel seemed equally willing to call a truce. "Sounds good to me."

They turned and walked down the hospital corridor toward the cafeteria. Before they had gone two steps, Delia slipped her arm around Rachel's waist and gave her a sideways hug.

Rachel returned the sisterly embrace, matching her stride to her sister's shorter step.

"I have no business criticizing you, Rachel. Why do you let me get away with it?" Delia said.

"Maybe because I know I deserve it."

Delia stopped and pulled her sister over to the wall where they could speak without being heard by orderlies and nurses and visitors walking the corridor. "That sort of thinking is what kept us victims. I thought you'd gotten over all that."

Rachel pulled herself free. "Maybe you

have. I . . . I've been meaning to talk to you for some time, Delia. Maybe now is the wrong time, but I don't know when I'll see you again." She glanced down at Delia, who was several inches shorter than her, opened her mouth to speak, and closed it again. "I need a cup of coffee first, all right?"

"All right," Delia agreed.

As they walked down the cafeteria line, Delia sent a worried glance in Rachel's direction. Her sister, the congressman's wife, looked stunning, sophisticated, and aloof, the kind of woman every man stared at, but only the most self-assured dared approach. She seemed both more harrowed and more pugnacious than Delia remembered her being the last time they had seen each other.

On impulse, Delia took an icy pint carton of orange juice to go with her hot tea. Her stomach growled at the sight of food in the cafeteria line, and she picked up a plastic-wrapped bagel to fill the emptiness inside.

The sisters found a table near the window that overlooked the hospital patio and sat down across from each other. Rachel emptied a packet of Nutrasweet into her coffee, and Delia dipped her tea bag up and down several more times in her Styrofoam cup before adding sugar and lemon.

"I want to divorce Cliff," Rachel blurted out.

Delia froze with the straw in her orange juice halfway to her mouth. She set it back down again. She looked at Rachel and saw things she hadn't noticed—had purposely ignored?—at first glance. Carefully applied makeup covered the shadows under her sister's eyes. She was more than slender; she was thin. Her shoulders were taut, and her fingers moved nervously, mercilessly ripping the sweetener packet into tiny shreds.

"I thought you two looked happy together the last time I saw you," Delia said. "That was only a year ago. Can so much have changed since then?"

"He . . . I . . ." Rachel took a shuddery breath. "What you saw—what I let you see— is what Cliff wants everyone to see. We're the perfect family. He loves me, I love him." Rachel snorted with disgust. "It's all a lie, Delia. None of it is true."

Delia raised an astonished brow. "I never cared much for Cliff, but I thought you loved him."

"I did. Sometimes I think I still do. But we've had problems since the day we got married."

"For thirteen years? Why on earth are you still married to him?"

Delia watched the slow flush climb her sister's throat, as Rachel stared down at her square-cut acrylic nails.

"I've been thinking about it a lot, lately. Why I would stay, I mean." She glanced up at Delia, but couldn't maintain the eye contact and looked down at her hands again. "I . . . I was so surprised anyone would be attracted to me . . . I mean . . . I was sloppy seconds and—"

"You were *what?*" Delia exclaimed.

"Shh! Keep your voice down."

"Explain what that means," Delia demanded furiously.

"What man would want someone like us, Delia? After what Da—after what happened to us. When Cliff first looked at me I thought I'd died and gone to heaven. He was so handsome and so smart and so popular. What could he possibly see in me?

"I wouldn't go out with him at first." She paused and chewed on her bowed upper lip. "Maybe that's what kept him interested. I don't think many girls turned him down. He kept after me to go out with him, until finally I did.

"Then, I wouldn't sleep with him. You know why."

Delia knew exactly why. It was the reason she had kept herself from Marsh. So he wouldn't find out she was not a virgin.

Rachel surprised her by saying, "Because I knew what it would feel like, that it would hurt. So I didn't see why I should do it.

"But I loved the kissing, Delia, and the holding and the closeness and all the rest. So I kept going out with him. Until one night Cliff said if I didn't do it with him, that was it, that we would have to break up.

"I think he thought I would give in. I almost did. But I couldn't, Delia. I just couldn't."

Delia stared at her sister with stricken eyes. She had left home without giving a second thought to what would happen to Rachel. She had been too distraught to do much thinking at all in the beginning, and later she had thought that with Ray John gone, Rachel's problems would be over. Things hadn't been going on as long between Rachel and their father, so she had figured there was probably less damage to Rachel's self-esteem.

She had been naive. No, worse, she had been stupid to think Rachel hadn't suffered every bit as much as she had. Maybe more, because Delia had despised Ray John for years before his death. Rachel had not.

"A week later, Cliff proposed," Rachel continued. "It never occurred to me that he was marrying me because he thought he was getting a virgin. I swear it, Delia. I thought he loved me. He acted like he did. He didn't want me talking to any of the other boys, and he was always there to walk me home from the library or take me to dinner.

"I thought he spent so much time with me because he wanted to be with me. I didn't realize it was because he wanted to make sure I wasn't seeing anyone else."

"He was possessive?" Delia asked.

"Is. Is possessive," Rachel corrected. For the first time she took a sip of her coffee and made a face as she swallowed. "Ugh. That's cold already."

"Do you want to get some more?"

Rachel shook her head. "I'd rather finish this while I have the courage to get it said.

"Anyway," Rachel said, "you can imagine what happened on our wedding night when Cliff discovered he wasn't the first. He went crazy, Delia. Absolutely insane. He wanted to know who had . . . had screwed me. He wanted the guy's name. You know I couldn't tell him, Delia. I would die first. I . . . I thought he was going to kill me," she whispered.

"He *hit* you?" Delia asked, aghast. "That bastard *hit* you?"

"Calm down, Delia. I deserved it, I suppose."

Delia's eyes widened in alarm. "No woman deserves that sort of treatment, least of all a bride. You should have left him right then and there."

Rachel shook her head sadly. "Cliff told me that I belonged to him. We were married, and we would stay married. He already had his political career planned, and he didn't want a messy divorce in his background. But he told me he would make sure I never . . . never . . ." Rachel swallowed and forced out, "spread my legs for another man again.

"I knew I would never do anything like that. I thought everything would be all right. Because I loved him. And he loved me.

"But it wasn't all right, Delia. He saw flirting where there wasn't any. He saw betrayal where it didn't exist. If I so much as smiled at another man, he would fly into a rage.

"The first time I told him I was going to leave him, he promised he would stop hitting me. He promised he would change. He was very sorry, Delia."

Tears welled in Rachel's eyes. "I believed him. I needed to believe him. He's always sorry, Delia. But the hitting hasn't stopped.

"Maybe I would have let it go on . . . if he hadn't hit me in front of Scott."

"Nooo," Delia moaned.

The skin stretched tight across Rachel's cheekbones as she continued, "I won't let my son grow up seeing his father hitting his mother. I can't bear it."

Delia's stomach churned with acid. She looked down at the uneaten bagel in front of her. There was no way she could choke it down now.

"Rachel, I'm so sorry," Delia said. "I should have seen what was happening. I should have tried to help you sooner."

The way Mama should have seen what was happening to you? Had she been as willfully blind as her mother? It didn't seem possible she could have made the same mistake as Hattie. But she had.

Delia reached out and clasped Rachel's hand across the table.

Rachel's grip tightened. "When I told Cliff I planned to divorce him, he threatened to take Scott away from me. He can do it, Delia. He knows a lot of important people. I want to be free of Cliff, but I won't give up my son to him."

"You won't have to," Delia said grimly. "I have a few influential friends myself." Because Delia had gone to law school in Texas, she had friends who had become Texas judges. And a few more who had become sharp lawyers.

"Have you hired an attorney?" Delia asked.

"That's another problem," Rachel admitted. "Cliff controls all our money."

"You don't have any of your own stuck away somewhere?"

"We put everything in an account with Cliff's name on it."

Delia stared at her sister, not understanding how Rachel could have let herself become a victim again. "Why didn't you come to me sooner, Rachel? Why have you let this go on so long?"

"I didn't want to burden you with my problems."

"*Burden* me?" Delia's throat ached. "Dear Lord, Rachel, you're my sister. I know I probably haven't said it much, but I love you. I'd do anything for you."

The tears brimming in Rachel's eyes spilled over. She pulled her hand free of Delia's to grab a napkin and dab at the corners of her eyes. "I'm sorry, Delia. I guess I've pretty much made a mess of things."

"You haven't done anything wrong. Cliff's the villain here. You're not going back to him again."

"I have to go home. I have to get Scott."

Delia frowned. "All right. To get Scott. Then you get right back on a plane and come back here."

"I'll try."

"Don't try. Do it."

"That's easy for you to say, Delia. You're not like us ordinary mortals. You never doubt yourself."

Delia snorted a denial. "Mother won't be out of the hospital for a while," She said. "You can stay at the ranch until you figure out where you'd like to live. If you need money, I have enough to tide you over until the divorce is final and you get back on your feet." She raised a hand to cut off Rachel's protest. "I know it isn't a perfect solution, but I won't take no for an answer."

"I don't want to live at the Circle Crown," Rachel said.

"I don't relish the prospect of going back there any more than you do. But maybe it's time we laid Ray John's ghost to rest. What do you say?"

"You'd stay there with me?" Rachel asked.

"For a few days, anyway," Delia said.

Delia saw Rachel's gaze shift to a spot above and behind her. She turned to see what had caught her sister's attention.

Marsh North stood there, a smile on his face, a cup of tea in his hand. "Hello, Delia." He put a respectful finger to his Stetson. "Mrs. McKinley."

Delia's fingernails creased her Styrofoam cup. She forced herself to relax and said in a remarkably calm voice, "What brings you here, Marsh?"

"I came to see you."

A frothy wave of pleasure rolled over her, despite her determination to treat this chance encounter as nothing out of the ordinary. She wished she hadn't just spent the night sleeping in a chair. She lifted a hand to brush at her hair, pulled it down, then went ahead and sifted her fingers through the tangles. It was a nervous gesture, and she smiled so Marsh wouldn't see that was how she felt. Nervous.

She should have contacted him long ago. But she hadn't. She wasn't sure exactly what she ought to say or do. This didn't seem the right time to bring up the past. But it hung there in the air between them.

Meanwhile, Rachel responded with the aplomb one might expect of a politician's wife. "Please join us, Mr. North." She scooted over so that Marsh could sit next to her, across from Delia. He slipped his hat off and laid it on the table.

"Marsh," he corrected.

"Then you'll have to call me Rachel."

Delia was busy absorbing impressions of Marsh.

He seems taller than I remember. Broader in the shoulders. His hair is still too long, still sun-bleached, but a darker shade of brown. He looks tired.

He had crow's-feet around his eyes, and deep lines bracketed his mouth. A scar cut through his right eyebrow, and another scored the edge of his mouth. A man aged better than a woman, Delia thought. All those character lines only made him look more ruggedly handsome.

"What are you doing here?" Delia repeated.

"I came back to Uvalde to get my daughter through high school. I got custody of her when my ex-wife died six months ago."

"I heard." At his raised brow she explained, "Rachel told me." She paused, feeling awkward because it sounded like she had inquired about him when she hadn't. But it would be dishonest to suggest she hadn't wanted to know the information, because she had. "I meant," Delia said, "what brings you to the hospital today? Is someone you know sick?"

"To be frank, I came to check on your mother."

Delia shot him a confused, searching look. "Why would you be checking on her?"

"I was at the ranch when she had her heart attack." He paused and said, "Actually, I think I caused it."

❧ *Chapter Nine* ❧

Marsh couldn't believe how beautiful she looked. Over the past two decades, memories of Delia Carson had been like a rash that erupted at inconvenient times, irritating, prickly, sometimes painful. He had made a habit of reading the *New York Times* just to keep up with what was happening where she lived. He had seen the articles when she became a candidate for judge, watched her take a stand in print for what she believed, and drunk a toast to her election success in a smoky Oriental bar in Korea. He hadn't seen her for twenty years, but it felt as though they had parted only yesterday. The attraction between them was as uncomfortably powerful now as it had ever been.

"Would you mind explaining that comment you just made?" Delia said. "In what way were you responsible for Mother's heart attack?"

Marsh met Delia's gaze and was startled to realize she was looking right at him. The experience was disconcerting because in the past she had so seldom met his gaze directly. Even when she did, it had been for only brief moments before she retreated behind lowered lids. She wasn't hiding now. Almost the instant the thought occurred to him, she lowered her eyes to her hands, which framed a Styrofoam cup.

Hiding again, Delia? What made you nervous? Are you still as attracted to me as I am to you? Or is there something else? What is it that's kept you away from me all these years?

"I made the mistake of thinking your mother had come to terms with the issues that caused Ray John Carson's death," Marsh said at last. "I was wrong."

Marsh got the violent reaction he had been seeking from such a provocative statement, but it came from Rachel, not Delia.

The congressman's wife choked and coughed without stopping for several seconds. "Coffee went down the wrong tube," Rachel gasped when she could speak again.

Marsh turned back to Delia in time to catch her shaking her head at Rachel. When she saw him looking at her, the gesture stopped abruptly. What was that all about?

"At any rate," he continued, "I'm glad your mother survived the incident," Marsh said. "Will the surgery this morning correct her problem?"

"Dr. Robbins says it will," Delia said. "He said he recommended bypass surgery two years ago, but Mother refused to have it. Now she doesn't have any choice."

"I don't understand why she didn't do it earlier," Rachel said.

"According to Dr. Robbins, she didn't want to give over management of the ranch to some stranger during the month to six weeks she'll need to recuperate," Delia said.

"Thank goodness you're here now," Rachel said.

"I can't stay that long," Delia said sharply.

"Why not?" Marsh asked.

"I have responsibilities. I have to be back in court."

Rachel looked at Delia wide-eyed. "Who's going to take care of Mom?"

"You're a more logical choice than I am," Delia said to her sister. "You're going to be here."

"Maybe," Rachel said. "Maybe I'll be here."

"You aren't going to back off from what we discussed, are you?" Delia asked.

"No, but I might not be able to come back right away," Rachel said.

"It sounds like you two have a problem," Marsh said. "Maybe I could be of some help."

Delia frowned. "I don't see how."

"I'm living close by, and I know the ranching business. Maybe I could fill in at the Circle Crown until your mother's on her feet again."

"We couldn't ask you to do that," Delia said.

"Why not?" Rachel asked. "If Marsh has been kind enough to offer, I don't see why—"

"Because I said we can't, that's why," Delia snapped.

Her eyes were hidden from him again. What was she so afraid of? Marsh wondered. He shrugged nonchalantly. "If you don't want my help, you don't want my help."

"If you won't let Marsh help, Delia, what are we going to do?"

Marsh watched Delia swallow hard before she looked him in the eye and said, "I'll have to stay myself. At least until I can hire a manager."

She had seen the trap too late and fallen into it. But he wasn't going to help her out. Not when he had her exactly where he wanted her.

"Thank goodness that's settled," Rachel said. "I hope you'll excuse me, Marsh. I want to see Mom before she goes into surgery. Want to come, Delia?"

"I've already spoken to Mother. I'll meet you in the waiting room in a little while."

"All right."

Marsh scooted out of the booth to let Rachel pass.

"Thank you for offering to help, Marsh," Rachel said once she was on her feet with her clutch purse tucked under her arm. "I know Delia appreciates your offer as much as I do."

"You're welcome," Marsh said with a smile.

"See you soon, Delia," Rachel said before she turned and walked away.

Marsh couldn't help following Rachel with his eyes. She had turned into a stunningly beautiful woman. But Rachel's beauty didn't hold a candle to the fire he saw in Delia's eyes when he sat back down across from her.

"You tricked me," she said as soon as Rachel was out of earshot.

"I made an offer. You refused."

"You knew I couldn't accept your help," Delia said. "Not after everything that's happened. I owe you too much already to be taking anything more from you."

"Will you have trouble getting the time off?" Marsh asked.

Delia grimaced. "I have some vacation coming. And I can ask for a leave of absence. But the timing isn't terribly convenient."

"Why is that?"

"Let's just say a certain district attorney will be doing cartwheels when he hears I'm off the bench for a while, and it irks me to give him what he wants."

"Is that the only reason you don't want to be here?" Marsh asked quietly.

Delia avoided his gaze. She took a deep breath and let it out slowly. When she looked up into his eyes, he was stunned at what he saw. The pain made his breath catch.

He reached out automatically to touch her, to comfort her, but she pulled her hand free of his.

"Don't touch me. Please. This is hard enough without . . ."

He wished he didn't feel so much for her. Especially when Delia seemed in such a damned awful hurry to get back to New York.

She was avoiding his gaze again. He reached out and gently raised her chin with a forefinger until she was looking at him. "Conscience bothering you, Delia?"

"What I did was unforgivable. I shouldn't have left you to face those charges alone. I'm sorry, Marsh." A sigh of relief quivered through her. She edged back until she was free of his touch. "I didn't realize how much I needed to say that."

"I won't say I wasn't upset when you left," Marsh said. *That was a whopping understatement.* "As it turned out, I didn't end up facing anything. The charges were dropped."

"Because I wasn't there to testify."

Marsh shook his head. "No, even before that. Someone came and talked to Sheriff Davis. Someone made him believe Ray John Carson had committed suicide. The sheriff told me I was no longer a suspect in Ray John's death, and that the rape charges had been dropped."

"But who . . . ?"

"You figure it out." Marsh rose from the booth, retrieved his Stetson, and settled it low on his brow. "I've got some business to take care of in town. I'll check back later to see how your mother's surgery went." He hesitated and said, "Unless you'd like me to stay?"

She shook her head. "No. I . . . I need some time to think."

"That offer of help stands," Marsh said. "If you need anything, give me a call." A grin flashed. "Anything," he said with an exaggerated leer, "means anything."

Delia made herself laugh at Marsh's blatant sexual invitation, doing her best to hide the shiver of excitement she experienced at the

thought of being held in his arms and kissed
. . . and loved the way they had never had a
chance to love. "Get out of here," she said
with a hard-won smile.

Feeling as though the world had tilted on its
axis, Delia watched Marsh walk away. Marsh
was obviously willing to take advantage of
their forced proximity to have a long-delayed
love affair with her. She had to admit the idea
was tempting. She had often, over the years,
wondered what it would have been like to
have sex—Would it be making love at this late
date?—with Marsh.

She didn't fool herself that it could ever be
more than a brief affair. She had her life. He
had his. He would never settle down again,
and she could never settle for a wandering
man.

She couldn't. Wouldn't.

But there was so much about him—about
the man he had become—that she admired.
She had followed his work with *The Chronicle*.
His investigative articles were incisive, artic-
ulate, insightful. He had seen so much of the
world, and done his part to help right wrongs
by exposing them to public scrutiny. He was
seldom in one place for very long, it seemed,
heading from one trouble spot to another.

She had been tempted more than once to
contact him, but had chickened out. In the beginning because she wasn't ready to see him
yet, and then because she had learned he had
a family. She hadn't even known she was still
harboring a secret desire to marry him until

she discovered he was married to some other woman. The news had struck her like a punch in the gut. It had taken her a while to recover. She had finally fallen in love with a Manhattan attorney, Averill Matthews, but it hadn't worked out. An astute man, Avery had figured out her heart wasn't free to love him.

And Marsh was so lucky to have a daughter . . . who might have been theirs, if fate had not intervened.

Delia tried not to think of might-have-beens. It was unproductive and disheartening. She focused on the facts.

She had a demanding career she loved and wasn't willing to give up. Marsh had the same. Their lives had no chance of intertwining except intermittently. When her mother no longer needed her, she would return to Brooklyn. When his daughter graduated from high school he would fly away to some trouble spot somewhere. End of story.

At least she had cleared her conscience. At least she had said she was sorry.

Delia frowned. She had heard long ago that the charges against Marsh had been dropped, but she hadn't investigated how it had happened. She had always assumed it was because she hadn't been there to testify. But according to Marsh, someone had come to the sheriff's office and cleared his name.

Why had he brought it up? What was it he wanted her to figure out?

She racked her brain to think of a person who could have known enough to confirm Ray John's suicide and clear Marsh at the same time. Someone with enough credibility for the sheriff to believe him . . . or her.

Rachel? Rachel hadn't even known Delia was pregnant. Who else was left?

Mother?

Delia's arm hairs lifted.

It wasn't possible. Her mother was the one who had wanted to press charges against Marsh in the first place.

Who better to clear him with the sheriff?

Why would Mother help clear Marsh?

Because she knew the truth.

She didn't believe me. She called me a liar. She took Ray John's side.

At first. But she had time later to think about it. Maybe she started to believe you.

Why didn't she tell me so? Why didn't she send word to me, asking me to come back home?

Delia rose abruptly from the booth and headed for the hospital waiting room to meet Rachel. She had cast her mother in the role of villain for too long to believe Hattie Carson could have been wearing a white hat all these years. Nor could she believe her mother would have allowed her elder daughter to believe the worst of her for so long without seeking to correct the situation.

"You'd better live, Mother," Delia muttered under her breath as walked briskly down the hospital corridor. "We have some talking to do when you're able."

Delia was stiff when she rose from the waiting room chair to greet Dr. Robbins. It was nearly three-thirty in the afternoon. Several times she had feared something must have gone wrong, but the nurses had assured her the surgery was commencing on schedule. The elderly doctor's surgical greens were patched with sweat, and clumps of gray hair stood askew where he had pulled off his surgical cap. His shoulders sagged wearily.

"Your mother came through the surgery just fine," Dr. Robbins said. "She'll be in recovery for quite a while, and then we'll keep her sedated so she can rest. You should go home and rest yourself. I'll have the nurse give you a call when Hattie's ready for visitors."

"You're sure she's all right?" Delia asked.

"The surgery was a success," Dr. Robbins said. "But your mother's heart has some scarring. She's going to need a lot of help and support in the coming weeks and months."

"Months?" Delia said. "Doctor, I was only planning to be here a couple of weeks."

"Then you'd better hire someone to take over for you. Your mother isn't going to be able to manage the Circle Crown on her own for a long time—if ever again."

"I thought you said there was only a little scarring from the heart attack," Delia challenged.

"This isn't the first attack," he said.

"What?"

"She had an attack two years ago. That's when I first recommended the surgery."

"Why didn't you tell me about this sooner?" Delia asked.

"I'm not sure I ought to be telling you about

it now," Dr. Robbins said. "Hattie is going to be madder than a wet hen when she finds out. But I like the old bird, and I'd hate to see her try to do too much too soon."

"If she takes care of herself, is she going to be all right?" Delia asked.

"Her heart will work better after the surgery. But it's never going to be as strong as it was."

Delia turned to make eye contact with Rachel, who was on the pay phone in the hall with Cliff. How were they going to get Hattie to slow down? How were they going to find someone they could trust to manage a ranching empire the size of the Circle Crown?

"My sister and I will wait at the ranch to hear from the nurse," Delia said. "You've got the number there?"

"I'm sure we do," the doctor replied. "Call me if you have any further questions."

Delia shook his hand. "I will. Thank you, doctor."

The doctor had left the waiting room by the time Rachel hung up the phone. "What did the doctor say?" Rachel asked.

"Mother's going to be fine. We'll be able to see her tomorrow morning."

"Thank God. I told Cliff Mom wasn't out of surgery yet, and I had to stay one more day. He wasn't happy, but he agreed. At least we'll have one evening together before I have to leave. What do you want to do?"

"I want to go home," Delia said. She meant to Brooklyn. But that wasn't possible. "To the

Circle Crown," she clarified, "to shower and change clothes."

"All right," Rachel said. "I'll follow you in my rental car."

"Afterward, how about if I buy you dinner at the Amber Sky?" Delia suggested.

"Chocolate chiffon pie for dessert?" Rachel asked with a grin.

Delia laughed. "Sure."

"You've got a deal!"

Delia glanced at her watch as she drove up to the back door of the Circle Crown, pounded the steering wheel as she realized the time, and swore, which did nothing to ease the sudden anxiety she felt. She hopped out of her rental car and waited for Rachel, who had been following her, to pull up beside her in another rental car. She knocked on Rachel's window, waiting impatiently for the car's electric system to roll it down.

"It's 4:00 P.M.! I had no idea it was so late. I've got to call Janet right now if I want to catch her before she leaves for the day."

"The door's open," Rachel said. "It always has been. Make a run for it, Delia. I'm heading upstairs to change into something I can wear to the Amber Sky without looking like a city girl."

Delia left her sister sitting in her car and hurried inside. The phone call was necessary, but also provided an excuse to go inside without Rachel on her heels asking how it felt to be back, a way to get past the first awkward moments home with her attention focused on

something else besides the home she had left
twenty years before.

But even the smells were familiar—tamales
in the kitchen as she passed through, and after
twenty years, gunpowder in the hall as she
passed her father's gun room. That had to be
her imagination, but the odor was sharp
enough to pinch her nostrils. Memories were
hard to shake.

She headed for the phone in her mother's
office. That room had the fewest memories,
but also the worst ones. She hadn't expected
them to bombard her from the doorway.

It was as though time had stood still. She
saw her mother sitting at her desk writing
checks, and herself standing in the doorway
scared to death, needing to tell her mother of
Ray John's perfidy.

She remembered the mild irritation in her
mother's glance when Delia interrupted her,
and the dawning horror as Delia said, in soft,
halting words, what she had come to say.

Her mother had risen from her chair, her
face splotched with red, the whites of her eyes
visible, and headed toward her. Delia had
been expecting comfort. She had gotten a vi-
cious slap instead.

"Liar! Take back those filthy lies!"

Reeling from the slap, she had protested,
"I'm not lying, Mama!"

Her mother had grabbed her hair and
yanked hard enough to bring tears to her eyes.
"It's that North boy. He's the one who's been
doing these things to you. He's the one who
got you pregnant, and you need someone else

to blame for behaving like a slut. Well, I won't have it! Marsh North can't help himself to my daughter and get away with it. I'm calling the sheriff. I'll have that boy arrested."

"It wasn't Marsh," she said, hanging on to her hair close to her scalp, trying to ease the pain, numb with disbelief. "It was Daddy. And it isn't only me he's been bothering. It's Rachel, too."

Her mother's eyes had narrowed in fury. "You wicked, loathsome child! Take back those filthy, disgusting lies!" The spittle had flown from her mother's mouth, landing on her face.

Delia wiped at it now. But her face was dry. She rubbed at her scalp, at the spot where the hair had nearly been yanked out. But that was remembered pain.

Her heart thundered in her chest. The room was empty. All that had happened long ago. She located the phone on the desk, forced herself to cross to it, and punched in the number for her office in New York with trembling fingers.

"Janet," she said. "I'm glad you're still there."

Nothing much new was going on, except the *Times* had called to confirm some statistics.

"What kind of statistics?" Delia asked, sliding into her mother's chair behind the desk.

"Number of trials scheduled, number of pleas granted, that sort of thing," Janet said. "Said they'd been in touch with the DA and he had given them numbers and did you have anything different."

Delia rubbed at the wrinkles in her brow. What was the *Times* after? Had they called Sam Dietrich, or had Sam called them? Frank's warning came back to her.

Watch your back, Delia.

What the hell was going on? There wasn't much Sam could do to her. She hadn't done anything that wasn't by the book. Except she had a few more trials scheduled than the other judges. Delia's mouth curled wryly. About twice as many, to be exact. That might be unusual, but there wasn't anything *wrong* with it. So where was the *Times* headed?

"The *Times* reporter still wants to talk to you. Do you want me to give him your number in Texas?" Janet asked.

Delia wanted to know what was going on, but she expected to be at the hospital most of the time for the next few days, and if the reporter didn't reach her by phone, knowing reporters, he would show up on her doorstep. "No. I'd rather not have him hounding me here."

She hung up the phone, picked up a pencil, and nervously rapped it against the old oak desk. Her stomach was churning. She wondered where she could get hold of a copy of tomorrow's *Times* in Uvalde. Not that she expected to see her name in print, but it couldn't hurt to keep her eye on the damned thing.

She sighed and pushed herself upright. Maybe that churning in her stomach had something to do with not having eaten much of anything for twenty-four hours. She was hungry. The Amber Sky beckoned.

✑ *Chapter Ten* ✑

The Amber Sky was almost full when they arrived. It looked smaller than Delia remembered. She eyed an old codger wearing a
sweat-stained white straw hat and scuffed
cowboy boots who had a toothpick hanging
from the corner of his mouth. At least the
crowd was the same.

The single fan in the ceiling was turning, but
despite the closed orange blinds, the air-
conditioning unit was struggling vainly to
counter the heat of the setting sun.

The café had a familiar feel that made Delia
think she had come home at last. She wished
Peggy Voorhees hadn't moved away to Cali-
fornia. She could have used another friend in
town. The people she and Rachel passed on
the way to their table either avoided her eyes
completely or gave her a too-effusive greeting.
She was home, all right.

They ended up at a table near the back of
the café that gave them some privacy. Delia
ordered chicken-fried steak smothered in

white gravy, mashed potatoes, and green beans, with iced tea to drink, and Rachel said, "Make it two."

"I'm so glad Cliff didn't insist I catch the five o'clock flight today. I've missed talking with you."

"I've missed you, too," Delia said.

"I hope Cliff doesn't create a scene when I tell him I'm serious about a divorce. What if he won't let me leave?"

Delia gave her sister a stern look. "He can't lock you in."

"He can get a restraining order to keep me from taking Scott," Rachel said. "He threatened to do it once before when I said I was leaving him."

"On what basis? Have you abused Scott?"

"Heavens no!"

"Neglected him?"

"No."

"Any excessive use of drugs or alcohol?"

Rachel remained silent. She turned to stare out the window at the traffic on Highway 90. Delia had to admit it was a better choice than the godawful blue-green wall over the counter.

"Rachel?"

Rachel glanced at her with wary eyes. "I . . . I've been on medication for a while, Delia. For depression. Prozac, actually."

Delia made a small moaning sound.

"And some pills to help me sleep."

"You take sleeping pills?"

Rachel nodded. "I've also been seeing someone, a psychiatrist. A while back . . . before Scott . . . I took a bottle of pills."

Delia stared in horror at her sister. They spoke on the phone at least twice a month. Rachel hadn't even hinted at this kind of trouble.

Rachel stared at her hands, which were knotted in front of her. "I wasn't really going to kill myself, Delia. I was just so unhappy. I thought Cliff might pay more attention if . . ." Her lips curled in the mockery of a smile. "Anyway, it didn't work. He kept it out of the papers, and I started seeing the psychiatrist."

"Why didn't you tell me?" Delia said, searching her sister's face. "Why didn't you let me help?"

"I couldn't." Rachel tucked her hands under the table where Delia couldn't reach them. "Don't you see, Delia? It was my problem. I had to solve it myself."

"But I'm your sister!"

Rachel shook her head. "You left, Delia. You had your own life, and I wasn't a part of it."

Delia wanted to put her arms around Rachel. More than the table kept them separated. Delia felt for the first time that she didn't have the right to comfort her sister, or to seek comfort from her. She had known Rachel was out there somewhere, but she had been too busy running from the past to be there for her sister. Lord, Lord, it was time the running stopped.

Delia thought of the bed she had barely glimpsed in her room at the Circle Crown and realized she was going to have to sleep there, to face what had happened there, and somehow let go of it once and for all.

"I know why you left," Rachel said. "I know you blame yourself for what happened to Daddy. But Delia . . ." Rachel stared at her, wide-eyed and breathless. "It . . . it wasn't your fault."

Delia rubbed her brow. "I know that, Rachel."

"You do?" Rachel asked, surprised.

It was not her fault that Rachel had murdered their father. Except that she should have done something sooner to stop Ray John. At least she would find a way to help Rachel this time before it was too late.

"The past doesn't matter anymore," Delia said, meeting Rachel's gaze. "What matters is how we're going to get you and Scott away from that madman you're married to. Maybe taking Scott and running isn't the best plan. Maybe we should think about this a little more."

Rachel tucked in a wayward strand of hair. "Are you saying I should stay with Cliff? Not try to leave again right away?"

Delia caught the look of despair in Rachel's eyes. She laid her open palm on the table and waited for Rachel to put her hand in it. When she did, Delia gave it a reassuring squeeze. "Only until I have time to talk to some of my friends here in Texas and see what we can do. Is there anything else I should know, Rachel? Anything else that might make it possible for Cliff to take Scott away from you?"

Rachel lowered her eyes and tried pulling her hand free.

Delia wouldn't let her go. There was

something else. Delia was afraid to ask, but she had to know. "What is it?"

"I don't think Cliff would bring it up. Because he might have to talk about what happened before."

"Before what?" Delia asked.

Rachel raised her eyes. "Before I held an empty gun to his head and pulled the trigger."

Delia's eyes slid closed, and she swallowed hard. "Like Daddy used to do?"

Rachel nodded miserably. "I only wanted to scare him. Because he had beat me. I wanted him to know if he did it again, I would kill him. And I would have."

"Would you? Really?"

For a long moment, Rachel was silent. Then she sighed. "I don't know. I wouldn't want to, because then I would lose Scott for sure. Scott is the most important thing in the world to me, Delia. But I might, if I had to. I know you'd take good care of Scott for me, wouldn't you? You're his godmother. And I know you love children."

"Please don't talk like that, Rachel. It scares me."

"I'm sorry, Delia."

"Is there anybody else you've confided in?" Delia asked. "Anyone who knows what Cliff has done to you? Anyone who could testify in court?"

"The psychiatrist."

"Has he seen the bruises?"

"She. She's seen them."

"And you told her how you got them?"

Rachel nodded. "But I don't have any proof,

Delia. Cliff never hit me when anyone was around to see. And I hid the bruises when I was in public. I . . . I was ashamed."

Delia stared at an amateurish painting of a single live oak hanging on the wall for sale along with other equally woeful paintings by local artists, avoiding the pain in Rachel's eyes. "I haven't been a very good sister, Rachel. But all that's going to change. I envy you having Scott, but I don't want to end up raising my nephew."

"You envy me, Delia? I always thought you were happy with your career. You're a judge, for heaven's sake. That's an incredible accomplishment. If you want to know the honest truth, I envy you."

"Want to trade?" Delia said with the hint of a smile. "I'll take Scott. You can have my gavel and robes."

Rachel managed a grin. "You're welcome to Cliff, but I think I'll keep Scott." The grin faded. "Will I be able to, Delia? Keep Scott, I mean, and still get away from Cliff."

"You will," Delia promised. "I'm sure we'll figure out some way to manage it."

Delia was eating the last bite of her buttermilk pie—a candy-sweet mixture of vanilla, sugar, buttermilk, and eggs that she liked even better than the café's famous chocolate chiffon—when Marsh walked into the Amber Sky. Not walked, precisely. Stalked. Or stomped. Or tramped. He was obviously in a bad mood and searching for someone. She hoped it wasn't her.

She saw the moment he recognized her among the dinner crowd, because he headed directly toward her.

"What do you suppose Marsh wants?" Rachel asked.

"I don't know," Delia murmured. "Why don't you ask him when he gets here?"

Rachel laughed. "He hasn't taken his eyes off you since he saw you. I don't think he'll even know I'm here."

Sure enough, when Marsh reached the table he focused his gaze on Delia and said, "Billie Jo didn't come home on the school bus. I can't find her."

Delia was at a loss. What did Marsh expect from her? She didn't even know what Billie Jo North looked like. His next words provided her answer.

"Where did you go when you were her age? Where is she liable to be?"

The live oak. The flush came fast and hot to Delia's cheeks.

"She wouldn't be there," Marsh said, easily reading her mind. "I don't think," he added a second later. He shifted his weight onto one hip, pulled off his hat, ran a frustrated hand through his hair, put it back on, and tugged it down again.

"Sit down, Marsh," Delia said. "While I think."

He jerked a chair out, turned it around, and straddled the turquoise padded seat with his arms across the painted black wooden back.

"The bus passed by the house without stopping. I got worried and came looking for her. The damned school didn't even know whether she got on.

"They were quick enough to tell me she got into another fight today. How the hell she could do that when she was already on suspension, I'll never know."

"*Another* fight? Suspension?" Billie Jo was certainly following in her father's footsteps, Delia thought.

"Yeah, well, that's a whole other story," Marsh said. "Anyway, I had to wait around at school for the bus driver to finish his rounds to ask him if he'd dropped her somewhere else. He said she never got on the bus in the first place. So where the hell did she go?"

"It's too early for the movies," Delia said. "And it's too cold for tubing. Is there a game room somewhere?"

"It went bankrupt a month ago," Marsh replied.

"Is there something going on after school she might be involved in?" Rachel asked. "A play or a club?"

"I searched the school from top to bottom. She wasn't there."

"Could she be with friends?" Delia asked.

Marsh rubbed at the shadow of beard that had accumulated since morning, then pressed the heels of his hands against his eyes. "I don't know. If she has friends, I don't know who they are."

Delia frowned and exchanged a look with Rachel, who shrugged. She didn't have any suggestions. But it seemed heartless to leave Marsh to search on his own.

"Would you like me to drive around with you? We could ask around at the Sonic Drive-In and McDonald's and Taco Bell and Pizza Hut to see if anyone's seen her," Delia offered.

Marsh lowered his hands. "Thanks," he said gruffly. "I'd appreciate that."

"Can you drop me off at the ranch after we find her? That way Rachel will have the car to get home," Delia said.

"Sure," Marsh agreed. "Anything."

He sounded desperate. Uvalde was a small, safe, friendly town, but Delia knew there were always isolated incidents where some stranger drove through a small town and a young woman disappeared.

"Do you mind if I go with Marsh?" Delia asked Rachel. "I might not get back in time for us to spend much time talking before you have to leave tomorrow."

"I think we've discussed everything that needs to be discussed for the moment," Rachel said. "Don't worry about me. Just find Billie Jo."

A moment later Delia found herself sitting on the tattered red leather bench seat of a familiar '57 Chevy pickup. Memories bombarded her. Good ones, mostly. Of a sky with a million stars. Male and female flesh dappled by sunlight streaming through the branches of an ancient live oak. Steamed-up windows. And the grind of gears and rattle of loose metal as Marsh set the rusted-out truck in motion.

"I'm surprised you still have this old rattle-trap," Delia said.

"I left it home when I ran away," he said. "Hitchhiked to Houston with a semi trucker and hopped an oil tanker for the Middle East. Luckily, fate took over in the form of an Arab oil embargo that brought a horde of American journalists past my hotel door. I ended up doing a little investigative work on the side for one of them. Which turned into a little more work. The rest is history."

She kept her eyes lowered as she admitted. "I've seen some of your stuff. It's good."

When he didn't say anything, she looked up and found him staring at her. He looked surprised. And pleased. She felt a flush creeping up her throat. She opened her mouth to make some sort of excuse or explanation for having followed his work and realized that would only make things worse.

"What about you?" he said. "Where did you end up when you left town?"

"Actually, I didn't go far. A good friend of my father's—my real father—lived in San Antonio. Nash Hazeltine is—was—my godfather. He was a rodeo clown, so he was on the road most of the time. I stayed with his wife, Lydia, and finished high school in Alamo Heights."

"Pretty nice area of town for a rodeo clown."

"Nash had family money. He and Lydia paid to put me through college and law school. They were both very generous with me."

"You keep using the past tense."

"My third year of law school at UT in Austin Nash died in a car crash on his way to a rodeo in Nacogdoches."

"I'm sorry."

"I still keep in touch with Lydia. She's remarried. They were very good to me."

They had arrived at the Sonic Drive-In, which was west on Highway 90 from the Amber Sky. Marsh drove into one of the few remaining spaces and looked around at the collection of teenagers in cars and pickups. "I don't see her," he said.

Delia opened the door and stepped down. "Let's go ask if anyone knows where she might be."

"She'll kill me," Marsh said, "for checking up on her."

"If she didn't want you to check up on her, she should have phoned, so you wouldn't worry."

Marsh cleared his throat. "We . . . uh . . . don't exactly have that kind of relationship."

Delia's brow furrowed. "What kind do you have?"

"She sort of takes care of herself without much help from me."

"You're still her father. She should have known you'd worry. Let's split up, so we can do this faster," Delia said.

Marsh was grateful for the respite from Delia's probing questions. When he had realized Billie Jo wasn't on the bus, he had been mad at first, thinking she was sulking somewhere, punishing him for getting her into trouble at school. Or maybe afraid of what he would do when he found out she had been in another fight.

As the daylight hours waned, his anger had faded and the worry had grown. What if something bad had happened to her? What if someone was hurting her right now? He had seen too much in his lifetime not to have a very vivid imagination.

He thought of all the ways he had failed Billie Jo as a father. Being gone so much overseas when she was little. Seeing her so seldom once he and Ginny were divorced. Sending a birthday card when he remembered, a Christmas card with money, but not a gift he had picked out himself. He thought of the promises he had made once upon a time about the kind of father he would be.

His kid would get lots of hugs. His kid would know he—except it had turned out to be a she— was loved.

He didn't think he had touched Billie Jo since he had met her in Logan Airport in Boston after Ginny's death. He had wanted to hug her. The forlorn teenager had looked like she needed a hug. But when he reached for her she had ducked under his arm and headed for the baggage carousel, muttering something about his luggage.

Since then, they had been two strangers living in the same house. He hadn't known what to do to break down the barriers between them. He had no practice being a parent. He had no role model to follow.

That wasn't precisely true. He could remember listening to his grandmother's stories, being hugged by her, being tucked into bed by her.

But Billie Jo was sixteen. You didn't tell stories to a sixteen-year-old or tuck her into bed. And she looked mortified every time he even hinted he might like to give her a hug.

Marsh leaned against the roof of a shiny red Ford Taurus with mag wheels and stooped down to speak to the teenage boy in the driver's seat. "Have you seen Billie Jo North since school let out?"

"Naw. Is she in some kind of trouble?"

Marsh realized he might be creating more than a few problems for his daughter by asking about her like this. "No, just trying to locate her," he said. "If you see her, tell her to call home."

"Is there some kind of emergency?" the girl sitting next to the boy leaned over to ask.

"No, just looking for her."

Marsh repeated the same questions up one side of the Sonic at a Ford Bronco, Chevy pickup, VW Bug, and ancient Ford Fairlane, while Delia went down the other side. They met at the walk-up order window.

"Any luck?" Marsh asked.

Delia shook her head. "No one's seen her. Let's go to Taco Bell and ask there."

They repeated the same procedure at Taco Bell and McDonald's and Pizza Hut with no success. It was long past dark. They drove around for a while looking up and down the streets in town, but saw no sign of her.

"Maybe she's gone home," Delia suggested. "When was the last time you called?"

"It's been a few hours." Marsh stopped at the Mid-Town Gulf station next to the courthouse on Main Street and used the pay phone. The phone at the ranch rang until he heard himself on the answering machine asking the caller to leave a message. He felt a stab of fear and channeled it into anger, which was more familiar and made him feel less terrified.

"If you're home, Billie Jo, pick up the goddamn phone," Marsh said. He felt Delia's hand on his arm and realized Billie Jo wasn't likely to respond to that sort of language, not to mention his angry tone of voice. Especially if she had run in the first place because she was afraid of what he would do to her for getting into trouble again at school.

"Look, Billie Jo," he said in a calmer voice. "I'm just worried about you. So if you're home, please pick up the phone."

Marsh waited. He heard the whir of the answering machine but nothing else. His stomach knotted. And knotted again. He slammed the pay phone receiver back on the hook. "Damn it! If she's home, she's not answering the phone."

"Maybe we should go to your place and wait for her there," Delia suggested. "We aren't doing much good driving around in circles."

"You'd come home with me?"

"Why not?"

Marsh could think of a couple of good reasons. For one thing, he was ashamed of the way the place looked. It hadn't been in very good shape twenty years ago, and it looked even worse now. There were a couple of antiques—his sleigh bed and a copper-plated dry sink with a hand-painted porcelain bowl, the pitcher for which had been broken long ago. But the rest of the furnishings were early Sears—a red Formica-topped, chrome-legged table and padded, chrome-legged chairs in the kitchen; a sagging sofa and a ragged, overstuffed chair in the living room; and some rugs that covered the worst-worn spots in the hardwood floors.

He could blame the run-down condition of things on his father, but Delia would see that the linoleum in the kitchen had been worn down a lifetime ago, and the watermarked rose paper had been there half a century.

For a second thing, he didn't think it was such a smart idea to be alone with her. Nevertheless, he wanted—needed—her to come home with him. To keep him from going crazy with fear while he waited. To keep him from turning that fear into anger when his wayward daughter finally showed her face. And to help him get through the night if she didn't.

When they reached the house, it was dark.

Marsh bit back a groan of frustration and despair. "Where the hell is she?"

"She'll come home when she's ready."

"How soon will that be?"

"When she's ready," Delia repeated.

"Wait here until I get the back porch light on," he told Delia. But when he opened the mud porch door she was at his shoulder and followed him inside the kitchen. He reached for the knotted string over the kitchen sink and winced as the bare seventy-five-watt bulb blinded him.

As soon as his eyes adjusted, he headed for the refrigerator, dropping his hat on the antler rack along the way. He gestured Delia toward the chrome chair with the most intact plastic seat. "Make yourself comfortable. Want a Pearl? Oh yeah, you don't like beer. Billie Jo has about a case of Diet Coke in here. How about one of those?"

"Sure."

"Want a glass and some ice?"

"No, the can is fine."

He popped the lid and handed her the Coke, then stepped back to the counter and set the cap on his beer against the Formica and hit it with the heel of his hand. The metal cap went flying and landed in the chipped porcelain sink. He took a long drink, needing the alcohol more than the liquid refreshment. Needing to keep space between him and Delia, too aware of her, of the fact she was here in his house, and they were alone.

He watched her glance around when she thought he wasn't looking, saw her appraising, judging. And knew what conclusion she would be forced to draw.

"It isn't much," he said bitterly. "But it's home."

"It could be very—"

"Operative words," Marsh interrupted. "Could be. It isn't much right now, though. Right?"

"You said it. I didn't."

"Discretion. Diplomacy. Qualities I would expect to find in a judge."

Delia's back stiffened, but she said nothing.

Marsh didn't know why he was so intent on provoking her, but he couldn't seem to help himself. Maybe if she stayed angry, she would keep her distance. Because he sure as hell was having trouble keeping his.

"There's been so much to do around the ranch—fence to mend, machinery to fix, fields to plow, cows to be inseminated—I haven't really gotten around to the house."

"It could use a woman's touch," Delia said, and then blushed delightfully.

"I've always thought so," he said in a husky voice.

"What time is it?" she asked.

Marsh was frozen for a moment watching her throat move as she took a long swallow of Coke. He glanced at the microwave clock. "It's nearly eleven-thirty."

Delia set the Coke on the table. "Maybe we should call the police."

He rubbed the back of his neck. "I hate to do that. It'll be all over town if I do, and if she is just out with a friend, or staying away to avoid me . . ."

"Why not just ask the Uvalde police chief to have his men keep an eye out for her while they drive around town? The county sheriff can do the same."

"It's worth a try." He picked up the phone and made the calls. The police chief was co-operative, but Sheriff Koehl had other fish to fry.

"Koehl has other priorities," Marsh said disgustedly as he hung up the phone, "unless I'm willing to make a formal missing person report." The former deputy's pride had been dented by that incident twenty years ago, even if all had been forgiven—because the statute of limitations had run—by the time the prodigal returned.

Marsh sieved his hand through his hair. "God, I'm a rotten father."

"What makes you say that?"

"Isn't this incident proof enough?"

Delia shook her head. "It looks to me like Billie Jo is as much to blame here as you. She's the one who got in trouble. She has to learn to face the consequences of her actions."

"Like you did?" Marsh asked quietly. "Seems to me you ran away, too."

Delia's brow furrowed, and her eyes searched his face. "Why are you doing this?"

"Doing what?"

"Purposely insulting me."

Marsh set his longneck on the counter. "Does the truth hurt that much?"

"There were extenuating circumstances."

"There always are." He took a step toward her and watched her grip the nearest chair, as though to use it as a barrier between them. She was wearing a pair of aged, butter-soft jeans, a sleeveless white silk shell, and snakeskin cowboy boots. He didn't stop until he was standing behind her, his hands at his sides, not touching her at all.

He could feel her heat.

He closed his eyes and breathed deeply. He

could smell the lavender shampoo in her hair. Why did it have to be lavender, of all scents?

He slid his hands around her waist from behind and felt her quiver. He laid his palms flat on her abdomen and pressed, and she leaned back into him, her buttocks nestled against his groin. She laid her head back against his chest, and he watched her eyes drift closed.

He lowered his head and kissed her throat beneath her ear. "Delia," he murmured against her skin. "You taste good."

He expected her to jerk away at any moment, to flee as she had those long ago days, to tease him with a taste of her and deny him the feast. She remained languid in his arms.

He took more. A nibble on the lobe of her ear. A love bite at her shoulder.

She made a moaning sound in her throat. But she didn't try to escape.

His genitals drew up tight in anticipation.

He slid his hands upward toward her breasts and felt the nipples, pebbled and pointy beneath the silk. Her breathing faltered as he circled the tips with his fingers.

"My turn to tease," he murmured in her ear.

Marsh turned her in his arms and lowered his mouth, oh so slowly, toward hers. He gave her plenty of time to realize the folly of what they were doing. He gave her a dozen chances to say no.

Her liquid eyes spoke volumes, but her lips didn't move.

Then he had what he wanted. Her lips soft and pliant under his. He brushed against them briefly—more teasing—and heard her mur-

mur of protest. Then he claimed her mouth, rougher than he wanted to be, because he needed too much. Anger tethered for years broke free as he forced her mouth open with his tongue and thrust deep.

You should have been mine long ago. We should have had these years together. You shouldn't have run from me.

He mastered his anger and stifled the resentment he had left unacknowledged for so many years, intent on enjoying what he had, for as long as he had it.

Where he had expected resistance, there was none.

She opened to him, her body arching toward him in imitation of his tongue thrusting in her mouth. He grabbed her buttocks with one hand and pulled her tight against him, grinding their bodies together, groaning with the exquisite feel of her with only a few layers of denim and cotton to keep them apart.

It wasn't close enough.

"I want you. I want to be inside you," he said raggedly.

His mouth clamped onto hers without giving her a chance to reply. He wasn't taking no for an answer. She shouldn't have started this if she didn't intend to finish it.

Moments—minutes?—later he tore his mouth away and laid his forehead against hers, his heart ricocheting around in his chest, gasping breath as though he had run a marathon. His body ached. He needed to be inside her *now*. So far, he hadn't asked, he had taken. But he wanted more. He wanted everything.

He wanted what she had never given him.

To his dismay, he realized he wanted—needed—her to be willing. He wanted to be sure she knew what she was doing. And that she wanted it as much as he did.

"Say yes, Delia. Please say yes."

She sighed tremulously. The refrigerator hummed. His pulse hammered in his ear.

"Yes," she whispered. "Oh, yes."

He made a growling sound in his throat, an animal claiming its mate, and swept her up into his arms. She gave a startled cry of alarm and then laughed, a bubbly, happy, excited sound that made his own lips curve in response.

"What are you doing?" she said.

"Carrying you off to my den, where you can't escape me," he said, burrowing his nose against her throat and biting and sucking hard enough to make her moan. Her arms clung to him, and he felt the sexual tension in her body.

He lifted his head to study her in the harsh light of the naked kitchen bulb. She looked a little dazed, a little frightened. Her cheeks were flushed with heat, and her lips were pouty from the kisses he had already given her. He couldn't resist tasting her again.

He felt her fingers tangling in the hair at his nape and shivered at the touch. He broke the kiss as he headed down the hall to his bedroom with her in his arms. The light from the kitchen was diffused in the hall, and her eyes gleamed like an animal in the dark.

He swore under his breath when he saw that his bedroom door was closed. He didn't want to set Delia down even to open the door, so he angled her and wrestled with the knob and shoved the door open with his shoulder.

He headed for the bed, intending to lay her down, but halfway there she pulled his head down and kissed him.

Her tongue traced the seam of his lips, and as he opened his mouth, slipped inside. The sheer eroticism of what she was doing stopped him in his tracks.

He let her legs slide to the floor because he wanted to feel her against him. He spread his legs and tucked her between them, lifting her enough to fit them together.

He felt her unbuttoning his shirt and shrugged his way out of it as she dragged it down his arms. He hindered her efforts to completely remove the shirt, because at the same time he was pulling her shell out of her jeans.

"Turn on the light," she murmured against his lips. "I want to see you." Her hand slid down the front of him as her mouth suckled one hard male nipple.

The top of his head was about to come off. She couldn't want to see him half as much as he wanted to see her. All of her.

He tore himself away and grabbed for the light on the bedside table, nearly knocking it over before he managed to turn it on. It took a moment for his eyes to adjust to the light and two seconds more for his mind to register what his eyes were seeing.

Billie Jo squinted up at him. "Daddy?"

She was curled up on his bed, wrapped like

a burrito in his grandmother's patchwork quilt. She wriggled inside the quilt, freeing her arms so she could shove herself upright as far as her elbows. Her eyes were swollen and red-rimmed, as though she had been crying. A dozen balled Kleenex scattered on the bed attested to it. She stared bewildered at him for a moment before her gaze flickered to Delia. Her eyes widened in alarm, then narrowed on him.

He thrust a hand through his hair in agitation, faced with the knowledge that his daughter had caught him half-naked in his bedroom with a strange woman. The snug fit of his jeans left nothing to the imagination and made his intentions toward said woman perfectly clear.

"What the hell are you doing in here?" Marsh growled as he snatched his shirt up off the floor and slipped it on, leaving the tails to cover his arousal.

"What's *she* doing in here?" Billie Jo countered.

He ventured a glance at Delia and saw she was beet red with embarrassment and desperately finger-combing her hair and tucking her shell back into her jeans. Her efforts weren't doing much good to hide the state she was in. Her pupils were huge, and her nipples were visibly peaked beneath the silk.

He was glad as hell to know Billie Jo was safe. And equally irate about when and where she had turned up. Nothing was going to happen between him and Delia tonight for certain, and God knew when—or if—this opportunity would come again.

He turned his frustration and fury on his daughter.

"She's here," he said, "because we were looking for you all goddamn afternoon and evening. Where the hell were you? Why didn't you come home on the bus? And how did you get yourself in trouble again when you were already on suspension?"

"What do you care?" Billie Jo countered. "So long as I'm not in your way."

"What's that supposed to mean?"

"It means you never wanted me here in the first place. Now I see why! I'm obviously cramping your style." She tried getting to her feet, but the quilt kept her trapped on the bed like a fly in a web.

"Who I entertain and when I do it are none of your damn business," Marsh retorted defensively.

"Marsh, please," Delia said. "You're only making things worse."

He turned on Delia like a dog in a fight that ceases to know friend from foe. "This is none of your business," he snapped. "So stay out of it."

"Fine!" she snarled back. "I'll wait in the kitchen. When you're done acting like an idiot, I'd appreciate a ride home."

She hadn't taken two steps before he grabbed her arm to stop her. "Delia, I—"

She wrenched herself free. "I think you and your daughter have some things to discuss. Reasonably. Rationally. Calmly discuss."

"I get the point," he said irritably. He turned back to find Billie Jo sitting on the edge of the bed still wrapped in the quilt from the waist down, watching them with wide-eyed interest. He didn't know what to say to her. He didn't know where to start.

He turned back to Delia for help, but she had already left the room and closed the door behind her, leaving father and daughter alone together.

He leaned back against the door with his legs spread wide and his arms folded across his chest. "All right. You're not getting out of here until I've heard the whole story. So start talking."

"Daddy . . ."

"What?"

Her eyes floated with tears. Her chin quivered. She lowered her gaze to the hands knotted in her lap. "I'm so sorry," she whispered. "I didn't mean to get into another fight. It just . . . happened. I knew how disappointed you'd be, and I . . . I needed some time alone. To think." She looked up at him, her heart in her eyes.

He was across the room an instant later and lifted her, quilt and all, into his lap. "It's all right, baby. I'm here."

"Oh, Daddy." She gripped his neck tight and clung to him, pressing her face tight against his throat as she sobbed her heart out.

Marsh felt the sting of tears in his eyes as he clutched his daughter to him. He wanted to do the right thing. He wanted to say the

right thing. He wanted to be a good father. He
just didn't know how.

He brushed his hand over her mussed-up
curls, soothing her, offering what awkward
comfort he could. He crooned to her, not even
sure himself what he was saying. Until the
sobs quieted at last. Until she hiccuped and
sighed.

"How did you get back to the ranch?" he
asked.

"I hitched a ride."

He forbore telling her how dangerous that
was, at least for the moment, because he was
afraid the slightest harsh word from him
would make her burst into tears again.

"Can you tell me one thing?" he said. "Can
you tell me where you were all the time I was
looking for you?"

She hesitated, then said, "I was sitting under
the live oak by the Carsons' north pasture
gate."

"Why would you go there?" he asked.

"That's where Eula said the sheriff found
Delia Carson when . . . when she lost your
baby."

ᨃ *Chapter Eleven* ᨃ

One of the hardest things Delia had ever done was to leave Marsh alone with his daughter. She knew all the bad things that could happen to a teenage girl in the clutches of an angry father, all the harm and hurt and pain that could result.

But even at his angriest, Marsh had never laid a hand on Delia. And she knew from their discussions years ago that Marsh had planned, above all else, to be a better parent than his father. She had to believe he wanted to mend fences with Billie Jo. But it was hard to sit on the chrome chair at the kitchen table waiting, staring through the open window at the dark, quiet night, letting the breeze riffle her hair, wondering what was going on down the hall.

As the minutes passed and Marsh didn't join her, Delia's thoughts turned to what had happened between her and Marsh in the kitchen. And the hallway. And the bedroom before the light had gone on.

I must be out of my mind.

No, just crazy in love with the man. You always have been.

It felt so good. It felt so right.

What did you expect? That the fire might have gone out?

Why didn't he ever come after me?

Why didn't you go after him?

Both good questions. Neither of which Delia had a good answer for. There were explanations, of course.

During the first eight years after she left Uvalde, she had been in high school, college, and law school. She hadn't written to Marsh, hadn't let anyone know how to get in touch with her. And Marsh had simply disappeared. She had no idea where he was or what he had done with himself. She had been too confused and unhappy for the first few years to do more than survive.

When she had finally picked herself up and brushed herself off and started living again, she had been too driven to reach her professional goals to worry about Marsh. Much. It hadn't been worry, actually. More like a constant yearning for a dream that was never going to come true.

She had started following his work when he was hired by *The Chronicle,* a budding national newspaper that, along with *USA Today,* was among the first of its kind. It had been a way of connecting to him without meeting face-to-face. Even then, she had still been running away. She had been afraid to see him again. Afraid of what he would say, what he would do. Afraid he had stopped loving her. It would have hurt too much to know that for sure.

"Penny for your thoughts?"

Delia started when she heard Marsh's voice. She felt his hands on her shoulders before she could turn around. She closed her eyes and groaned as his thumbs found the tight muscles in her neck. "God, that feels good."

"It's been a rough day for you."

"And you." She tried to get up, but he pressed her back down and kept up what he was doing. It felt too good to make him stop. Which was exactly why she should have stopped him. "What time is it?" she asked.

"Midnight."

"I should be going."

"Not yet. You haven't told me what you were thinking."

"I was thinking about you. Is that what you wanted to hear?"

"It's a good start. What else?"

She took a deep breath and said, "I was thinking how scared I was all those years of seeing you again."

His hands stopped what they were doing, but his grip tightened. "You were scared?"

She nodded.

"Why? I loved you, Delia."

She heard the pain in his voice. She angled her body so she could look up at him, and his hands fell away. Once they did, she stood and moved away from him, toward the sink.

Running again, Delia. Stop it. Stop running.

She turned and faced Marsh. His eyes were sunken with fatigue and oh, so wary. His hair was standing every whichaway. His shirt was tucked haphazardly back into his Levi's. He shouldn't have looked so appealing. Or so desperately vulnerable.

Her heart lodged in her throat, making speech impossible. Being with Marsh made her feel whole again, as though a missing part of a jigsaw puzzle had been slipped into place.

Delia became aware of the refrigerator humming, of a steady drip hitting the old porcelain sink, of Marsh's gray eyes staring intently at her.

She took a deep breath. "I'm so sorry I ran away."

He smiled, a gentle curve of his lips, but his eyes were unbearably sad. "I know."

She swallowed over the lump in her throat. "I wish . . ."

He opened his arms and she stepped into them and he folded them around her.

Delia felt Marsh's arms tighten around her. "I called *The Chronicle* once looking for you," she said.

"I never got any message."

"I didn't leave one."

"Why not?"

She pressed her cheek against his shoulder. "Too scared."

"Of what?"

"That you wouldn't want to see me."

He made a sound in his throat. "God, Delia. I never stopped thinking about you." Marsh's lips pressed against her temple, then her cheek, and finally sought her mouth.

Her eyes slid closed again as her lips met

his in a kiss of frustration and need and forgiveness.

"It's been an incredible day," she said against his lips, when they finally broke apart to breathe.

Marsh chuckled ruefully. "You can say that again."

"Is Billie Jo all right?"

He nuzzled her throat beneath her ear. "I tucked her into bed. She was practically asleep before the light was out." He lifted his head and looked her in the eye. "She's heard the rumors about us. It's what she's been fighting about at school."

"Oh, no."

"She was at the live oak all afternoon and evening. Thinking."

"Did she say what she was thinking about?"

"Not precisely. If I had to guess, I'd say she doesn't want to believe the gossip about us she's heard at school. But she didn't come right out and ask me for the truth, either."

"Maybe she's afraid of what the truth might be."

Marsh put his hands on her shoulders. "How can I tell her the truth, Delia? If I didn't get you pregnant, who did?"

"I see," Delia said, curling her arms protectively around herself and backing away from him. "It always comes back to Ray John, doesn't it? Take me home, Marsh."

"Who killed Ray John, Delia?"

Delia froze. "He killed himself."

"Suicide?" Marsh shook his head. "That

bastard was too selfish to do any of us that kind of favor."

"It was an accident," Delia said breathlessly. "You saw for yourself how he was always pointing a gun at somebody's head and pulling the trigger."

Marsh raised a disbelieving brow. "Are you saying that's what happened?"

"I wasn't there at the time," Delia snapped. "How should I know?"

"Weren't you?"

Delia felt suffocated, like someone had a hand over her mouth and nose. She took a gulping breath of air. And another. Marsh knew something, had found out something. But only three people knew the truth. She was sure none of them had talked. So how could he possibly know? "What are you saying, Marsh? What are you suggesting?"

"I don't believe Ray John Carson killed himself," Marsh said. "I think he was murdered."

"Take me home." Delia was already headed for the door.

"Can we talk about this?"

She was out the kitchen door and headed for Marsh's pickup, nearly running. "There's nothing to discuss."

She yanked hard on the door to the old pickup, got a helping yank from Marsh to open it, and pulled it closed behind her. The window was already down, and she stuck her elbow in it to keep Marsh from leaning in. She would rather have stuck her head out. She felt like throwing up.

"All right," Marsh said, moving around the

pickup and slipping behind the wheel. "I'll let it go for the moment. But the issue isn't going to disappear, Delia. It'll be right there between us until you deal with it." He ground the gears as he sent the pickup clanking down the rutted dirt road that led off the North Ranch.

Delia's brow furrowed as she considered what Marsh had said. She angled herself so her back was braced against the door, and she was facing him with one leg tucked under her. "Is that what you think has kept us apart all these years? You think I ran away because I knew my father had been murdered?"

He kept his eyes on the highway. "The idea occurred to me. I wouldn't have blamed you, Delia," he added quietly.

Delia couldn't believe what she was hearing. "You think *I* killed Ray John?"

"It makes sense to me."

"I only wish I'd had the courage," she said bitterly.

As soon as she finished speaking, Delia realized what she had done. Her heart clutched. If she hadn't killed Ray John, that left only two other people in the house who could have— the one who had actually committed the murder and her mother.

Marsh couldn't know Rachel was a suspect, but knowing him, he would ferret out the truth . . . unless she stuck firm to the suicide theory. "He . . . he killed himself," she said softly.

"There were no powder burns on his hands."

"How could you possibly know that? Why would you even think to check?"

He glanced at her, then back at the highway. "I can't help it if my job has taught me to question things. I looked up the coroner's report a few weeks back. I would have been out of luck, except there's a little old gray-haired lady in records who hasn't thrown anything away for thirty years.

"Only scant traces of gunpowder showed up on Ray John's hands, not what should have been there if he were the one with his finger on the trigger. Most likely, he was struggling with someone when the gun went off.

"Something fishy had to be going on for that to be kept secret by the authorities. All I can figure out is that you confessed to the sheriff what Ray John had done to you, and he decided it was justifiable homicide and spared everybody the expense of a trial."

"I . . . I never spoke to Sheriff Davis."

"Then who did? Only somebody who knew the truth could have told the police what happened. Who does that leave?"

Delia let out a slow breath. *Rachel. And Mother.*

But Mother had forbidden Rachel to say anything. And Mother wouldn't have gone to the sheriff herself, because she hadn't believed the truth about Ray John.

Had Rachel struggled with Ray John over the gun? Is that how he had been shot? Or had someone else been there that morning? Someone stronger. Who else besides herself and Rachel hated Ray John enough to want him dead?

She perused the harsh planes of Marsh's face in the eerie green light from the dash. She hesitated, then said, "Are you telling me you killed him?"

He glanced at her and smiled. "I wanted to. I would have been glad to. But I didn't."

"Then who did?"

"Figure it out, Delia."

"Have you?"

He nodded. "I think so."

Who else had wanted Ray John dead besides herself and Rachel? She had no intention of raising suspicion about Rachel by mentioning her name. "It couldn't have been Mother," Delia murmured.

"Why not?"

"She loved Ray John. She didn't believe the things I told her about him. And she was upstairs with me when the gun went off."

Marsh shot her a startled look. "She was?" His brow creased. "But who else could have gone to the sheriff and gotten me released? And why did Sheriff Davis tell me Ray John had committed suicide, when he couldn't have had information back yet from the coroner to prove it one way or the other? No, Delia. Sheriff Davis had already made up his mind what story he was going to tell the public. And it wasn't the truth."

Marsh pulled up to the back door of the Carson mansion. He didn't turn off the ignition, just let the truck idle noisily. A light burned in the kitchen. Another was on in a room upstairs.

"Looks like Rachel's still awake," he said.

Delia glanced up at the lighted window. "That's my bedroom light. Rachel must have left it on for me. Maybe she thought I'd forget where everything was after all these years of being gone." *And maybe she remembered that Ray John liked it dark.*

"Welcome home, Delia," Marsh said.

"Thank you, Marsh."

"I'd like to come visit Hattie when she's home from the hospital," Marsh said.

"I'll let you know when she's ready for company." Delia didn't know why she was having such a hard time getting out of the pickup. She couldn't shake the feeling that once she said good-bye to Marsh she might not see him again. Which was ridiculous, because he lived on the property right next door, and she wasn't going anywhere for at least a week.

"Be seeing you around," Marsh said.

"All right." She hesitated, unmoving.

He reached over and caught her nape and angled her toward him. His mouth covered hers hungrily, as though he were starving, and she were sustenance. As abruptly as he had captured her mouth, he let her go.

"Good night, Delia."

Still, she sat frozen. She could taste him. Her lips were damp from his. Her body felt hot and liquid inside.

"Would you like to go somewhere?" he said in a ragged voice.

"Where?"

Marsh laughed huskily and dragged her into his lap to kiss her mouth and nose and eyes. "Damn it, Delia, I want you so bad I hurt. But I refuse to check in to a motel in town, and we won't have any privacy at either my place or yours. That leaves the front seat of this pickup or the cold hard ground. That isn't how I want to make love to you for the first time."

"I wouldn't mind."

Marsh groaned and pressed his mouth to her throat, while his hand grasped her breast and squeezed. "Don't say things like that, or I'm liable to take you at your word."

"When did you get so sensible?" she complained, nibbling at his ear. The feeling she would lose him, that something would happen to steal him away before they ever had a chance to love one another persisted. And made her daring.

"Take me to the live oak," she whispered in his ear. "The grass is soft there. No one will bother us."

He shoved her off his lap so fast she nearly fell on the floor. She was still scrambling onto her side of the bench seat as he whirled the pickup and headed down the dirt road that led to the north pasture gate. He kept both hands on the wheel for the whole bumpy trip to the live oak, which was a damned good thing, because he was driving recklessly fast. He didn't once look at her or say another word.

Delia figured he was as worried she might

change her mind as she was that he might get cold feet.

When they arrived, Marsh turned off the key. The truck rumbled for another three seconds before it finally died.

The quiet was profound. At first. Delia made out the sound of crickets. And the soft rustle of the live oak as the wind whispered through its leaves.

Now that they were here, Delia suddenly felt awkward and uncertain. She stepped out of the truck and left the door hanging open. The overhead light didn't work. The moon and stars created silvery shapes and shadows.

Delia heard Marsh get out of the pickup and come after her. She stood with one hand on a limb of the live oak and looked across the fence line at the spot where she had taken the spill from her horse.

"This should feel strange or wrong," Delia said. "We haven't seen each other for twenty years before this morning." She turned to face Marsh. "But it doesn't. It feels like I never left, like all the years between never happened."

His eyes glittered. "They happened."

"You sound angry . . . bitter."

"My life turned out differently than I'd hoped."

"Not better?"

"I love Billie Jo," Marsh said. "I love my work. But I don't know that my life's better than it would have been if I'd stayed right here at home and married the woman I loved."

Loved. Past tense. "I'm here now. And I'm yours."

"For how long?" Marsh asked.

"For as long as we have." She couldn't promise him more than that. When he didn't answer right away, she was afraid it wasn't enough.

At last he said, "I'll take what I can get."

His mouth was soft on hers, surprisingly gentle. Hungry without being urgent. "I don't want to hurry," he murmured against her lips. "I want to take my time."

"Take all the time you need," she said, her mouth smiling beneath his. "I've got all night." She realized as she said the words, that it wasn't nearly enough. But it was all they had for certain.

"We'd better not waste a moment, then," Marsh said, sweeping her up in his arms.

She gave a startled shriek as he swung her around in a circle, but he kept it up until she was giddy with laughter.

"Put me down," she pleaded. "You're making me dizzy."

He slid her down the front of him and hugged her tight. His smile was brilliant in the moonlight. He looked happy and excited, playful as a teenager. "You're lucky I have a blanket behind the seat of the pickup, Carson, or your ass would be in grass," he teased.

"The sooner you get it, the sooner you get it. If you know what I mean," she teased back.

He gave her a smacking kiss and let her go. He ran for the truck, rooted around behind the seat for the blanket, and came running back.

She already had her boots and socks off and was standing barefoot in the dewy grass by the time he returned.

"You're supposed to wait for me," he said, spreading the brown wool army blanket out on the ground.

"The grass feels good," she said wiggling her toes.

Both of them dropped to their knees on the blanket, and he had her prone under him a few moments later. Two seconds after that he had her out of the silk shell.

"What happened to going slow?" she said with a delighted laugh.

"Next time," he said as his mouth latched onto her nipple through her lacy bra.

Delia moaned and arched toward him.

She had thought it would be over quickly, and it was true they were naked in no time. But Marsh seemed intrigued by the sight of her in the moonlight.

"You're so beautiful, Delia. More beautiful than I remembered. And your skin is so soft." His hands twined in her hair and spread it out around her face. "I wish your hair were longer. It's so silky. I want to wrap myself up in it."

"Ray John used to say that."

She was sorry the instant the words were out of her mouth.

Marsh stiffened. His eyes never left hers as he continued to caress her hair. "I wish I had known sooner, Delia. I would have killed him for you."

"Then I'm glad you didn't know," Delia

said. "It wouldn't have been a fair exchange—your life for his."

He grabbed handfuls of her hair, holding her captive for his kiss. "It's me, Delia. It's Marsh."

She felt like weeping. "I know, Marsh. I'm sorry I mentioned his name. Only—"

"It's this place, Delia. It has too many memories."

"I always loved coming here," Delia confessed. "I loved being with you. You made my life bearable. You gave me hope."

"I want to make love with you, Delia. Without any ghosts to haunt us."

"I don't think of him often. But I thought you should know—because you always liked my hair long—the reason I cut it."

"I'm glad you told me."

But they both knew she would never grow her hair for him. He would never have a chance to wrap himself in it the way he wanted. Ray John had stolen that small dream, as he had stolen larger ones.

It was a miracle she and Marsh had managed to find each other in the first place. A miracle they had found each other two decades later.

"Make love to me, Marsh. I've waited so very long to feel your arms around me again."

"I want to be inside you, Delia. I've wanted it for a lifetime."

They had waited twenty years for this moment. Suddenly neither of them was in any hurry. They took the time to discover each other, after all.

Delia wasn't able to get enough of touching Marsh, the springy black curls on his chest, the sinewy muscles in his arms and shoulders, his taut buttocks.

And he touched her, with adoration and desire.

"Do you like that?" Marsh asked.

Delia moaned.

"Was that a yes?" Marsh asked.

Delia laughed.

"Was *that* a yes?" Marsh asked.

Delia kissed him, sweetly, softly on the mouth. "Oh, yes. That was definitely a yes." She touched him, and he groaned.

Before she could ask, he gasped, "Yes!"

It had been right to come here where it all started. Where they had once met as two people who loved each other. Where they had spoken of their hopes and dreams.

Her hands tightened in Marsh's hair as he kissed his way down her belly, lifted her with his hands, and loved her with his mouth and tongue.

Nothing had ever felt so exquisite. Nothing had ever been so devastating. Nothing had ever made her feel so complete.

He mantled her sweat-slick body as the shudders of ecstasy faded. She liked the firm, solid weight of him. She wrapped her arms and legs around him and held him close while her breathing returned to normal. She tasted herself on his lips when he kissed her.

"I want to be inside you," he murmured. "I need to be inside you. Are you protected?"

"What?"

"Are you going to get pregnant if we do this?"

Delia's face heated. How silly to be embarrassed. She should be glad he had asked. She should have asked a few questions herself. "I'm on the pill. To regulate—"

"Then I won't need this," he interrupted, pitching a condom aside.

Where on earth had he gotten that? Delia wondered.

"I don't have anything you can catch," he said in response to her incredulous look.

"I never thought you did. Neither do I," she added hastily.

He chuckled. "That's a comfort. But to tell you the truth, Delia, this would be worth dying for."

It was the sort of thing a man said in the heat of the moment. But when Delia looked into Marsh's face, she was jolted by the realization that he meant it.

She reached between them with her hand and led him to where they both wanted him to be.

Delia met Marsh's gaze steadily as he drove himself in to the hilt. His eyes slid closed, and he made a satisfied sound in his throat. She moaned as he withdrew slightly before thrusting again.

He loved her with his mouth and his hands and his body. And she loved him back. It was a spiritual joining of body and soul that lifted Delia to heights she had never known existed. It wasn't only her physical being that felt exalted, it was her innermost self.

When Marsh spilled his seed inside her, she felt a terrible sense of loss. Because the moment was so fleeting. Because their togetherness couldn't last. Because there was no fertile ground in which his seed could take root.

She wasn't aware of the tears until Marsh began to kiss them away.

"Don't cry," he murmured. "It was beautiful, Delia. It was more than I ever dreamed it could be."

He spooned her against his groin and wrapped the blanket around them. "Let me hold you for a little while."

His hand was already on her lips to still her protest.

"Just a little while," he pleaded.

They stayed there all night. He loved her twice more. They dressed in the light before dawn, and he drove her back to the Circle Crown.

"I have to be home before Billie Jo wakes up," he explained.

"I should try to get in before Rachel knows I've been out all night," she said.

They didn't speak of what had happened between them during the night just past. They didn't speak of the future.

When they arrived at the back door to the Carson mansion, Marsh left the engine running. The lights were still on in the kitchen and her bedroom.

This time she shoved the truck door open and stepped out before she spoke. "So long, Marsh."

"So long, Delia."

She pushed the pickup door closed as quietly as she could and ran for the house without looking back. She heard Marsh back up and turn the truck for home.

When she opened the kitchen door, Rachel was sitting at the table waiting for her.

"Have a nice night?"

Delia headed for the refrigerator to hide the heat in her cheeks. "What are you doing up so early?" She retrieved a carton of orange juice and poured herself a glass.

"I have a plane to catch in a few hours," Rachel said, taking a sip from the coffee cup in front of her. "And I want to go by the hospital to see Mom before I leave."

Delia leaned back against the sink and looked around her. She peered down the hall at the entrance to Ray John's gun room. "Being here feels familiar and strange at the same time."

"This house has that effect on me, too," Rachel said. "And I've been back to visit several times since I got married. I didn't sleep well last night."

"You weren't worried about me, were you?" Delia asked.

Rachel smiled. "No. I heard Marsh's truck drive up last night. When you left with him, I figured you wouldn't be back before morning. Thinking about confronting Cliff was enough to keep me awake."

"I'm sorry we didn't have more time to talk," Delia said.

Rachel arched a disbelieving brow.

Delia laughed. "All right, I'm not at all sorry

about the way I spent the night. But I do wish we'd had more time together."

"We'll have a lot more time in the future. After I leave Cliff." Rachel rose and set her cup in the sink, then headed down the hall. "If I don't go get into the shower pretty soon, I'm going to miss my plane again."

"Rachel," Delia called after her.

Rachel paused and looked over her shoulder.

"Thanks for leaving the light on in my room last night."

The sisters exchanged a look that said everything without saying anything.

"You're welcome," Rachel said.

✎ Chapter Twelve ✎

Marsh slipped back into the house without making a sound. He had left the truck at the end of the lane, afraid the rackety thing would wake Billie Jo. He tiptoed down the hall, opened the door to her room, and glanced inside.

She was still sound asleep, wrapped in her blanket like a bug in a rug.

He padded back down the hall to the kitchen, filled a teakettle with water, and set it on the stove to boil.

Then he let himself think about what had happened last night.

He had made love to many other women in the past. He had even had marathons of sex that left him feeling enervated. But nothing in his memory had ever come close to what he had experienced last night.

He conceded the fact he had loved Delia all these years without admitting it to himself. In sheer determination not to mimic his father's mistake, he had lived a full life. But he realized now he had only been filling up the desperately long days and months and years without her. When all was said and done, he was as much a one-woman man as his father.

He had suspected that sex between him and Delia would be satisfying. But he had not expected to feel so much. He had not expected his need for her to be so great. He had not expected to feel so wrenched by the thought of letting her go this morning.

What if she returned to New York and left him behind? How would he live the rest of his life without her? Was he willing to pull Billie Jo out of school in Uvalde and leave the ranch so he could go after Delia in New York?

A knock on the door forced him from his reverie. He wanted it to be Delia. He yanked the door open, half-expecting to find her there, although he couldn't think of a reason why she would be.

A tall, gangly teenage boy with shaggy black hair and sad brown eyes stood at the kitchen door dressed in cutoffs, enormous Nikes, and a sleeveless black Rolling Stones T-shirt cut off to reveal a muscular midriff. "Is Billie Jo ready?"

"Who are you?" Marsh asked. And what was he doing here?

"I'm Todd Hendrickson, sir." The boy had his hands in his back pockets and shifted from foot to foot. "I . . . uh . . . gave Billie Jo a ride home yesterday. I'm . . . uh . . . we're going tubing on the Frio today."

"Isn't it a little cold for that?" Marsh said. What did Billie Jo think she was doing, making dates with boys without asking his permission?

"The . . . uh . . . sun's been real warm the past week."

Marsh stared at the kid. He'd give the boy credit. He wasn't running. "Who all's going?" Marsh asked.

"A whole bunch of us from school, sir."

At least he was still in school. "She's asleep," Marsh said.

The kid's face fell. "Oh."

Marsh took mercy on the boy. "Come on in and make yourself comfortable while she gets dressed."

"Uh . . ."

Marsh held open the screen door. "We might as well get acquainted." He saw that was the last thing the kid wanted, but it wasn't possible for the boy to run now without losing a lot of teenage face.

"Uh . . . Yes, sir." He pulled a Colorado Rockies baseball cap off as he stepped inside and shoved it into his back pocket.

Marsh liked the "sirs" because it meant the boy had been raised right, but they made him feel his age. The boy refused a cup of tea, and Marsh didn't have coffee. He poured the kid a glass of apple juice and set it on the table. "Have a seat while I go wake her up."

He didn't wait to see whether Todd did as he'd been told. He was too busy thinking about what he was going to say to Billie Jo. He was a little surprised at himself, that he hadn't sent Todd away. That must mean he intended to let Billie Jo go out with the boy.

The thought of his innocent daughter anywhere near a boy with healthy teenage hormones was unnerving.

He knocked twice and opened the door. "Billie Jo?"

She mumbled something, turned over, and curled right back up again.

He entered the room and closed the door behind him. Otherwise the sound of their voices would carry right down the hall to the kitchen.

He sat beside her on the bed and gave her shoulder a nudge. "Wake up, Billie Jo. You've got company."

Her eyes opened a crack. "Daddy? It's Saturday. I don't have school."

"Todd's here."

She bolted upright like a jack-in-the-box. "Todd?" She glanced at the Boston Bruins clock beside her bed. "It's almost eight o'clock!" she exclaimed. "You didn't send him away, did you, Daddy?" She was already out of bed and scrambling around the room grabbing cutoffs and stepping into them and pulling them up under the huge T-shirt she had slept in.

"Whoa, pardner," he said, grabbing her on her way by him. "We have a few things to discuss first."

"I can't talk right now, Daddy. I'm late."

"Sit!" he said, tugging on her arm.

She plopped onto the foot of the bed, her arms crossed mutinously across her chest. "You aren't going to tell me I can't go, are you, Daddy? That wouldn't be fair. Todd is the first person I've met I can talk to. We're not going to be alone. We're going with a bunch of kids from school."

"Not Eula, I hope," Marsh muttered.

Billie Jo flushed. "She won't be there. I asked. You have to let me go, Daddy. Please."

He was worried about how she would get along with the other kids. What if someone brought up his past? What if Todd got some bright idea that she was as wild as her father had been? What if Todd tried to make a move on her, and she got her feelings hurt, or worse?

"How well do you know this Todd fellow?" Marsh asked.

"He's the quarterback of the football team. His father is foreman of a mohair ranch north of town," Delia said. "His mother is president of the school board."

Marsh frowned. Not the type of parents who would want their son dating a trouble-maker at school, the daughter of "that wild North boy." "And they approve of Todd taking you out?"

She shifted uneasily. "Not exactly."

"What, exactly?"

"He said his mother would die if she knew he wanted to go out with me." Her North chin jutted. "But he said he didn't care. That he liked me better than any other girl he's ever met. So you have to let me go with him, Daddy."

Marsh saw heartache down the road for his daughter. Maybe it would be better if he kept her home today. One look at her eyes, and he

knew he wasn't going to change her feelings
for Todd by keeping them separated.

"If he tries anything, you have to promise
me you'll spend the rest of the float with the
girls."

Billie Jo started to throw herself into his
arms, but caught herself, leaping up from the
bed, instead. "Thank you, Daddy. Thank
you!"

She ran to her dresser to search for the right
shirt to wear.

"Don't forget to brush your teeth," he said.

"I won't."

"What about breakfast?" He could see she
was torn, that the last thing she wanted was
breakfast, and that she knew he wanted her to
eat something.

"Could you make me some toast? I'll take it
with me."

"All right. I'll tell Todd you'll be ready in a
few minutes."

"Daddy," she said.

He turned back.

"Don't let him leave."

Marsh grinned. "Don't worry. If he hasn't
already run, he isn't going to now."

Marsh had very little time to grill Todd before Billie Jo showed up in the kitchen doorway. He felt his chest tighten at the sight of
her face when she looked at Todd. Her eyes
were bright with joy.

"Hello, Todd."

Todd rose so fast he bumped his knees on
the tabletop. "Hi—" His voice broke and he
had to clear his throat. "Hi, Billie Jo."

If his daughter was smitten, so was the boy.

He wished so much for Billie Jo to be happy, wanted so badly for her not to be hurt or disillusioned. But there was nothing he could do except stand back and let her live her life.

And be there if she needed him.

"You two have fun," Marsh said.

As they headed out the door, Marsh saw Todd relax, certain for the first time that he was going to escape with his prize.

"Yes, sir. I'll take care of her, sir."

"You do that, Todd," Marsh replied.

They were almost out the door when Billie Jo turned back and rose on tiptoes and gave him a kiss on the cheek. "I love you, Daddy." Then she hurried after Todd, letting the screen door slam behind her.

They left a trail of dust as Todd's brand new, chrome-wheeled black Chevy pickup headed down the rutted road.

Marsh made himself a cup of tea and stood there holding it until his aching throat eased enough that he could swallow again.

∽ *Chapter Thirteen* ∾

"I know I've been gone almost a week, but I don't think I'll have to be here much longer," Delia told her secretary. "Tell the *Times* reporter I'll be back in New York in a couple of days, if he can just hold his britches."

"Shall I quote you?" Janet asked.

Delia laughed. "Make me sound judicial, please."

"Right, boss," Janet replied.

Delia hung up the phone feeling anxious. Something was going on. She was tempted to call Frank Weaver and ask if he had any idea what it was, but if Sam Dietrich wasn't involved in the *Times* investigation of her, she didn't want to get him involved.

She sighed, then used her palms to push herself upright from the chair before her mother's desk. It was time to go check on her mother.

Hattie had stayed in the hospital only four days following surgery before coming home, against the advice of her doctor. In the twenty-four hours since her return to the Circle Crown, Delia had more than once bitten her tongue to avoid an argument. It felt like her mother was intentionally provoking her.

Delia arranged the bedcovers under her mother's arms as she listened to a litany of things she should have done and hadn't, determined not to lose her temper as she had at the hospital.

"No, Mother, I haven't called Dardus yet."

"If you don't order feed now, you're going to run short," Hattie said.

"I'll get in touch with him this afternoon," Delia promised.

"Call the Cattlemen's Association and tell them I won't be at the meeting next week in San Antonio, that you'll be there in my place."

"I'm not sure I'll be here next week," Delia said.

"Why not?" Hattie demanded.

"I have a job, Mother."

"Right now, your job is taking care of the Circle Crown."

"I'm looking for a ranch manager—"

"I won't have a stranger meddling in my business!" Hattie said.

"He won't be a stranger, he'll be an employee," Delia said patiently.

"The Circle Crown will be yours someday, Delia. I don't understand how you can turn your back on it."

"I have other plans for my life, Mother."

"It's my fault, I suppose. I should have included you more in ranch business when you were growing up. At the time it seemed more important to prove to you girls I could do it myself."

Delia raised a disbelieving brow. "You could run this ranch blindfolded with your hands tied behind your back."

"I suppose it might have looked that way to you. Nothing was ever simple. And I was determined to manage entirely on my own. I had something to prove to my father."

"He's been dead since long before I was born," Delia pointed out.

Hattie snorted. "Just because someone's dead doesn't mean they don't still control how you live your life."

Delia couldn't argue with that.

"I always knew I could run the Circle Crown better than my two younger brothers," Hattie said. "But till the day he died, Tucker Carson couldn't conceive of his cattle kingdom being run by his daughter. He willed the Circle Crown to John Carl and Jimmy—till fate stepped in and gave it back to me."

Delia knew the story. Her uncles, John Carl and Jimmy, had tried to beat the Burlington and Rock Island across the tracks in a brand-new Ford Thunderbird—and lost. Hattie Carson had been queen of the Circle Crown ever since.

"I've been proving my father wrong for forty-two years," Hattie said. "I don't intend to let a little heart attack stop me from making it forty-three."

"If you don't slow down, you won't last another year," Delia warned.

"Would you care?"

The question brought Delia up short. Her mother sat waiting for Delia to give her an answer that could only hurt her. "You need to rest, Mother."

"You haven't answered my question. Would you care?"

"I'm here, Mother. Let's leave it at that."

"For how long. And why did you come? I must admit I was surprised. Pleased. But surprised."

"This isn't the right time to be discussing these things," Delia said.

"There may not be much time left," Hattie said quietly.

Delia found herself caught by her mother's intent, silvery blue gaze. "When you're completely recovered from your surgery, we'll talk." There was so much she wanted to ask and hadn't, because she was afraid of the answers she might get.

"I don't want to wait," Hattie said.

"You don't have any choice," Delia replied.

She made a quick escape from her mother's bedroom. She felt like screaming. Like running and running until her side ached, and she couldn't run anymore. She arrived at the barn without realizing that was where she was headed.

Her palomino gelding had died several years ago, but there were several quarter horses in the stalls. She picked a sleek chestnut with a white blaze and stockings, saddled the animal, and kicked it into a lope as she headed across the pasture.

She knew where she was going long before she got there.

The live oak was unchanged. Twenty years was the twinkle of an eye to the ancient tree. Delia stepped down from the saddle and let her mount graze as she settled herself on the ground with her back against the immense tree trunk.

She had learned more about her mother this morning than she had known about her in all the years she had lived at home. It was easy to see the demons that had driven Hattie to devote herself to the Circle Crown. Her mother had succeeded in proving Tucker Carson wrong. But at what price?

The similarities between what her mother had done and her own life were shatteringly apparent. She had devoted herself to punishing men like Ray John Carson. And given up her dream of helping kids. And becoming a wife and mother.

Hattie didn't seem regretful of the choice she had made. Delia wasn't so certain she had chosen correctly.

Seeing Marsh again had been like pouring alcohol on a raw wound—cleansing, but searingly painful. There was a hole inside her that only he could fill. And she wanted a child— Marsh's child—so much sometimes it hurt just to think about it.

Maybe it was too late for Hattie to change, but Delia was still young enough to make different choices. The question was, did she have the courage to risk grabbing for the brass ring one more time? And could she handle the disappointment if it once more eluded her grasp?

Aside from the simple question, "Does Marsh still love me?" there were serious logistical problems to a relationship between someone whose work was in New York and a rancher settled in southwest Texas. Were they insurmountable problems?

Delia took a deep breath of fresh Texas air. Life was precious. She wasn't going to waste another moment living it without love. There just had to be a way to make things work between her and Marsh.

And if he doesn't love you anymore?

She couldn't feel the way she did about Marsh if her feelings weren't returned. He still loved her. She knew he did. It was simply a matter of getting him to acknowledge his feelings.

She hoped.

For the rest of the day, Delia left the tending of her mother to Maria, the housekeeper, while she concentrated on taking care of Circle Crown business.

There was more than enough of it to keep her busy.

Calving would begin any day. Delia saw from the ranch books that her mother had hired extra help to get through the season. It appeared, however, that Hattie usually supervised the help. Which meant that chore was going to fall to Delia.

Unless she could find someone else to do the job. Despite her mother's objections, she was determined to find someone to take over management of the ranch.

She spent long hours poring over ranching magazines and journals, looking through the advertisements in the back to see if someone was seeking a position in ranch management. She found far more ads looking for help than offering to provide it.

She had put out the word in the surrounding community that the Circle Crown was looking for a manager, but so far no one had come forward. Except Marsh. And she refused to consider his offer seriously. That was a temporary solution at best.

Besides doing all the ranch business, Delia was also keeping a close eye on Rachel. Cliff had been more than perturbed with his wife for being gone an extra day. They had quarreled the evening Rachel arrived home and, according to Rachel's account to Delia on the phone later that same evening, Cliff had raised his hand to Rachel just once before she leveled him with a vase of cut flowers.

"You should have seen the stunned look on his face, Delia," Rachel had said with a laugh. "Dripping wet and draped in gladiolas and too stunned to move. I got out of the way before it occurred to him to hit me again."

That had been the extent of the violence between them, but Delia remained worried that her sister might be forced to do something dire before she managed to get away from Cliff.

Delia usually called Rachel each day right after she called her office and checked on her mother, which allowed her to give Rachel comfort and reassurance and get a little comfort and reassurance herself. She dialed Rachel's home phone in Dallas from memory.

It rang twice before a child's voice said, "Hello?"

"Scott, is that you? It's Aunt Delia."

"Hi, Aunt Delia. It's me, Scott."

"Is your mom around?"

"She's in the garage saying good-bye to Daddy. He's going to cut a ribbon. Do you want to talk to her?"

"Sure. When she's through with your dad."

Delia heard a loud, "MOMMY! Aunt Delia's on the phone!" Scott came back on and said, "I'm playing with the Power Rangers you gave me. They're the best!"

"I'm glad," Delia said. "Your mom told me that's what you wanted most for Christmas besides a bicycle."

"I didn't get a bicycle," Scott said, "'cause Daddy said I'm too little. Mommy said I am, too, big enough. But Daddy said no 'cause—"

Delia interrupted, not wanting to put Scott in the position of telling her things that weren't her business. "Who's your favorite Power Ranger?"

"I like Tommy. He's the white tiger, only I liked him better when he was the green dragonzord."

"The what?" Scott repeated himself, but *dragonzord* didn't make any more sense the second time, so she just said, "Really?"

"Yeah, he's neat. But Kimberly sucks."

Sucks? Did six-year-olds know what that meant? "Oh?"

"She turns into this stupid pink bird thing. Oh, here's Mommy."

She heard Scott say, "I'm telling Aunt Delia about Power Rangers."

And Rachel answer, "Go play now while I talk on the phone." A second later Rachel said, "Hi. Has Scott been chattering your ear off?"

"No, he's a delight. But Mother's been driving me crazy. It feels like she's purposely trying to provoke me every time she opens her mouth," Delia said.

"You know how much she hates relying on anyone else for anything. It's what kept her so busy the whole time we were growing up. It must be awful for her to know she can't do it all herself anymore. I suspect you're bearing the brunt of her frustration."

"If you say so," Delia conceded, twining the phone cord around her finger. She was sitting in her mother's swivel chair, at her mother's desk, from which Hattie Carson had run the Circle Crown. What Rachel said made a whole lot of sense. But it didn't make Hattie's jabs any easier to handle. "I'm not sure how much more of this I can take. She's going to push me too far, and I'm going to blow up."

"Would that be so awful?"

"I don't like her, but I don't necessarily want to give her another heart attack," Delia said.

"Have you found anyone yet to manage the ranch, so you can go back to New York?" Rachel asked.

"Not yet. You could do it, you know. Once you leave Cliff, that is."

"I don't want the job," Rachel said. "I have other plans."

"Like what?"

"I want to go back to school and become a veterinarian. There are a couple of good vet programs in Texas, but nothing close enough to Uvalde that I could live at the ranch."

"I had no idea you had aspirations in that direction."

"I didn't before you left home," Rachel said. "After that . . . I sort of got sidetracked when I married Cliff. Speaking of which, how are things going, Delia? Have you talked to any of your friends? How do things look for me?"

Delia grimaced. She had talked to several judges she knew. None of them were very encouraging about Rachel's prospects. Unbelievable as it was, Cliff's abuse of Rachel wouldn't keep him from getting joint custody of his son if there was no record he abused Scott. That wasn't the worst of what Delia had discovered.

"The attorneys I spoke with are worried what will happen if Cliff brings up your suicide attempt and the fact you pointed a gun at him—even an unloaded one—and pulled the trigger. That behavior, together with your current use of Prozac and sleeping pills, could be all Cliff needs to prove that you're unstable and that he should have sole custody of Scott."

Delia waited for Rachel to say something. "Rachel?"

"I won't give up Scott. I won't let Cliff have him. No matter what I have to do." Rachel's words were desperate, but her voice was utterly calm.

The hairs stood up on Delia's arms. "Don't do anything you'll be sorry for—"

Rachel hung up the phone.

"Damn it, Rachel! Don't you dare do anything stupid!" Delia tried getting her sister back on the phone. The line was busy.

Delia heard her mother calling to her in a voice that was commanding, even as frail as she was. She ignored her at first, thinking Maria would take care of whatever Hattie wanted. Then she remembered Maria had gone to town for groceries.

"Delia, my water pitcher is empty."

How could that be possible? Delia wondered. She had seen Maria take a full pitcher of water upstairs before she left. Unless her mother had accidentally spilled it. Or dumped it out on purpose.

"Delia? Bring me a glass of water. Can you hear me? I know you can hear me. Why don't you answer me?"

Delia desperately punched in Rachel's number. The busy signal buzzed irritatingly. She hung up and dialed again. Same response. She tried to think what she should do. Whom she should call.

She could call Cliff and warn him his life might be in danger. But there was no way she could betray her own sister. If she didn't call, and Rachel killed Cliff, her sister might end up in jail for life, or worse. Texas was famous for hanging its villains.

"Delia! Damn you, answer me!" Hattie cried sharply.

There was no sense pretending she couldn't

hear her mother. Hattie's bedroom door was open, and the sound carried easily down the stairs to Hattie's office, where Delia was frantically dialing and redialing Rachel's number.

"Delia!"

"I'm coming, Mother!" she yelled back. She slammed down the phone and hurried to the kitchen to get a glass of ice water, then held it balanced in front of her as she practically ran up the stairs.

No matter what she says, I won't argue with her. I won't let her make me angry. I have to remember she's sick. She's feeling impotent and angry. I'll give her this water and listen to whatever she has to say, and then I've got to figure out what to do about Rachel.

Delia was halfway up the stairs when she heard a knock at the kitchen door. It was a toss-up whether to go on up to her mother's room or back down to answer the door.

The thought it might be Maria with her hands full of groceries made her turn around. Maria could take the glass of water to Hattie while Delia unpacked the groceries. It was the coward's way out, but Delia didn't care. It would give her a few moments of peace to decide what to do about Rachel.

She yanked open the kitchen door and found Marsh standing there, a folded newspaper wedged under his arm. "What are you doing here? I said I'd call when Mother was ready for visitors."

"I came to see you."

Delia was unbelievably glad to see him . . . and wished he hadn't come. She hadn't allowed herself to think about Marsh—or Marsh's suppositions about how Ray John had died—because she didn't like the conclusions she reached when she did. So she hadn't called him, even though the doctor had conceded Hattie could have visitors for brief periods if she didn't let herself get upset.

"You look like you can't make up your mind whether to let me in or shut the door in my face."

She grabbed Marsh's arm and tugged him inside. "Maybe you can help."

"What's wrong?" Marsh said.

"Everything!"

Marsh took the glass of water from her and set it on the tile counter with one hand, while he tucked the folded newspaper section in his back jeans pocket with the other. When both hands were free, he gripped her shoulders to steady her. "Is Hattie all right? Has she had another attack?"

"Worse."

"She's dead?"

Delia shook her head.

"Something's wrong with you?" he asked sharply.

"I'm fine."

"Spit it out, Delia. I'm not a mind reader."

"It's Rachel. I think she's going to kill Cliff."

"What?"

Delia grasped handfuls of Marsh's shirt with her fists. "You heard me! I think she's going to kill her husband!"

Marsh tugged her hands free of his shirt and held them in his own. "What makes you think she'd do anything so drastic?"

She's put a gun to Cliff's head before. She's killed before. Delia couldn't say that aloud, but she raised her eyes to Marsh's face, anxious to convince him of the urgency of the situation. Everything came out in a rush. "I was talking to her on the phone, and I mentioned there was a possibility she could lose custody of Scott in a divorce proceeding, but before I could tell her nothing was certain, she hung up on me."

"From this you deduced she's going to kill Cliff?" Marsh asked skeptically.

"You don't understand."

"I sure as hell don't."

The words had an eerily familiar ring and the two of them stood frozen as they recalled when he had said them before.

Hattie's voice knifed down the stairs. "Delia! Where are you? What's going on? I'm getting up!"

"Don't get up, Mother!" Delia shouted from the kitchen. She pulled her hands free and walked toward the doorway so her voice would carry better. "Marsh North is here to visit. I'll be right up with your water."

Delia retrieved the glass of water from the counter and started down the hall. When Marsh didn't follow, she turned and said, "Are you coming?"

"Sure," he said, shaking his head in confusion. "Why not?"

It surprised Delia how fortifying it felt to have Marsh at her back. Maybe with him in the room, her mother wouldn't provoke an argument.

"About time you got here with that water,"
Hattie said when Delia arrived at the doorway
to her room.

"Marsh is here, Mother. He came to visit. Is
that all right?"

"Don't know why he'd bother."

"I wanted to make sure you're all right,"
Marsh said at Delia's shoulder.

"I'm stuck in bed for another week at least,"
Hattie grumbled. "Doctor's orders." She sat in
the center of the four-poster bed like a queen
on a throne, pillows piled up behind her to
keep her upright. She fiddled with the bow at
the throat of her quilted pink robe.

Delia felt Marsh's hand in the center of her
back urging her into the room. "Here's your
water, Mother," she said, handing the glass to
Hattie.

"Set it on the table there," Hattie said, waving it away. "Pull up a chair and sit down,
North."

Delia had been dismissed. Hattie hadn't
been thirsty at all. Like a child that cries when
it's ignored, Hattie had simply wanted Delia's
attention.

Besides an upholstered chaise lounge that
matched the curtains and the Egyptian cotton
bedspread, the only other chair in the vicinity
was a bent willow rocker. Marsh picked it up
from the corner and set it next to the bed before he settled his large frame comfortably in
it and crossed his ankle over his knee.

"How are you, Mrs. Carson?" Marsh asked.

"I've been better," Hattie said.

Delia set the glass down on the table beside

the bed and stepped behind Marsh, out of the way. If she had thought she could get away with it, she would have left the room. She was frantic with worry about what Rachel might be doing at this very moment. Her mind was buzzing with possibilities for contacting her sister.

"I believe I owe you my life," Hattie said.

Delia's ears perked up. "What are you talking about, Mother?"

"Maria told me how you gave me CPR," Hattie said to Marsh. "If not for you, I'd have been long dead by the time the ambulance showed up."

Delia saw the flush high on Marsh's cheeks as he protested, "Anyone would have done the same."

"I doubt it," Hattie said. "Anyway, I owe you a favor, North. What can I do for you?"

That was just like Hattie, Delia thought, offering to repay a personal favor in business terms. "I'm sure Marsh doesn't want anything from—"

"There is something you can do for me," Marsh said.

Hattie raised an eyebrow. "Name it."

Marsh hesitated before he spoke. "Maybe I should wait until you're feeling better."

"Does this have anything to do with what we were discussing the last time we spoke?" Hattie asked.

Marsh nodded.

"Go ahead and ask."

"I'd like you to tell me how Ray John Carson died."

Delia gasped. "Marsh, that's enough! Everyone knows Ray John committed suicide."

Hattie's piercing gaze stayed riveted on Marsh's face. "Figured it all out, have you?" Hattie said.

"I think so."

Hattie's mouth twisted in a bitter smile, and she gave a cackling laugh. "Maybe I will," she said. "Maybe it's time I did."

Delia stood frozen, listening with disbelief to her mother's bizarre conversation with Marsh. Her mother couldn't possibly intend to expose Rachel's crime to an investigative reporter. There was no statute of limitations on murder.

Hattie winced and grabbed at her chest. She took several hitching breaths and moaned.

"Now look what you've done!" Delia said as she hurried to her mother's side.

At the same time, Marsh rose from the rocker and supported Hattie, who was having trouble staying upright on her own. "Do you need a doctor?" he asked.

"No," Hattie gasped. "I'm fine."

"You should be resting, Mother." Delia rearranged the pillows behind Hattie, helping her to lie down.

"Plenty of time for that later, child. We need to talk," Hattie said.

"Not now," Delia said, her voice sharp with anxiety. "Later. When you've rested."

"All right," Hattie agreed. "But North is right, Delia. I should tell you what happened."

"I already know what happened," Delia said.

Hattie shook her head. "You saw what I wanted you to see."

Delia paused, stunned and confused.

"Get out of here and let me sleep," Hattie said. "Come back later."

Delia felt disoriented. What did her mother mean? Delia had heard the shot, seen Rachel with the gun in her hand. She stood staring at Hattie until Marsh grasped her arm and drew her away.

He put a firm, reassuring hand around her shoulder and ushered her downstairs to the kitchen.

"I think you could use a cup of tea," he said.

"I'll make it," she replied, moving around the kitchen putting the teakettle on the stove and getting tea bags from the canister on the counter. She turned to face Marsh with her back to the sink.

He was leaning against the back door with his arms crossed. "Are you all right?"

"No. What did you mean by confronting Mother like that?"

"Hiding from the truth won't make it go away."

"How do you know what the truth is?"

"I don't, but Hattie does. All you have to do is listen."

Delia put her hands to her ears. "I don't want to listen. I've had my fill of handling crises."

Marsh grimaced. "I'm sorry to hear that, Delia. I wish I didn't have to do this right now, but I don't think it can wait." He drew the newspaper from his back pocket and held it out to her. "It's the op-ed page of the *New York Times*."

Delia frowned and took the paper from him. She was having the *Times* delivered to the ranch, but it arrived late in the day. Her blood ran cold as she read the headline: BROOKLYN'S HANGING JUDGE: TOO TOUGH, OR TOO INEXPERIENCED?

She scanned the article and certain phrases leaped out at her.

> *Won't cooperate to keep the system operating. Refuses to accept plea bargains agreed on by the DA and PD. Inefficient ratio of trials to plea bargains. Woman with a personal ax to grind. Should be relieved of her responsibilities, or better yet, resign.*

The article pointed out she was one of the youngest judges ever elected to the Brooklyn Supreme Court and suggested she had needed more seasoning than the bare minimum ten years' experience as an attorney required before taking such a responsible position. The article mentioned she was on a personal leave of absence and finished, *It would be better if The Hanging Judge stayed in Texas, where they're more used to vigilante justice.*

Delia raised stricken eyes to Marsh. She had thought she had more time before something like this happened. She had thought the *Times* would wait until its reporter could talk to her. It was hard to speak past the Gibraltar-sized lump in her throat. "Sam Dietrich is behind this. He wants me out, and he saw a way to do it and earn some political points along the way."

"Are the accusations true?"

"How can you even ask?"

"I'm a reporter. It's my job to ask questions. Are the accusations true?" When she didn't answer, he said, "The only way I can help you is if I know the facts. Are the accusations in that article true?"

"No. Yes. Some of them."

"Well, I'm glad we got that straightened out," Marsh said with a rueful smile. "Maybe we should sit down with a cup of tea and discuss this some more."

Her shock at the attack on her by the *Times* was quickly followed by anger. "Sam Dietrich isn't going to get away with this!"

"Who's Sam Dietrich?" Marsh asked.

"It's a long story."

"I've got time to listen."

"Something more pressing needs my attention right now," Delia said curtly.

"More pressing than your job? More pressing than your life's work?"

"Didn't you hear what I said when you came to the door? At this very moment my sister may be looking for Cliff McKinley with a gun in her hand. I have to find a way to reach her. I have to find a way to stop her."

Delia felt frantic inside.

Upstairs her mother waited to reveal the truth about Ray John Carson's death. She was terrified of what she was going to hear. And she had realized too late the seriousness of Frank Weaver's warning to watch her back.

She had a fight ahead of her to keep her job. And unless she could think of something fast, her sister might end up murdering a U.S. Congressman.

"Let me help, Delia," Marsh said. "What can I do to help?"

"Hold me," Delia said. "Just hold me."

Marsh's strong arms closed around her, and Delia laid her face against his muscular chest, finding a haven of solace as he rocked her and crooned soothing words in her ear. Marsh's comfort gave her the brief surcease from worry she needed to allow her to pause and think.

Suddenly, she lifted her head and said, "I've got it!"

"What?"

"A way to help out Rachel."

"What?" Marsh repeated.

"Cliff is going to get an urgent call at his office in Dallas requiring him to go *immediately* to Washington. Rachel can escape with Scott while he's gone. All I have to figure out is who I know with enough clout to make such a request, and then get hold of Rachel to explain everything to her."

"What if somebody from the *Washington Post* offers to do a feature article on the congressman at work?" Marsh suggested. "He'd have to be in Washington for that."

"Perfect! That's the kind of publicity no politician can turn down, especially not somebody as ambitious as Cliff. Once Rachel gets here with Scott, I can help her make Cliff keep his distance while we get the divorce proceedings started and work on the custody issue."

"What about going back to work? I thought you planned to be out of here as soon as you could find someone to manage the Circle Crown. That seems even more important in light of that attack on you in the *Times*."

"New York can wait and wonder," Delia retorted. "I don't have to prove anything. I shouldn't have to defend myself. I haven't done anything wrong."

Marsh shook his head. "More than one innocent person has been convicted by public opinion," he said. "Lord help you if the rest of the press jumps on the bandwagon."

"I can't leave now, Marsh. It simply isn't possible. They can't pillory me if I'm not there, can they?"

"Depends on how anxious this DA fellow is to see you kicked off the bench."

"The plea bargains Sam Dietrich offered me were absurd, Marsh. If I didn't know better, I'd think the man was getting paid off," Delia said.

Marsh's eyes narrowed. "Really?"

"He was asking for ridiculously light sentences for violent crimes and multiple offenders. In fact, Sam came to me about a case the day I left New York. A boy from a gang in Flatbush, Leroy Lincoln, killed another kid in a drive-by shooting. The evidence against him was overwhelming. Sam wanted five years probation with review in eighteen months.

"That's no more than a slap on the wrist. The way the system works, in eighteen

months the DA's office will recommend the
kid be released from probation because he's
been a model citizen. End of case. Meanwhile,
grass has barely grown over the victim's
grave.

"Is it any wonder I won't go along?" Delia
said.

"Have you ever thought maybe Sam *was*
getting paid off?" Marsh asked quietly.

"By a street hoodlum? Where would a kid
from Flatbush get the kind of money it would
take to bribe the Brooklyn DA?"

"There's money in drugs."

"You don't really think Sam might be dirty,
do you? I worked with him a lot of years before I became a judge." She rubbed her nose
thoughtfully. "I never saw any of these sweet
deals then."

"Maybe he kept the cases he was fixing
away from you. It would explain why he
wants to get rid of a brand-new judge who
won't go along with him," Marsh said.

"I would never be able to prove it," Delia
said.

"Let me work on it for a while," Marsh said.

"Don't you have responsibilities keeping
you busy here in Uvalde?"

"Of course. But even though I've been on
hiatus from work, I like to keep up with
what's going on in the world. I'm connected
by phone and fax and computer modem to all
sorts of sources. I can work on this in the eve-
nings from home."

"I appreciate the offer, Marsh."

"My pleasure," he said. "Shall I call my friend at the *Post* now?"

"Let me try to reach Rachel one more time." Delia picked up the phone in the kitchen and dialed Rachel's number. This time it rang. And rang.

"Her answering machine must be turned off," Delia said, her heart in her throat. "She's not at home, or she's not answering the phone. Scott wouldn't let it ring. Unless she's telling him not to answer it."

"Give me the phone." Marsh called his friend with the *Post* and asked for the favor. The conversation left little doubt that Marsh and his "friend" had once been intimate. "How do I know what kind of feature you can sell to your editor?" Marsh said. "Use your imagination. Thanks, Jan. I appreciate it."

He hung up the phone.

"Who's Jan?" Delia asked, insatiably curious and, to her dismay, jealous at the thought of Marsh with another woman.

"Janelle Perkins. I met her when the communist government fell in Czechoslovakia."

Delia raised a brow. "And you became very good friends?"

Marsh smiled. "I haven't fallen in love with anyone but you, Delia. I never said I'd been a monk."

Delia was surprised by the admission. "What about Ginny?" she said. "You loved her, didn't you?"

Marsh riffled his hair with his hands. "I married Ginny because I wanted to prove to myself that I was over you. I thought I loved

her. It wasn't the same as what we had. I used
my job as an excuse to stay gone, because we
fought too much when we were together. The
marriage ended long before it was over."

"I'm sorry."

"It wasn't your fault."

"I'm the one who ran away."

Marsh's lips tilted in a wry smile. "I wasn't
far behind you. No, Delia. I'm entirely to
blame for my mistakes."

"And I'm to blame for mine?"

"You're putting words in my mouth."

The phone rang, and Delia quickly picked it
up. "Hello?"

"Is that you, Delia?"

Delia's heart caught in her throat, and she
looked at Marsh with eyes widened by fear.
"Yes, it's me."

"This is Cliff McKinley. What the hell have
you been saying to my wife?"

৩ *Chapter Fourteen* ৩

"Where are you, Cliff?" Delia asked.

"I'm at the office. Do you think I'd make a call like this from home, with Rachel hanging over my shoulder yammering at me? My wife doesn't open her mouth these days without your name coming up. This interference in our personal lives has got to stop, Delia. Do you understand?"

"I understand you've got a problem, Cliff, and Rachel's the one who suffers for it."

"What the hell does that mean?" Cliff demanded.

"You hit your wife, Cliff. You need help."

Delia took the phone away from her ear while Cliff harangued her in language no self-respecting man—let alone U.S. Congressman—ought to be using. When the phone seemed quiet again, she put it to her ear and heard Cliff discussing another call with his secretary.

"I have to take a call from the *Washington Post*," Cliff said importantly. "If you know what's good for you, you'll stay out of my life from now on."

"Or what?" Delia challenged. "There's nothing you can do to hurt me, Cliff."

"From what I saw in the *Times*, you're already in plenty of trouble. Give me a hard time, and it'll only get worse."

"Is that a threat?"

"Call it what you like. Just leave me and my wife alone."

The phone went dead.

"I take it that was the esteemed congressman from Texas," Marsh said, taking the phone receiver from Delia's limp hand and hanging it back on the wall.

"It was," Delia said. "He threatened me. He said he'd make trouble if I don't stay away from Rachel. Can he do that, Marsh?"

"Probably. He's got friends, too, Delia."

Delia retrieved the phone and called Rachel's home number. It rang, and this time the answering machine picked up, but Delia didn't feel comfortable leaving a message after her call from Cliff. "Where do you suppose she's gone? How am I supposed to get her on a plane headed in this direction if she won't answer the phone!"

Delia slammed the phone back on the wall so hard the bell inside rang.

"Do you feel better now?" Marsh asked.

"Don't patronize me," Delia snapped, pacing the length of the kitchen and back again. "This is serious."

"I never thought it wasn't."

"I don't know a soul in Dallas I can call to

go check on her," Delia said miserably. "What good does it do to get Cliff out of town if I can't reach Rachel?"

"How about if I fly up there and bring her and Scott back with me?"

Delia stopped pacing and stared at Marsh. "I couldn't ask you to do that."

"Why not?"

"I'm not sure Rachel would come if you asked. If anybody goes, it should be me."

"You can't leave your mother alone right now. And you can give me a note for Rachel, explaining the situation."

Delia could ask Maria to stay overnight while she flew to Dallas, but the housekeeper had family of her own. Marsh's offer was tempting. "What about Billie Jo?" Delia asked.

"She's old enough to stay by herself." Marsh frowned thoughtfully and amended, "It would be better, though, if she could stay with you."

"You know I have the room, if you don't think she'd mind."

"She'll do as she's told," Marsh said. "But no, I don't think she'd mind. In fact, she's fascinated by you."

"She is? Because I'm a judge?"

"Because you lost my baby."

As far as Delia could tell, Billie Jo North was not the least bit pleased to be spending the night at the Carson mansion. The sulky pout hadn't once left her face since Delia had picked her up after school. Delia had kept up a one-sided conversation while she cooked supper and served it to Billie Jo at the kitchen table. It was hard to imagine herself that young. But Billie Jo was the same age Delia had been when she ran away from home.

The teenager had been twirling the same few strands of spaghetti around her fork for the past five minutes. She hadn't eaten ten bites of her supper.

"I can make something else, if you don't like spaghetti," Delia said.

"I'm not hungry," Billie Jo said.

Delia didn't know a teenager who wasn't always starving, but she didn't contradict the girl.

From out of nowhere, Billie Jo asked, "Are you in love with my dad?"

Delia's jaw dropped. "What?"

"You were going to go to bed with him. Are you in love with him?"

The girl's frankness left her momentarily speechless. If things worked out the way Delia hoped, Billie Jo would become her stepdaughter. That thought was both delightful and daunting. There was nothing wrong with admitting how she felt about Marsh. Except she would have liked to tell him before she told anybody else.

"Yes, I love him," she said.

The girl let out a long-suffering sigh. "I thought so." She set her left elbow on the table and dropped her cheek into her palm. "Boy, this is a mess."

"What's a mess?"

"Dad wasn't too happy getting stuck with

me in the first place, and he sure isn't going
to want me around if he's getting married
again."

"Marsh and I haven't talked about marriage." They hadn't even talked about love in
the present tense, but hey, why worry about
details at a time like this. "I know your father
wouldn't give you up for anything—or anyone."

Billie Jo eyed her doubtfully. "I don't know
how you can say that. He can hardly wait to
get me through high school so he can go back
to his stupid newspaper."

Delia felt her stomach knot. "He hasn't said
anything about that to me."

"He's probably planning to send me off to
a girl's school somewhere in the Northeast
when he marries you," Billie Jo said glumly.
"That's what I thought he'd do when Mom
died. I was surprised when he didn't. I should
have known this wouldn't last."

Delia knew exactly how Billie Jo was feeling.
She knew what it was like to be abandoned by
someone you loved. To feel a little hope that
you might get back what you lost, only to realize you might be left alone again. She had
given Billie Jo the only comfort she could. But
if things worked out between her and Marsh,
and she had anything to say about it, Billie Jo
would be living with them.

"Do you like it here in Uvalde?" Delia asked
Billie Jo.

"I didn't at first. Now that I've met this boy
at school . . . It's not so bad."

Thunder rumbled in the distance.

"Sounds like it's going to rain." As Delia spoke, she heard the first splatters of rain against the kitchen windows. It quickly turned into a deluge.

Because of the drought, every drop of water was welcome. So Delia was surprised to hear Billie Jo's "Oh, no! Rain!"

"What's the matter?" Delia asked.

"The roof leaks. At home, I mean. We had a storm once before, and it was awful. I have to go and set out some pots to catch the rain, or everything will get ruined. We need to go *now!*"

Delia rose hesitantly from the table and carried her plate to the sink. "I'm sorry, Billie Jo, but I can't leave my mother alone." She racked her brain to think of a friend she could trust to take Billie Jo home and couldn't come up with a name. Maria's family only had one car, and her husband worked nights. At times like this, Delia missed her old friend, Peggy.

"I'll call Todd," Billie Jo suggested, hurrying to the wall phone in the kitchen. "Maybe he can give me a ride home."

"Who's Todd?"

"The boy from school I mentioned. Daddy knows him." Billie Jo called, but Todd wasn't able to help. He had talked back to his mother at supper, and she had taken away his truck keys.

Billie Jo turned to Delia, her expression crestfallen. "Todd can't do it."

"Maybe the rain damage won't be as bad as you think," Delia said.

"It will!" Billie Jo cried. "You don't know

what it's like. There are drips *everywhere!*" Billie Jo wrung her hands. "You have to take me home. You *have* to! My things will be ruined, if you don't."

Delia's heart went out to the girl. She made a sudden decision. "Give me a minute to check on Mother. Then we'll go. I can be gone long enough to set out some pots. But you won't be able to stay and watch them fill up," Delia said with a smile.

"Thank you," Billie Jo said. "Thank you so much!"

Delia ran upstairs and peeked in at her mother. The remnants of Hattie's dinner sat on a tray near the bed. Delia saw in the dim light from the lamp near the door that her mother was sleeping peacefully. With any luck, she would never know that Delia had been gone. Delia quietly picked up the supper tray and carried it back downstairs with her.

"Mother's asleep," she said. "Let's make this quick."

They used umbrellas to race from the kitchen door to Delia's rental car and laughed at each other's soaking wet clothing once they were safe inside.

"We might as well have skipped the umbrellas," Delia said. "The rain's blowing sideways."

Delia made the trip to Marsh's home in record time. She was careful not to speed, but she pushed the limit. The road up to the house had turned to mud, and the car skidded as she hit the brakes at the back door.

Billie Jo was out of the car in a flash and

scampering for the mud porch. It wasn't
locked, and she shoved her way inside the
house before Delia was even out of the car.
Delia hurried after her, leaving the useless um-
brella behind.

Her hair was dripping wet by the time she
reached the door and let herself in. She took
one look at her snakeskin boots and realized
why Marsh had a mud porch. She found Billie
Jo's muddy boots lying discarded outside the
kitchen door and pulled hers off, too. She
wiped her muddy hands on a towel hanging
from a nail on the back of the house and
headed inside.

Billie Jo was squatting in front of a cupboard
beside the stove. Pots and pans rattled as she
pulled them free and stacked them behind her.
Delia picked one up and set it on the kitchen
table under a steady drip which had already
created a small puddle of water. As far as she
could tell, that was the only leak in the
kitchen.

"Where are the towels?" Delia asked. "I'll
wipe up this water."

"In the hall closet, near the bathroom," Billie
Jo said.

Delia left Billie Jo gathering pots and pans
and headed down the hall. She nearly slipped
and fell, which was how she found the second
leak. She turned on the hall light, stared at the
wet floor, then looked up at the ceiling, before
retreating to the kitchen for another pot.

Billie Jo held an armful of pots, and Delia
took one from the top of the stack.

"These are mine," Billie Jo said. "Get your own."

"Emergency," Delia said with a grin. "Flood in the hall."

Billie Jo didn't argue further. She crept along the edge of the hallway where it was dry and slipped into her bedroom.

Delia inspected the hall ceiling, trying to find the source of the drip. A drop of water plopped onto her forehead. She stepped back and set the pot on the floor and waited. The next drop hit near the edge of the pot. She centered it and headed to the linen closet for towels to clean up the mess in the kitchen and hall.

Once she found the towels, Delia realized she and Billie Jo needed to be dried off, too. She wiped her face and briskly towel-dried her hair, leaving the towel around her shoulders as she headed for Billie Jo's room with another towel for her.

She knocked on the closed door and waited until Billie Jo said, "Come in."

The room reminded her a lot of her own teenage bedroom. Pictures and dried flowers and notes were taped to the mirror over the dresser. The lamp beside Billie Jo's brass-railed twin bed had apparently been with her a long time, because it featured Cinderella in her ball gown. Clothes were layered over the back of a wicker chair by the bed. A tumble of shoes lay in the bottom of the closet. The bed hadn't been made.

Billie Jo looked at her expectantly.

"I thought you could use a towel to dry

off," Delia said, "so you don't get a chill."

Instead of giving the towel to Billie Jo, Delia spread it out and draped it over the girl's head. Their fingers tangled as Delia helped Marsh's daughter dry her hair.

A moment later, Billie Jo's hands dropped to her sides, and she stood unmoving, letting Delia finish the job.

When Delia pulled the towel away, Billie Jo glanced at her and then at her hands, which had knotted in front of her.

"My mom used to do that," Billie Jo said. "Dry my hair with a towel like that after she washed it, when I was a kid."

Delia folded the towel to give herself something to do with her hands so she wouldn't reach for Billie Jo. Marsh's daughter so obviously needed a hug, and so obviously wouldn't have accepted one from her.

"You must miss your mother a lot," Delia said softly.

Billie Jo tried to shrug as though it were no big deal, but couldn't pull it off. "Yeah," she said, her heart in her eyes, her voice a bare whisper. "I do."

Billie Jo's glance slid to a photograph beside the bed.

"Is that a picture of your mother?" Delia asked, gesturing with her chin.

"Yes."

"May I see it?"

Billie Jo picked up the color photograph of a smiling young woman with windswept, curly blond hair standing at the helm of a yacht and held it out to her. "Daddy thinks I look a lot like her."

She did. Except for the shape of her eyebrows and her square chin, both of which she had gotten from Marsh. "Your mother was very beautiful," Delia said. Unbelievably beautiful. Delia felt a spurt of jealousy and nipped it in the bud. The woman was dead. And Marsh had divorced her years ago.

A loud *plop*, as a drop of water landed on the small writing desk in the corner, reminded them why they were there.

"I'd better get that water wiped up in the hall," Delia said, handing the picture back to Billie Jo.

"I'll come help you when I'm done here," Billie Jo said.

"Use this to wipe up any extra water you find." Delia thrust the folded towel at Billie Jo and headed back into the hall.

Nobody had a perfect life, Delia thought as she dropped to her knees to wipe up the water from the hall floor. There were always trials and tribulations to be overcome. They just took different forms in each family.

She wondered if Billie Jo would let her become another mother to her. She wondered if she would even get the chance.

Billie Jo still hadn't come out of her bedroom by the time Delia was done. "How are you doing?" she called down the hall.

"Fine," Billie Jo called back. "Did you check Daddy's room?"

"Not yet." Delia had been in Marsh's room once before, but she couldn't have described it

to save her life. She had been too busy being
embarrassed to form any impressions. She was
surprised at how neat it was. Her eyes were
drawn to the quilt on the bed.

She reached out to touch the motley collection of fabrics and colors and realized it was
sopping wet. She had already starting stripping it from the bed when Billie Jo arrived in
the doorway.

"Uh-oh," Billie Jo said.

Delia stopped what she was doing. "Uh-
oh?"

"Daddy is absolutely insane about that
quilt. I was going to take it on a picnic one
time, and he made me put it back. He treats it
like it was made of gold, or something."

Billie Jo crossed to the bed and pointed out
a ragged spot on the quilt. "See that? Rats ate
it. Daddy said he was lucky that was all the
damage they did. I didn't realize till he found
it in the barn that he'd been looking for it ever
since we came back here.

"It's special, because it's made with pieces
of North history. Daddy said someday, when
I have kids of my own, it'll be mine."

Billie Jo paused, as though realizing how
much she had said and how corny it sounded.
"Anyway, I thought you should know to be
careful with it."

"It's sopping wet," Delia said. "I was going
to throw it in the dryer, so it doesn't get
moldy."

"The dryer doesn't work," Billie Jo said.
"We've been hanging things on the line out
back."

Delia finished stripping the precious quilt, whose history she knew as well as Marsh's daughter. Marsh had brought the quilt to the live oak one day and explained the story of each patch as his grandmother had told it to him. The ruined patch had been a piece of the dress his mother had worn on her first date with his father.

"We'll take the quilt with us, and put it in the dryer at my house," Delia said as she gathered it into a wet bundle. "See if you can find where that leak's hitting the bed and put a pot under it," she told Billie Jo, "while I take this out to the kitchen. That way we won't forget it when we leave."

It took them half an hour to put pots under all the leaks and wipe up all the water they could find.

"Was anything of yours ruined?" Delia asked.

"Some papers got wet, but they'll dry," Billie Jo said. "Thanks, Delia." She flushed. "I mean, Judge Carson."

"Delia's fine," Delia said with a smile. "I'm glad you made me come. I can see this would have been a disaster."

Why hadn't Marsh had the roof repaired? Even as she formulated the question, Delia thought she knew the answer. He must have been inundated with work on the ranch, and with the persistent drought, who could have imagined it would rain? Knowing Marsh, it had never occurred to him to hire someone else to do something he knew how to do himself.

Delia and Billie Jo emptied all the pots and pans one last time before they left. "If the rain doesn't stop, we'll make a quick trip back later to check on everything," Delia promised.

They pulled their boots back on, and Delia retrieved the quilt before they braved the rain again.

On the ride back to the Circle Crown, the sullen-eyed, silent teenager Delia had met at supper was replaced by one who talked a mile a minute and asked questions like she was the investigative reporter, instead of her dad.

"Have you ever been married?" Billie Jo asked.

"No."

"Why not?"

"I was engaged once, but we realized we didn't love each other enough to spend our lives together."

"Did my dad get you pregnant?"

Delia was so startled by the question she almost ran the car off the road. "No, he did not!"

"Oh." Billie Jo was silent for a few moments. "Whose baby was it?"

Delia didn't know what to say. She couldn't tell the truth. She didn't want to lie, either. "I can't tell you that, Billie Jo. Not without revealing some things that are still painful to me."

That shut Billie Jo up. For about a minute.

"So my dad didn't rape you?"

"He most certainly did not! I know the whole town believes he did, but it simply isn't true."

Billie Jo looked relieved for a moment. But came up with another question. "Then why did you run away?"

"Where did you get all this information?" Delia asked, astounded and perplexed.

"Eula Hutchins told me most of it. She found out from her mom, who's Sheriff Koehl's sister. So why did you run away?"

"I had problems at home, like a lot of kids do, but instead of staying and working them out, I took off."

Billie Jo ruminated on that for the rest of the trip back to the Circle Crown. "One more thing," she said as Delia turned off the ignition.

When she didn't speak right away, Delia said, "You might as well ask."

Billie Jo took a deep breath and said, "Is it true your mother killed your father?"

Delia's eyes rounded. "What? Where on earth did you hear that?"

"Eula Hutchins said—"

"I don't care what she said," Delia interrupted. "My mother had nothing whatsoever to do with my father's death. He was cleaning one of his guns, and it accidentally went off and killed him." Delia realized her hands were shaking. At least, that was the story she had clung to all these years.

"Let's go inside, and I'll show you where you can sleep." She shoved the car door open, grabbed the quilt from the back seat, and raced for the kitchen door, Billie Jo close on her heels. It wasn't really necessary to run, because the storm had passed overhead and gone, leaving only dripping eaves and the pungent smell of wet grass and fresh air.

Delia stuffed the quilt in the dryer before she showed Billie Jo to Rachel's room, where she would be close enough that Delia could keep an eye on her and far enough away not to disturb Hattie. "There's a TV room downstairs next to my mother's office if you'd like to watch, or there's a radio in here if you'd like to listen to music. The study—the room with the gun cabinets in it—has a lot of old books, if you'd like to read."

"I saw the guns in there," Billie Jo said. "Who do they belong to?"

"They belonged to my stepfather." Delia could not, for the life of her, understand why Hattie hadn't gotten rid of them. "If you need anything, I'll either be in my room right across the hall, or down the hall in my mother's room."

She left Billie Jo changing her clothes for bed and went to check on Hattie. Delia still hadn't gotten over Billie Jo's last question in the car.

Did your mother kill your father?

How did rumors like that get started anyway?

She heard Marsh's voice saying, *Figure it out, Delia.*

Her father had struggled with someone. Someone had come to the sheriff's office and explained Ray John's death and cleared Marsh's name.

Who's left, Delia? Just Rachel. And Mother.

Just Mother.

It wasn't possible for her mother to have fought with Ray John. Hattie had met Delia at the top of the stairs that morning and gone down with her.

Think, Delia. You heard the shot. You thought it was a dream. The scream didn't come until much later. Hattie had time to come back upstairs. Maybe Rachel was telling the truth. Maybe she did find the gun on the floor.

Delia found herself at her mother's bedroom door, her heart pounding so hard it hurt. It felt like she was standing on the edge of a precipice that was crumbling under her feet, and any second she was going to fall off.

The moment of truth had come. There was no putting it off any longer.

Delia reached out and grasped the doorknob and opened Hattie's door enough to peer inside. Her mother was still asleep. In fact, she didn't look like she had moved an inch since Delia had seen her last. Delia gave a chicken-hearted sigh of relief. She had a respite. The showdown could be put off one more day.

Tomorrow. Tomorrow she would learn the truth.

Delia was pulling the bedroom door closed again when an alarm went off in her head.

Hattie hadn't moved an inch.

Delia shoved the door wide, turned on the overhead light, and hurried to her mother's side. Hattie's face looked bloodless under the bright light. Delia reached with trembling fingers to touch her mother's throat. She found no pulse. Hattie's flesh was cold.

Delia refused to believe what her eyes were telling her. She laid her ear against her mother's chest, listening for her heartbeat.

''Wake up, Mother.'' She lifted Hattie by the shoulders, as though to sit her upright. Her head sagged sideways like a broken doll. Delia let go of her mother abruptly, and Hattie fell back onto the pillow, her body lifeless, flaccid.

Delia shook her head in disbelief. It simply wasn't possible. The bypass surgery had been a success. Hattie was supposed to get better. She had been resting comfortably.

And Delia had left her alone to go save a run-down house from a little rain.

She was dead before you ever left the house. She died sometime earlier in the evening. Without making a sound. Without crying out for help.

Delia felt like howling. She had been cheated. She hadn't made peace with her mother. She hadn't even spoken much with her, except to argue. There should have been more time. She should have had more time!

There were questions she had wanted to ask. Things she had wanted to say. Things Hattie had wanted to say to her.

Now it was too late. Too late.

Hattie Carson was dead, taking whatever secrets she possessed to the grave with her.

Delia reached for the Bible on her mother's bedstand, and it fell open to a page where Hattie had left a folded piece of stationery. The parchment was crisp, pure white, as though it had been put there recently. *Delia* was written in her mother's bold script across the front.

Delia carefully set the Bible down and opened the note.

I forgive you. Can you forgive me?

Delia stared at the words until her eyes blurred with tears. Oh, God. Oh, dear God. How had her mother known she needed forgiveness? How had her mother known she still loved her all these years, even though she hated what her mother had done?

Delia slowly crushed the note in her hand. She looked at her mother lying there so peacefully, as though she were merely asleep. Hattie Carson wasn't a monster, just an old woman. Her mother. Her repentant mother.

Can you forgive me?

Delia's chin quivered. "I don't know, Mama," she whispered. "I don't know."

✎ Chapter Fifteen ❧

"After the cardiac catheterization, I realized there was considerably more damage to your mother's heart from the second attack than I'd hoped," Dr. Robbins said. "Surgery was necessary if she was to have any kind of functional life. Hattie opted for it, despite the risks." Dr. Robbins took a breath and let it out. "We almost lost your mother on the table. That's why the surgery took longer than expected.

"I never mentioned any of this before, because Hattie specifically requested that I not discuss her condition with her family. When I spoke to her after the surgery, I told her she only had a few months, maybe a year to live, and that she ought to tell her children. But you know Hattie."

Delia rubbed her temples with her thumbs. Yes, she knew Hattie. "Thanks for telling me, Dr. Robbins."

Hattie's doctor had come to the Circle Crown with the coroner and the ambulance that had taken her mother away to Morten-son's Funeral Home. Mortensons had been burying Carsons ever since the two families had traveled west from Pennsylvania together in 1877 and settled in Uvalde.

"Would you like me to prescribe something to help you sleep?" Dr. Robbins asked.

"No, thank you," Delia said.

"Give me a call if you need me." The doctor laid a comforting hand on her shoulder before he left her alone in the parlor and let himself out the front door.

He was the last to leave of those who had come to carry away the mortal remains of Hattie Carson, and the house fell silent.

"Delia?"

Delia turned and saw Billie Jo standing at the entrance to the parlor in a thigh-high T-shirt, one bare foot atop the other.

"Is everybody gone?" she asked.

"Yes. I'm sorry for all the commotion, Billie Jo."

"It's all right. I mean, how could you know . . . I'm sorry about your mother."

"Thanks, Billie Jo." Delia sighed and looked at her watch. "It's only eleven, but how about a midnight snack?"

Billie Jo grinned crookedly. "To tell you the truth, I'm starving. I hardly ate any supper."

"I noticed," Delia said with an answering smile.

It seemed the most natural thing in the world to slip an arm around Billie Jo's waist as the two of them headed down the hall to the kitchen. What surprised Delia was Billie

Jo's arm curving around her waist in return. It dawned on her that Billie Jo knew how much she needed the comfort, because she knew what it felt like to lose a mother.

The two of them raided the refrigerator and filled the tile counters with sandwich-making stuff. They carried their creations and a glass of milk apiece over to the table and sat down to eat.

Delia was ravenous. She hadn't consumed any more at supper than Billie Jo. Amazing how one sought the solace of food—and offered it—in times of sorrow. It was probably some primordial, instinctual thing, Delia thought, as she swallowed a large bite of ham and cheese, some reaffirmation of the need to keep on living in the midst of death.

Billie Jo kept the conversation going with descriptions of Todd and their tube trip down the Frio. She was entranced with the boy, and no detail of their day together was left undiscussed.

"Todd lost his older brother Jeff in a car accident a year ago, so he knew exactly how I felt about losing my mom without warning," Billie Jo said.

Like Delia had lost hers.

Billie Jo shot a mortified look at Delia, obviously sorry for having brought up the subject of death, which everybody knew should be avoided at all costs in a situation where someone had just died and which, therefore, inevitably came to mind.

Billie Jo took a bite of her sandwich and concentrated on chewing.

Delia had opened her mouth to say something, anything, to break the awkward silence, when the kitchen door swung open and Rachel stepped inside.

"Rachel!" Delia was on her feet and headed for the door in two seconds flat. Before she reached Rachel, Marsh stepped inside holding Scott, who was sound asleep against his shoulder.

"Marsh!"

"Daddy!" Billie Jo cried, jumping to her feet and heading toward him. "You're back!"

A confusing series of hugs and kisses and exclamations followed while Scott, who Rachel said had been awake during the whole plane flight and most of the drive to Uvalde, slept through it all.

"How did you all get back here so quickly?" Delia asked Marsh, her arm around Rachel.

Rachel answered for him. "I was packing when Marsh rang the doorbell. I'd already made up my mind to leave Cliff. I'm sorry I hung up on you like that. I had no idea you would be so worried, but I didn't answer the phone again because I was afraid it might be Cliff, and that I might give everything away on the phone—that I meant to leave him, I mean."

"I'm glad you're here. Don't worry, Rachel. We'll work everything out."

"I think Scott needs a bed," Marsh said. "Where would you like me to put him?"

"Mrs. McKinley can have her bedroom back," Billie Jo offered, "and I'll go home with Daddy."

"I'll show you where it is," Rachel said to Marsh, heading toward the hallway that led upstairs. "You stay and finish your sandwich, Delia."

"Rachel, wait!" There wasn't any way for Delia to say it except to say it. "Mother's dead. She died in her sleep earlier this evening."

She watched the blood drain from Rachel's face, saw the grim look appear on Marsh's. Her sister set a palm against the kitchen wall to steady herself.

"Dr. Robbins said her heart was failing, and that she knew it but decided not to tell us about it," Delia said. "He was here earlier with the coroner. Mother's been taken to Mortenson's Funeral Home."

For a moment Delia thought her sister was going to be all right. They had both already grieved once for Hattie Carson, only to find that she wasn't dead, after all. This second death, coming after the false alarm, seemed unreal somehow. Like the story of the little boy who cried wolf, it was difficult to believe Hattie was really gone this time.

Delia saw the moment her announcement sank in. Saw Rachel reel as though she had been physically struck. Saw her face crumple and her mouth stretch wide in an ululating wail of grief.

Scott half roused against Marsh's shoulder in a subconscious response to his mother's cry of distress.

"I'll take Scott upstairs and put him to bed," Marsh said, "so you two can have some time together."

"I can show you where Mrs. McKinley's bedroom is," Billie Jo offered. She led her father down the hall, leaving the two sisters alone in the kitchen.

Delia laid a comforting hand on Rachel's back and felt her shudder. A moment later, Rachel turned to her, and they clutched each other tightly.

Delia felt numb, too battered by everything that had happened in the past week to feel anything more. She simply held on to Rachel while her sister cried, her own eyes dry, her throat aching.

Some time later, Marsh reappeared at the doorway to the kitchen with Billie Jo. "Scott's asleep upstairs. I'm going to take Billie Jo home. I'll talk to you tomorrow, Delia." He hesitated a moment and sought out Delia's gaze before he said, "If you need me before then, give me a call."

He ushered Billie Jo quickly through the kitchen, not waiting for a reply from Delia. There wasn't really much she could say. It was only after he had closed the kitchen door behind him that she realized he hadn't offered condolences on Hattie's death.

Rachel sank into one of the kitchen chairs and dropped her head onto her crossed arms facing away from Delia. Delia sat down next to her and reached out to touch her arm, so Rachel would know she was there.

"I never really felt like I knew Mama," Rachel said, reverting to the childhood name she had used for her mother. "It was as though she lived on a mountain so high that even if I climbed forever, I could never reach her. Did you ever feel like that?"

"Um-hm," Delia agreed.

"Daddy was different."

Delia's jaw tightened reflexively. She and Rachel had not discussed Ray John Carson once since the day he had died.

"Daddy could be so funny," Rachel mused. "He used to play with me and hug me and kiss me . . . I mean when I was really little. Before . . . before the other." Rachel turned her face toward Delia. "Why did he do those things to us, Delia? What was wrong with him?"

"I don't know."

Rachel turned her face away again, staring at a Timmons Feed and Grain Store calendar hanging on the wall with the days crossed off in black marker.

Delia noticed the Xs stopped on the day she had come home, as though that was the day all those Xs had been leading up to. Of course, the real reason there were no more Xs was simply that Hattie had gone into the hospital.

Six days ago. Not even a week.

But enough time to turn her life upside down.

The refrigerator hummed. The wind brushed a branch of the old live oak against the kitchen window.

"Mama didn't mean to do it, Delia," Rachel murmured. "It was an accident."

"Do what?"

"Kill Daddy."

Delia stared at Rachel, who remained unmoving with her face turned away. "Sit up and look at me, Rachel."

Rachel pushed herself upright as though her upper body weighed a ton. She stared at Delia, her eyes dazed, her lower lip swollen where she had been chewing on it, her mascara streaked by tears.

"Repeat what you just said."

Rachel stared blankly at her. "What? That Mama killed Daddy?"

"Damn it, Rachel! Don't play dumb with me." Delia's hands clenched into fists on the table.

"I'm not, Delia. Why are you so upset?"

"What do you mean by saying Mama killed Daddy? Why would you say such a thing?" Delia demanded.

"I was there when she pulled the trigger," Rachel said simply.

Delia's brows arrowed down. She shook her head in confusion and disbelief. "Why didn't you ever say anything? Why didn't you tell me?"

"Mama made me promise I wouldn't say anything to anyone."

Delia felt betrayed. "You should have told me. I'm your sister. I was entitled to know."

Rachel shook her head. "I couldn't, Delia. Please understand."

Delia didn't understand. How could Rachel have kept such a secret for so many years? "Will you tell me now what happened? Or are you going to keep it to yourself a little longer." Delia couldn't help the sarcasm in her voice, even though she could see it upset Rachel.

"I'll tell you whatever you want to know."

"Sure, now that it's too late to say anything to Mother," Delia snapped.

"Do you want to know, or not?" Rachel snapped right back.

"Just tell me the damned story," Delia said.

"All right. Stop yelling at me and I will." She pulled a strand of hair from her no longer perfect coif and twisted it agitatedly in her fingers.

"I came down to the kitchen that morning because I was thirsty and wanted a drink of water. I had already put my glass down in the sink when I heard Mama and Daddy arguing in Daddy's gun room.

"Mama blamed herself for what had happened to us, because she had seen signs of what was going on and hadn't done anything to stop Daddy. She was really mad at him, Delia. And at herself for all the mean things she had said to you."

Why didn't she ever tell me? Delia wondered. *Why didn't she ever admit she believed me?*

"I heard Mama say something like 'You should be shot' and Daddy answered 'Put down that gun.' I got scared and ran to see what was going on.

"They were fighting over one of Daddy's guns when it accidentally went off. I called Mama's name, and she came running toward me to keep me from seeing what had happened to Daddy. I saw the gun on the floor, but Mama didn't stop to pick it up.

"She practically pushed me out of the room. She grabbed my hand and dragged me back upstairs and all the time she was whispering to me that I couldn't ever tell anybody what had happened—not anybody—or they would send her away to prison forever. She told me to stay in my room and not to come out until she came and got me.

"But I couldn't do that, Delia. I had to see what had happened to Daddy. I heard Mama on the phone, and I sneaked downstairs and . . . and that's when I screamed."

Who had Hattie called? Delia wondered. Not the sheriff. She had called him later. Who, then? Her lawyer, probably. Hattie had always had a level head.

"Didn't you know that all these years I've thought *you* killed Daddy?"

"Good grief, Delia. I told you at the time I didn't kill him."

Delia smiled cynically. "I wouldn't have expected you to admit to murder."

"No wonder you're so upset with me for not telling you the truth sooner. I'm sorry, Delia."

"I don't understand Mother at all," Delia said. "Why couldn't she have told me she believed me? Why didn't she admit she was wrong sooner and ask me to come home?"

"Maybe she felt like she didn't deserve your forgiveness, Delia. Or that you wouldn't give it to her, even if she asked."

Delia's throat squeezed shut. Rachel knew her well. As had Hattie. It was why she had left the note. Oh, yes, she was definitely Hattie's daughter. She had held herself aloof, no more willing to offer forgiveness than Hattie had been willing to ask for it. She had every bit as much stubborn pride as her mother.

And now it was too late.

The sob caught Delia by surprise. Grief she had held in abeyance as a final defiance of Hattie washed over her with all the power and devastation of a flash flood. Because she had refused to grieve, her grief when she allowed herself to feel it was a hundred times more terrible, because it was mixed with equal doses of guilt and shame.

Delia laid her head down on her arms at the kitchen table and cried. She was inconsolable, though Rachel tried to console her. It was as though all the tears she had never shed—for the loss of her innocence and Rachel's, for the betrayal and loss of her stepfather, for the death of her mother—had to be cried before she could move another step, before she could go on with her life.

Every time she managed to stop, she would lift her head and see the calendar marked with Xs and start crying again.

"Please, Delia, you're going to make yourself sick," Rachel said.

"I can't seem to st-hop," Delia sobbed.

She had no idea how long she had been sitting at the table crying when she felt herself being picked up and lifted into someone's lap. She opened her eyes enough to see it was Marsh. She sneaked a hand around his neck and clung, burying her face against his chest.

"It's all right, Delia," he crooned. "Rachel called and told me everything."

"Ma-ma killed Dad-dy," she sobbed.

"I know, sweetheart. I've known for a while."

"How?" she asked. "How did you know?"

"It was the only thing that made any sense. She was the only one besides you who could have gone to the sheriff. She was the only one who could have convinced him that Ray John committed suicide because she had threatened to expose him."

The sobs lessened, and Delia felt a strange calm settling over her. "I never forgave her," she murmured to Marsh. "I told her I never would."

Another sob. "I'm so sorry, Mama. I'm so sorry."

Marsh's arms tightened around her. "She knows, Delia. She knows."

"I should have cried or screamed or *something*. I should have made him go away. I should have told Mama."

"Shh," Marsh said. "It doesn't matter anymore. It's all over, Delia. It's all over now."

"Is she going to be all right?" Rachel asked anxiously. "Should I call Dr. Robbins?"

"I'll take her upstairs and put her to bed," Marsh said. "She'll be all right after she gets some sleep."

"Don't talk about me like I'm not here," Delia said irritably.

She heard Marsh chuckle.

"See what I mean?" he said. "She'll be back to her old cantankerous self in no time."

"Thank you for coming, Marsh," Rachel said.

"I'm glad you called," he said, rising with

Delia in his arms. "You'll have to show me where to go."

"I can talk," Delia said. "And I know where my bedroom is. If you'll put me down, I can get there myself."

Marsh and Rachel exchanged amused glances.

"Maybe you can," Marsh said, "but indulge me, will you?"

"I don't see why I should," Delia said petulantly.

"Stuff it, Delia," Rachel said. "Let the man carry you upstairs."

Delia gave Rachel a startled look, but settled meekly into Marsh's arms. "All right. Let's go."

"I'll be up in a few minutes," Rachel said.

Marsh headed up the stairs and then down the hall to Delia's room. He paused at the door while Delia hit the switch that turned the bedside light on. He crossed to the bed and leaned down to pull the spread and top sheet away before he laid her down. He pulled off her boots and tucked her feet under the covers, then pulled them up under her arms.

"Good night, Delia. I'll call you in the morning," he said as he bent over to kiss her on the forehead.

She caught his wrist and said, "Please don't leave yet."

He sat down beside her on the bed and brushed her bangs tenderly away from her forehead. "Do you want to talk about Hattie?"

She shook her head.

He waited expectantly, but when she didn't

speak, he said, "Thanks for coming over to save my house from the deluge."

"You're welcome."

"And for talking to Billie Jo. It seems you explained quite a few things to her that she's been wondering about."

"You're lucky to have her."

"I know."

Delia sighed. "What's going to happen to us, Marsh?"

"Whatever we want to happen, Delia."

"As soon as the funeral's over and I find someone to manage this place, I have to go back to New York. Especially with the accusations that have been leveled against me."

"I know."

"How do we make it work, Marsh, if I'm there, and you're here?"

"One of us will have to move."

"Are you saying you'll give up the ranch?"

His mouth tightened. "I can't go anywhere until Billie Jo's out of high school. She's already had too much upheaval in her life for me to move her again right away."

"It'll take another year and a half for her to finish high school."

"I know."

"What about your job at *The Chronicle?*"

"When my editor found out I was thinking about quitting for good, he offered me an opinion column, something I can write from anywhere. I'm going to accept it."

"Marsh, that's wonderful! That means you could move—"

"No, I can't. Not yet."

"So we wait another year and a half to be together?" Delia asked.

"You could resign from the bench tomorrow."

Delia rose onto her elbows. "You're kidding, right?"

"Why not? You can be a lot more help to kids in trouble as a lawyer here in Uvalde than you can sentencing teenage perps to probation or jail in New York."

"If I resign, it'll look like I did it under pressure from the DA's office. It'll look like I'm admitting that I'm incompetent. I won't do that, Marsh."

"Are you saying that if a cloud weren't hanging over your head, you'd be willing to resign?" Marsh asked in a soft voice.

Delia hesitated. Remembering all the years she and her mother had wasted, all the years she and Marsh had wasted, she took the plunge. "I love you, Marsh. I want to be with you. If the circumstances weren't what they are, I'd resign tomorrow. But you can see why that's impossible."

Marsh grinned and wrapped his arms around her and gave her a quick, hard kiss. "Will you marry me, Delia?"

Delia laughed. "This is a little sudden, isn't it?"

"I've been thinking about it for twenty years. Say yes."

He looked so excited, like a kid with his first bicycle. She hated to spoil his pleasure. But somebody had to be sensible. "Don't ask me now, Marsh. Not when things are so unsettled.

I can't say yes, even though I want to."

Marsh pulled himself free. "You can do anything you want to do, Delia. You told me so yourself, twenty years ago."

Delia's lips pressed flat. "I can't resign, Marsh. Not yet. Not until the accusations made against me in the *Times* get refuted or until I can prove them wrong."

"How long is that going to take? Another year on the bench? Two? Three? Thirteen?"

"It takes as long as it takes," Delia retorted.

Marsh stood. "We'll see about that," he said as he headed from the room.

"Where are you going?" Delia cried.

Marsh paused at the door. "To dig up proof that Sam Dietrich is making deals for money. The sooner I establish he's dirty, the sooner you can resign."

❦ *Chapter Sixteen* ❧

Marsh had never been so frustrated in his life. Everything he saw indicated Sam Dietrich was so clean he squeaked. There was no sign anywhere, in any bank account—foreign or domestic—that Marsh or a hacker friend of his had been able to locate, that Dietrich had accepted payoff money. His bank account matched his income from his job as the Brooklyn DA. He had property and investments, but nothing illegal, nothing even remotely stinky.

Marsh turned off his computer, leaned back in the timeworn leather chair, and put his boots up on a walnut desk autographed by the spurs of previous North scions. He rubbed his eyes, which were tired from a day spent staring at a blue computer screen. Billie Jo should be getting home from school any minute. He needed to start thinking about what he was going to fix for supper.

Marsh didn't have the will to get up and move.

He had been so sure he would find

something that would make it all easy. Delia would confront Dietrich and resign from the bench and come back to Texas and marry him. He snorted in disgust. So much for easy solutions.

To make matters worse, a second denunciation had been leveled at Delia in the *Times*, but in the guise of news, rather than opinion. Judge Carson hadn't made the front page, but there was a picture of Delia on page three in the front section, along with a brief article about her meteoric rise in the Brooklyn DA's office, her close friendship with Manhattan attorney and Democratic party mover and shaker Averill Matthews, and her even closer margin of election to the bench.

The Brooklyn district attorney was quoted as saying he believed the problem was "more the result of inexperience and inflexibility than incompetence. Judge Carson," the article continued, "was unavailable for comment."

The news article didn't make judgments; it purported to state facts. But the plain facts showed that Delia had twice as many trials scheduled as any other Brooklyn Supreme Court judge, and that overall her plea bargains were stiffer than those of other judges.

"They don't call her The Hanging Judge for nothing," Marsh muttered to himself.

He was sorry for Delia's sake that she had been attacked by the press. He was more concerned with how her troubles were going to affect their relationship. Without some evidence to prove Dietrich was manipulating the situation, Delia's only hope of clearing herself was to go back to work and let her work speak for itself.

That would mean the end of their chances of getting married right away and maybe for a long, long time. And because there was nothing certain about the future, maybe forever.

Marsh looked up and saw Delia standing at the door to his office with his grandmother's quilt folded over her arm. She was wearing a sleeveless white cotton shirt knotted at the waist, ragged, cutoff jeans, and Keds without socks. Her hair was bound up in a short ponytail. Except for the lines around her eyes and mouth—and the missing yard of hair—she could have been the girl he had met all those years ago. He felt a stab of wistful longing for the years they had lost.

"I knocked, but I guess you didn't hear me," Delia said.

"I was thinking." He rose and took the quilt from her and laid it over the back of the chair he had vacated. "Thanks for taking care of this for me."

"I know how much it means to you," Delia said.

It should have been the easiest thing in the world to take her in his arms and kiss her. It was what he wanted to do. He hesitated too long, and the moment passed.

She stepped back and said, "Did you find out anything?"

"No good news, I'm afraid. Why don't we go into the kitchen? We can talk while I start supper."

"What are you making?" Delia asked as

they walked back down the hall together.

"I haven't decided yet. Maybe you can help me make up my mind."

He opened the refrigerator and looked through it with Delia standing at his shoulder. Several plastic-wrapped packages of hamburger sat on the shelf, along with an equal number of packages of chicken.

"You should probably freeze some of this," Delia said.

"I want to divide it into serving-size portions first," Marsh said. "I just haven't found the time to do it."

He pulled out a package of hamburger. "Hamburgers it is."

"I'll split the rest of these into portions for you while you're cooking," Delia offered, "and wrap them for the freezer."

"Thanks," Marsh said. "I'd appreciate that."

It felt strange working in the kitchen with someone else. Marsh had never done it with Ginny, more because she didn't want him underfoot than because he wouldn't have been willing. It reminded him of a time when his grandmother had still been alive, and he had helped her with piecrust or cookie dough.

He wanted this quaint domestic scene to become reality. Considering what he had—or rather, hadn't—been able to find out about Sam Dietrich, that wasn't likely.

"Will you join us for supper?" Marsh asked. "I can make another burger."

"I wish I could, but I can't. I don't want to leave Rachel alone right now. I only stopped by to return your quilt and to find out what information you might have discovered about Sam."

Marsh met Delia's hopeful gaze and grimaced. "I can't find a thing, Delia. The man's clean as a whistle."

Delia turned away and finished wrapping a pound of hamburger. "I guess that settles that."

"Meaning?"

"Meaning I'll have to go back to New York as soon as I can get things worked out here."

Marsh wiped his hands on a towel and crossed to stand behind Delia. He saw her tense even before he circled her waist from behind and nuzzled her nape. He felt her shiver as he sucked on the flesh below her ear.

He turned her in his arms, and she snatched at a paper towel to wipe her greasy hands as he pulled her into his embrace. The towel fell to the floor as he captured her mouth with his.

He had been starving; she was a feast for the senses. He slid his tongue along the seam of her lips until she opened to him, and he thrust inside. Then she was his, and he took and gave and took some more. He backed her up against the sink and thrust against her, heard the animal sound she made in her throat and answered with one of his own.

He lifted her and set her on the counter and wrapped her legs around him.

The hamburgers sizzled.

So did he.

Marsh tore his mouth from hers and laid his forehead on her shoulder, gasping for breath.

"We have to stop. Billie Jo will be home any minute."

She took his head in her hands and brought his mouth back to hers and kissed him tenderly. It felt as though she were bidding him farewell.

Then she leaned her cheek against his and hugged him tight. "There has to be something ... some way," she said, "something else we can do." She leaned back, her worried gaze meeting his. "I can't give up this easily. I won't."

"I'm open to suggestions," he said, giving her kiss-swollen lips more of his attention.

She took his kisses, gave him a few of her own, then drew away, her brow furrowed in thought. "What else would make Sam deal with a bunch of felons besides money? What is he getting for letting them go? I know something's rotten. I just know it! But what?"

"Maybe we can figure it out by looking at the cases you think were fixed," Marsh suggested. "Perhaps there's a connection between them. How many do you think we're talking about?"

"The first outrageous plea bargain Sam threw at me occurred two months after I took my oath of office," Delia said. "I can count on one hand the number since. Leroy Lincoln would be number six."

"That takes two hands," Marsh pointed out.

Delia made a face at him.

"Can you get copies of the plea bargains and all the other pertinent information?" Marsh asked.

"I can have Janet—my secretary—fax it to me."

They both looked toward the screen door when they heard the squeal of the school bus brakes.

"Let me down, Marsh," Delia said, her color high.

"Kiss me first."

"Marsh—"

He kissed her, his tongue slipping into her open mouth to plunder it. Then he set her on her feet and held her steady until she had her legs under her again.

He was at the stove turning hamburgers, and Delia was at the counter wrapping the last of the chicken for freezing, when Billie Jo pulled open the screen door and stepped inside.

"Hi, kid," Marsh said. "How was school?"

"Fine." Billie Jo had stopped right inside the door, her ambivalent feelings about the scene she was witnessing apparent on her face.

Marsh felt like cheering when his daughter decided to be civil.

"Hi, Delia," Billie Jo said. "Did you come for supper?"

"No, I'll be leaving as soon as I finish here. I brought back your dad's quilt."

"Oh. Did it dry all right?"

"Like new," Delia reassured her. She washed her hands and used another paper towel from the roll standing beside the sink to dry them. She retrieved the paper towel on the floor and threw them both in the trash can she found under the sink, then turned to Marsh and said, "I'll call you when I get the information we discussed."

"I'll see you tomorrow anyway," Marsh said. In answer to Delia's raised brow, he reminded, "At Hattie's funeral."

"Oh. Sure."

Billie Jo held the door for Delia. "I . . . uh . . . I won't be coming to your mom's funeral with Daddy," she said. "Because . . . uh . . ."

Marsh watched Delia lay a comforting palm against Billie Jo's cheek. "I understand, Billie Jo," Delia said. "Don't worry about it." She gave Marsh one last glance over her shoulder before she left.

Marsh marveled at how well Delia understood his daughter. He should have realized that Hattie's funeral would evoke memories for Billie Jo of her own mother's death. There were lots of things he didn't know—was still learning—about his daughter. In all these months he hadn't talked to Billie Jo about Ginny's accident, waiting for his daughter to bring up the subject. But she never had.

What could he have said? That he had been shocked to hear about Ginny's death and dismayed to learn he was going to have responsibility for his teenage daughter? He could not—would never—admit that to Billie Jo. As he had feared, their first months together had been rocky. This past week they seemed to have turned some sort of corner. Talking to his daughter was easier; it certainly was not yet easy.

He could remember thinking that when he had a child of his own he would make sure he—she—would know she was loved. Hell. It sure was simpler to make those sorts of promises than to keep them.

"Hamburgers again?" Billie Jo said as she dropped her bookbag on the table and joined him at the stove.

"My culinary repertoire is limited," Marsh said. "There's always spaghetti or baked chicken."

"If I have baked chicken again anytime soon, I'm going to start clucking," Billie Jo said in disgust. She hefted herself onto the counter and sat eyeing him speculatively. "So, when are you and Delia getting married?"

Marsh dropped the spatula and burned himself retrieving it from the pan. "What?" He stuck his burned fingers into his mouth to cool them.

"I'm not blind, Daddy. I saw the hickey on her neck."

Marsh flushed. He wondered what Delia was going to say when she found it. He hadn't meant to put it there, but Delia hadn't been complaining when it happened. "We don't have plans right now to get married."

"What's stopping you?"

"There are . . . complications."

"You don't love her?"

"I didn't say that."

"She doesn't love you?"

"I didn't say that, either."

"So what's the problem?" Billie Jo asked.

"Delia's work is in New York," he said.

"Oh. I see."

"I don't suppose you'd be willing to move

to Brooklyn?" Marsh said, his lips twisting wryly. As soon as the words were out of his mouth, he knew he shouldn't have asked. It wasn't fair to his daughter to drag her halfway across the country because it was what he wanted. But he didn't take it back.

Billie Jo was silent a long time, biting at her lower lip with her teeth in the way that reminded him of Ginny, while she contemplated his request. Her answer made him feel proud of her and ashamed of himself.

"I'd move if you asked me to, Daddy. But I'd rather not. I'm kinda getting used to this place. I mean, all the stories you've told me about Grandma Dennison and Great-grandma Hailey are kinda neat. I like living in a house where Norths used to live a hundred years ago." She grinned and corrected, "Except when it rains."

"The roof's next on my list."

She continued as though he hadn't spoken. "Especially now that I've met Todd, it would be hard to leave hi—this place and go somewhere new and start all over."

Marsh had thought only of himself for a long time. He owed his daughter some stability. He owed her a little self-sacrifice.

Even if it means giving up Delia? Marsh felt a familiar ache in his chest. But he knew what his answer had to be.

"Don't worry your head about it," he told his daughter. "Delia and I will work something out."

Billie Jo's relieved sigh told him how much she had been willing to give up for him and made him feel even worse for having asked.

"Thanks, Daddy." She jumped down from the counter, grabbed her bookbag from the table, and headed for her bedroom. "I have to call Todd," she said.

"Supper will be ready any minute."

"Just to tell him we aren't moving," she shouted back down the hall at him.

Marsh realized then that Billie Jo had suspected what might be coming if he married Delia, maybe even dreaded it, without ever letting him know it. He should have asked how she felt sooner. He should have listened to what she had to say. He had a lot to learn about being a parent.

He wished Delia was going to be here to help.

He made himself consider, for the first time, the notion that she might not.

The morning of Hattie's funeral had dawned gray and cold for southwest Texas in January, but Delia, used to the frigid temperatures in New York, hadn't worn a coat. The wind was picking up, making it unpleasantly chilly at graveside.

The whole town and half the county had turned out at the Uvalde Cemetery—the older portion on the west side of Highway 90 where plots were still reserved for Circle Crown descendants—for Hattie's funeral. The Carsons were a prominent Uvalde family, so that wasn't unusual. Except Delia figured the crowd had come as much to ogle The Hanging Judge, and U.S. Congressman Clifford McKinley and his wife, as to pay their last respects to Hattie.

The plot was shrouded by a live oak, which rustled noisily, so the minister's voice was occasionally lost. Delia was having a hard time concentrating on what he said. She was burying her mother with unfinished business between them, but she had learned a valuable lesson from the experience: It was dangerous to let matters between herself and Marsh North lie unresolved. There were no guarantees in life. It was foolish to postpone living it with someone you loved.

She was meeting Marsh after the funeral to go over the plea bargains she thought were suspicious. They had to find some connection between them, some sign of wrongdoing by Sam Dietrich. Or else.

Or else what? Are you going to resign anyway to be with Marsh? Are you willing to do that? Are you going to let people think the worst of you?

Delia was unable to answer those questions.

The wind whipped at her new black dress with its high collar, which concealed the hickey Marsh had given her the previous day. She hadn't discovered the stupid thing until after the stores were closed last night. Actually, Rachel had pointed it out to her. She had been at first astonished, and then embarrassed. She had been so lost in what Marsh was doing to her that she hadn't felt him put it there.

Thank goodness for small towns. After needling Delia over her predicament, Rachel had called her friend, Madge Kuykendall, who had met them downtown at Madge's Boutique with the key to the store and helped her find something to wear.

Rachel stood beside her at Hattie's grave holding Scott's hand, looking beautiful in a black St. John knit despite her tears, which she dabbed at with a lace handkerchief. The six-year-old was becoming restless as the long-winded Baptist minister proved that everything in Texas was done bigger and better, even funerals. Congressman McKinley, looking sad and solemn, stood beside his wife.

Cliff's unexpected arrival in a black limousine after the start of Hattie's funeral had created quite a stir. Frankly, Delia had thought he would remain in Washington. On second thought, she had realized it would have looked odd—and been a political faux pas—for the congressman to miss his mother-in-law's funeral. It also gave him the perfect opportunity to come after his wayward wife.

When Rachel had told Cliff on the phone that she had left him and didn't intend to return to Dallas, he had been furious. He had told her he would come and get her. He had said he wasn't going to let her go. But there wasn't much he could do to her from more than a thousand miles away.

Well, he had taken care of the distance without much trouble. Trust Cliff to manipulate even their mother's funeral to his advantage. Delia knew her sister must be terrified, but there were no outward signs of her distress other than the tears she shed.

Delia didn't intend to let Cliff bully her sister—or take her away with him. She wasn't sure what she would do if he became physically violent. Rachel was safe so long as there were witnesses around to keep Cliff in line. But Delia was worried about what he might do when everyone left the cemetery, and they were alone again.

Delia sought out Marsh in the crowd. He was standing directly across from her in the second row of mourners. She made eye contact with him and was surprised to realize how well they could communicate with no more than that. He glanced at Cliff, then back to her, and nodded, and she knew she would not be left alone to deal with her sister's husband. With Marsh beside her, Delia was sure she could handle Congressman McKinley.

Rachel might have escaped in the push of people who wanted to shake Congressman McKinley's hand and express their condolences after the funeral, except Cliff slipped an arm around her waist and held on tight. Rachel sent an increasingly irritable Scott to wait for her in the car, where he had left his Power Rangers.

Cliff was patient with his constituents, and it wasn't until the last one had left with a smile on his face that he gave his full attention to his wife.

"Let's go get Scott and go home, Rachel," he said, heading toward the limousine, pulling Rachel willy-nilly along with him.

Rachel dug in her heels. "No, Cliff. Stop it. Stop!"

"Hold on, McKinley," Marsh said, stepping in front of the other man, Delia by his side.

"Who are you?" Cliff demanded.

"Marsh North."

It was apparent Cliff recognized the name. The congressman had made a point of acquainting himself with the press. "What are you doing here?"

"I'm a friend of Delia's. I moved back here recently with my daughter."

"It's nice to meet you, but if you'll excuse us, my wife and I are leaving," Cliff said.

"I don't believe the lady wants to go with you," Marsh said.

"I don't!" Rachel said.

"Shut up, Rachel!" Cliff ordered.

"Let her go, McKinley," Marsh said.

"Get out of my way." Cliff attempted to move forward.

Marsh stayed where he was, and Cliff came to an abrupt halt. Realizing he couldn't escape with Rachel, Cliff let her go.

The congressman turned to his wife and said, "I'm taking Scott home, Rachel. With or without you." He headed toward the car, where the little boy was waiting.

Rachel clutched at his arm. "Cliff, please, you can't—"

Cliff shook her off, but she grabbed at him again. He whirled and slapped her, then stood frozen, appalled at what he had done.

Delia gasped. She saw Marsh's hands ball into fists and reached out to grab him to keep him from attacking Cliff. "Marsh, don't!"

"You bastard," Marsh snarled at Cliff. "Why don't you try that with someone your own size." Marsh's body was taut with leashed anger. A muscle in his jaw spasmed as he clenched his teeth.

The congressman looked around quickly to see if anyone had seen him cowering from the other man. When he realized the area was abandoned, he turned back to face his three adversaries. "I'll do what I like," he retorted. "She's my wife."

Rachel stood with her head high, her face pale except for the red spot where Cliff's palm had struck her cheek. "Not for long," she said.

Before anyone could make another move, Delia stepped between Cliff and Rachel. "That's enough, Cliff," she said in a quiet voice. "Rachel isn't going with you, and neither is Scott. She's staying here and filing for divorce."

A look of such virulent hatred appeared on Cliff's face that Delia stepped backward until she came up against Marsh's muscular chest. His strength steadied her. "Let Rachel go, Cliff," Delia said. "Otherwise, it'll be all over the papers that you beat your wife."

"Are you threatening me?" Cliff said, his brows lowering ominously. "Let me return the favor. If you try smearing me, I'll make sure your sister ends up in an asylum. The woman's unbalanced. She drew a gun on me. She tried to kill herself. She should be put away."

Delia knew Cliff would make good on his promise, that there was every possibility he could. They were at a stalemate.

Cliff smirked at her and started to reach for Rachel. Marsh's voice stopped him.

"Congressman, perhaps you can explain

why a condominium in Alexandria with the deed recorded in your name has been occupied for the past two years by Miss Elizabeth Camp."

Delia gave Marsh a look no less startled than the one on Cliff's face. She turned to Rachel to see if she had known about Cliff's indiscretion, but her sister looked equally surprised.

Cliff's expression quickly became grim. "How did you—"

"Let's just say I have my sources, Congressman McKinley. Now, step away from your wife."

Cliff took a step backward and turned a malevolent look on Delia. "If you try to use that information against me, I'll ruin you."

"You can keep your little love nest, Cliff. So long as you give your wife a divorce and custody of her son," Delia said.

"He's my son, too."

"I'm sure appropriate visitation can be arranged," Delia said.

"Only if it's court supervised," Rachel said. Her skin was stretched tight over her facial bones. Her eyes burned with anger.

Cliff's face paled. "How can you do this to me, Rachel?"

"You did it to yourself, Cliff."

Cliff's chin jutted. He had lost, but he wasn't defeated. "You'll pay for this," he said to Delia. Then he turned and walked away.

Delia didn't exhale until the chauffeur closed the limousine door behind Cliff. She turned to Rachel and saw her sister's eyes were dry for the first time since the funeral had begun. "Are you all right?"

"I'm fine. For the first time in years, I'm just fine."

"Let's go home," Delia said. "Come with us, Marsh," she invited.

"I have some things I have to do," he said. "I'll talk to you later this afternoon, when we get together to go over those papers."

"Before you go, will you tell me how you found out about the condominium?" Delia asked.

"I'd be interested to know that, too," Rachel said.

"I figured as long as I was paying a hacker to look around at Sam Dietrich's bank deposits and real estate deeds, I might as well investigate the congressman, too." He shrugged. "It paid off."

"Thanks, Marsh," Delia said.

"Yes, thanks," Rachel said.

"My pleasure," he said with a smile.

"Scott must be getting restless. Will you be much longer?" Rachel asked Delia.

"No, I'll be there in a minute."

Delia stood silent until Rachel was gone. Then she turned to Marsh. "Thank you."

"I didn't do anything."

"You were there for me," Delia said.

"Of course I was there for you. I love you, Delia."

Delia's heart skipped a beat.

Marsh shook his head. "Damn. I meant to say it for the first time in a more romantic setting."

"This is fine," Delia said.

Marsh gave her a quick, hard kiss. "This afternoon," he said. Then he was gone.

Delia stared after him. This afternoon they would go over everything. Depending on what they found . . . choices would have to be made.

⟨ை *Chapter Seventeen* ⟩⟨

Delia arrived at Marsh's back door late the afternoon of Hattie's funeral just as Billie Jo was leaving. Todd was standing half in and half out of the screen door, holding it open for her.

"'Bye, Daddy," Billie Jo said, slinging her bookbag over her shoulder. "Todd will bring me back when we're done studying."

"Hey!" Marsh called as he slung the towel he had been using to dry dishes over his shoulder.

Billie Jo turned. "What?"

He opened his arms. "How about a hug?"

To Delia's amazement, the teenager loped back to her father, wrapped her arms around his waist, and let him give her a big, noisy bear hug.

"I love you, kid," Marsh said.

"I love you, too, Daddy."

An instant later, Billie Jo was on her way out the door. She paused long enough to say, "Hi, Delia," wink broadly, and add with a grin, "You and Daddy have fun!" before she grabbed Todd's hand and raced for his pickup.

Delia was still staring after them through the screen door with her jaw slack when she felt Marsh's arms surround her from behind. "Did I just see what I think I saw?" she asked.

"Billie Jo North with the son of the school board president? Yup. That's what you saw."

Delia turned within Marsh's embrace. "No. I meant the hug. And the 'I love you, kid.' "

Marsh flushed. "Oh. Yeah. Well. That's new. I'm trying it out to see how it feels."

"How does it feel?" Delia asked with a teasing smile.

"Good. Great."

"How about one for me?"

Marsh grinned and gave her a crushing hug. "I love you, Delia," he whispered in her ear. He let her go and said, "Well? What do you think?"

"I see what you mean," she said breathlessly.

Before she could say more, Marsh took her in his arms again. His mouth came down to cover hers. She dropped the soft leather briefcase she had brought and heard it hit the linoleum floor. A moment later Marsh lifted her into his arms and headed for his bedroom.

Delia didn't protest. Of course, he never left her mouth free long enough for her to get a word in edgewise. Even if she could have spoken, there was nothing she would have said to stop him. She loved him. He loved her. Their future together was precarious, to say the least. Every moment they had together was precious, to be savored and saved as a poignant memory that might be all she had of Marsh North for a very long time to come.

Marsh made short work of her boots and jeans and shirt, quickly stripping her. Her eyes devoured him as she returned the favor. Desire spiraled through her.

"I want you inside me," she said.

Need flared in his gray eyes as he lowered them to the bed, pressing her thighs apart with his knees as his body mantled hers. He drove into her in a single bold thrust.

Delia gasped and then groaned in satisfaction. Her hands slid from their grip on his shoulders into his hair, clenching handfuls of the silky stuff to pull his head down for her kiss.

She wrapped her legs around him and arched upward to seat him more deeply. Their tongues mimicked their bodies as he moved inside her, while his hand slid between them to caress her. An animal sound emerged from her throat as her body tightened in exquisite pleasure. In moments he had driven them both to the brink.

Just when Delia didn't think she could bear any more, he was gone, leaving her bereft. She murmured a sound of protest as he withdrew, blinking at him in confusion. "Marsh?"

"Shh," he said, his chest heaving, his body taut. "I want to take my time. I don't want this to end. I want to remember every moment of loving you."

Because it might be the last time? she wondered.

He made love to her breasts and throat and belly with his lips and tongue. His hands cupped her breasts and made of them a treasure to be explored. His mouth found its way to the heart of her, and she arched upward as she felt his silken hair against her thighs.

He made her feel exalted, revered, adored. Her fingertips grazed flesh that quivered beneath her touch, and her mouth followed where her hands led to return pleasure for pleasure.

It wasn't enough. She wanted them joined. She teased and taunted until he made them one again. She felt his urgency, his fear, and his need and answered with an urgency and fear and need of her own. Time was running out. This might be all they had. She wanted to crawl inside him and stay there, wanted to be a part of him, body and soul.

She felt the inevitable surge of her body toward completion of the sex act, the power of it driving her, making her aware of the impossibility of staying where she was. She had to move forward. She had to take the next step. There was no standing still. In this, as in all things, there was no holding on to the present. The future beckoned. The past and its promise was gone forever.

Delia clung to Marsh as her body arched in the throes of climax, heard his cry of exultation as he spilled into her.

She welcomed his weight on her, folded her

arms around him and held him close as he
nuzzled her throat, their spent bodies sweat-
slick and heaving for the air to keep them
alive.

"I'm too heavy," Marsh said as he slid
down beside her and tucked her close to him.

They lay quietly until their breathing eased.
Delia settled her head against Marsh's chest
and listened to his heart. It beat slowly now,
steadily, strongly.

"What are we going to do?" she whispered,
raising her head to meet his gaze. "I can't live
without you, Marsh. I don't want to live without you."

He pulled her atop him, and his arms tightened around her. "We're going to figure out
Sam Dietrich's angle. We're going to get your
name cleared. Then you're going to resign
from the New York bench and marry me."

Delia laughed at the determined look on
Marsh's face. "I see you've got everything
worked out."

"Damn straight." He shifted her away and
sat up. "We'd better get to it."

He rose, heedless of his nakedness. She admired the sight of his sleek back and buttocks
as he pulled on Jockey shorts and jeans.

She was dressed nearly as quickly as Marsh
was and followed him out to the kitchen,
where she had dropped the briefcase full of
papers her secretary had faxed to her. She
wished Marsh had put on his shirt. She found
the sight of him, bare-chested in low-slung,
well-worn jeans, entirely too distracting.

He caught her staring and grinned. "I'm

ready to look at whatever's inside that brief-case whenever you are."

She stuck out her tongue at him, and when he made a move to reach for her she backed off warily. "Marsh, we have to do this."

"I'm waiting on you," he said.

She didn't want to work, she wanted to play. But they didn't have the time. Reluctantly, she set her briefcase on the kitchen table and pulled out a lined yellow legal pad.

"I've made a chart of the six suspicious plea bargains," she said. "I thought it might help us to organize our thoughts."

She pulled a chair around and sat down next to Marsh as he looked over the information she had put together.

NAME	RACE	AGE	CRIME
1. Jaime Perez	Hispanic	19	Sale of a Controlled Substance (second offense)
2. Franklin Harris	White	40	Sale of Stolen Property (third offense)
3. Rosa Torres	Hispanic	18	Assault with a Deadly Weapon/ Attempted Murder
4. John Pisakowski	White	56	Armed Robbery
5. Ralph Washington	Black	22	Sale of a Controlled Substance (second offense)
6. Leroy Lincoln	Black	18	Murder One

"I thought I might find some simple, visible connection between the cases," Delia said. "Nothing jumped out at me."

"Let's presume, for the sake of argument, that Dietrich doesn't get paid off in money," Marsh said. "That he's using some other form of barter for payment."

"Such as drugs?"

Marsh shrugged. "Why not? It makes sense. Especially since the first of these plea bargains happens to be with a kid who sells drugs for a living. Or maybe Dietrich's getting some other kind of stolen goods as payoff," Marsh said, pointing to Harris's crime—the sale of stolen property.

He frowned. "Only, I can't see the Brooklyn DA accepting stolen goods. Too easy to trace. Besides, you can only use so many TVs and stereos and VCRs. There's always the possibility Dietrich is taking cash."

"Even if that premise works for the first and second plea bargains, what about the third one?" Delia asked. "Rosa Torres isn't selling anything except herself."

"She's a prostitute?"

Delia nodded. "She took a knife to her boyfriend when she caught him in bed with her girlfriend."

"What about some sort of gang connection between all of these cases?" Marsh asked.

"Perez is a member of the Snakes. Washington and Lincoln are part of the Black Boys. None of the others have any relation to gangs."

"Where do they all live? Any connection there?" Marsh asked.

Delia looked at her notes. "All the Blacks and Hispanics live in Flatbush. Pisakowski lives in Carroll Gardens. Harris lives in Park Slope."

"Figures," Marsh said. "But it doesn't help us much. What about prior offenses?"

"They all have them."

"So they've all been through the system before," Marsh mused. "Any of them get light sentences before? I mean, has Dietrich cut any of them any slack in the past?"

Delia looked hurriedly through the case files before she glanced up at Marsh. "No," she said, frowning. "Nothing as light as what he wanted me to agree to for these subsequent offenses, even though he was the DA for two of the previous cases."

"Which two?"

"Perez and Washington."

Marsh looked at the chart. "Perez was the first suspicious plea bargain Dietrich brought to you. So what did Perez find out about Dietrich between the first crime and the second crime that forced the DA to deal?"

"Maybe Perez saw Sam do something illegal," Delia suggested.

"Caught him buying drugs? Or sold drugs to him? And recognized him because he had seen him in the courthouse?"

Delia shook her head. "Sam Dietrich is too ambitious to do anything as stupid as buying drugs on the street. The man wants to be governor. He wouldn't make a buy directly. He'd get someone to do it for him.

"Besides, I've spent enough time around Sam that I think I'd notice if he was a user. There's no sign of it in his behavior. But I could easily be wrong."

Marsh scratched his nose. "There's no sign of it from his bank accounts, either. Drugs cost a lot of money."

"Maybe you didn't find the money in his bank accounts because he takes money from people to do deals, but spends it on drugs, rather than depositing it," Delia said.

"That assumption might work. As long as he got his payoffs in cash and stuffed it under a mattress until he spent it."

Delia made a face. "Not likely, huh?"

"I wouldn't say so. What about something Perez could have seen him do that wouldn't allow for a middleman."

"Like what?"

Marsh pointed to Rosa Torres. "Visiting a prostitute."

"Surely not. Sam could afford a better class of woman if he wanted one."

"Maybe he likes things done to him a nice woman won't do," Marsh suggested.

"I can't imagine—"

"What if Perez saw Dietrich with a prostitute doing something perverted?" Marsh said. "That would give him an incentive to deal, wouldn't it?"

"If that's true, what about the rest of these cases?" Delia said. "You're not going to suggest they all saw Sam breaking the law, are you?"

"I'm betting there's a connection between them somewhere. One of these perps holds the key to this puzzle. But we may have to go to New York to find it."

Delia raised her brows. "We?"

Marsh smiled wryly. "Would you mind if I came along?"

"I'd appreciate the help," Delia said. "But what about Billie Jo?"

"Do you think Rachel would mind keeping her at the Circle Crown for a couple of days?"

"I suspect she'd enjoy the company," Delia said.

"When are you heading back to New York?" Marsh asked.

"As soon as I've hired a ranch manager."

"How long is that going to take?"

Delia grimaced. "Your guess is as good as mine. I've got the word out that I need someone. Hopefully—"

The kitchen phone rang shrilly. Marsh answered it and stood listening for a moment before he started shaking his head. "Go turn on the TV in the living room," he ordered brusquely. "Rachel says there's something on the news about you."

Marsh had already hung up the phone and was two steps behind Delia as she hurried to the living room. She turned on the TV in time to hear a female news commentator say, "More accusations of impropriety have been leveled against Brooklyn's Hanging Judge. Sources say a crime committed against Judge

Carson in her youth has left her with a private ax to grind. The numbers speak for themselves. No other judge in the Brooklyn Supreme Court demands such tough sentences.

"But are they fair and impartial? That question has provoked an investigation of Judge Carson's courtroom practices by the state attorney general's office."

Delia turned to Marsh. "An *investigation*?"

"Shh. Let's hear the rest of it."

The camera cut to rumpled, tired-looking Assistant DA Frank Weaver standing on the steps of the Brooklyn Supreme Court Building. "All I know is Delia Carson was an excellent prosecutor."

"So she sent a lot of men to jail?" a TV reporter standing beside him asked.

"That's what I just said, isn't it?" Frank retorted. "But she would never—"

The reporter cut him off. "Back to you, Sherry."

"That's all on this breaking story," the TV commentator said. "We'll have more for you on the news tonight at ten. This is Sherry—"

Delia punched the TV off and whirled on Marsh. "Cliff had a hand in this! I know it!"

The phone shrilled again. Marsh headed down the hall to the kitchen to answer it with Delia right behind him. "It's for you," he said.

She stared at the phone for a moment before taking it from him. "What is it, Rachel? I see. Don't let them in. I don't know what I'm going to do!" she said. "Don't answer the door again. Don't answer the phone. Wait. I'll let it ring once, hang up, then call back, so you'll know it's me. Don't do anything till I get there."

Delia hung up the phone. "I have to go home."

"Reporters are calling the house?" Marsh asked.

"Two TV crews are squatting on the doorstep!" Delia paced the kitchen agitatedly. "What am I going to do now?"

"Are you asking for my advice?"

Delia lurched to a stop as Marsh stepped in front of her.

"If you're asking, here's my suggestion," he said. "Don't go home. Head straight for New York."

"Right now? Tonight?"

Marsh nodded. "The sooner we get to the bottom of Sam Dietrich's secret, the sooner we can show that Dietrich has a private reason for complaining about your work."

"What about the investigation that's being launched against me?" Delia said bitterly. "Exposing Sam isn't going to stop that."

"Why wouldn't it?" Marsh said. "If nothing else, it'll turn the spotlight on Sam instead of you."

"What about the charge that I'm tough on criminals because I have a private ax to grind?"

"Do you?"

Delia stood stunned, staring at him. "How can you ask me that?"

Marsh kept his gaze locked with hers. "Why are you so tough on criminals, Delia? Isn't it possible you're punishing a lot of other men for what Ray John did to you?"

"How can you even suggest—"

"Before you protest too loudly, think about it."

"I'm a good judge," Delia said defensively.

"I'm not saying you aren't. I'm only asking you to look inside yourself and ask honestly whether your strict pronouncements from the bench might not be influenced by what happened to you, by the fact you were once a victim yourself."

Delia felt tears stinging her eyes and nose. "I'm fair. Criminals should be punished."

"Because Ray John never was?"

Delia stared at Marsh, gritting her teeth to keep her chin from trembling. She had always known she wanted a role protecting the good guys from the bad guys, well aware that Ray John's behavior was what had motivated her to pursue a legal career. But had she been doing more than merely punishing criminals? Had she been avenging herself, as well, through all those harsh plea bargain arrangements, all those tough sentences?

She looked up at Marsh, the agony of acknowledging such a failing apparent in her eyes.

Marsh's arms closed around her, and she leaned her head on his shoulder. She felt Marsh's lips against her temple, reassuring, supportive.

"What if it's true?" she whispered. "What if I've been penalizing all those criminals for what Ray John did to me and Rachel? What can I do about it? I can't go back and change

anything now." She swallowed with difficulty
past the lump in her throat. "Maybe I don't
deserve to be a judge. Maybe I should hand in
my resignation."

Marsh took her by the shoulders and separated them. He smiled down at her. "Not before you prove yourself innocent of all
charges. Not before you prove that Sam Dietrich's complaints originate from attempts to
hide criminal behavior of his own."

"I've just told you I may be guilty of what
they say!" Delia protested. "I've been giving
out the harshest sentences I can."

"There's no law against that," Marsh
pointed out.

"Yes, but—"

"Have you ever committed any illegal act,
taken a bribe, solicited one, bargained under
the table—"

"Of course not!" Delia replied indignantly.

"Sweetheart, nothing else matters. Everyone's human. We all act from different motives. Yours only matter if you let them push
you into doing something beyond the legal
limits. You've never done that."

"But I let my feelings influence my decisions."

"Name me one judge who hasn't," Marsh
said. "You're no different from anyone else.
Personalities make a difference. You told the
public when you campaigned that you intended to be tough on criminals. All you've
done is keep that promise."

"But my reasons—"

"Are your own," Marsh said. "What's important is that you understand the motives for

what you do, not that they be revealed to everyone else. It's the suggestion of impropriety that got the attorney general involved. They're not going to find any, are they?"

"No."

Marsh's arms folded around her again. "Then nothing else matters."

Delia gave a tear-choked laugh. "I can't believe you just talked me out of resigning. I thought you wanted me to resign!"

"I do," Marsh said. "But I want it to be because you choose me. Not because you're forced into it."

Delia raised herself on tiptoes to kiss Marsh on the lips. "Thank you, Marsh."

"I haven't done anything."

"You're trusting me to choose a future together. I'd say that's everything."

His mouth came down to claim hers. They were both out of breath by the time he released her.

"Lord," he said, his heart thumping crazily, "if we don't get out of here soon, we're going to end up back in bed. Let me call Billie Jo before you talk to Rachel again and explain what we're doing. Then I'll call the San Antonio airport and find out when the next plane leaves for New York."

"There's no need for me to go back to the Circle Crown to pack," Delia said. "I have whatever I'll need in my apartment in New York."

"Good," Marsh said. "All we have to do now is expose whatever it is Sam Dietrich's trying so hard to hide."

✍ *Chapter Eighteen* ✍

Delia felt like screaming. Everywhere they turned in Brooklyn, she and Marsh had found a dead end.

Jaime Perez was dead, killed in a hit-and-run accident. Franklin Harris's parole officer hadn't seen him for three months. He thought Harris might have taken off for Florida, where he had relatives. Rosa Torres had been making regular visits to her parole officer, but he had no idea where she was if she wasn't at her address in Flatbush. He suggested Delia and Marsh try Sunset Park near the BQE—the Brooklyn-Queens Expressway—after dark. Rosa had been picked up for hooking there in the past.

Delia was walking arm in arm with Marsh along the famous Promenade in Brooklyn that had the best view of the Manhattan skyline across the East River—the one most people saw on postcards. Their late afternoon pace was leisurely. Their conversation was not.

"I'm going with you," Delia said.

"Sunset Park after dark is no place for a woman."

"Rosa Torres will be there."

Marsh rolled his eyes. "You know what I mean. Let me go get her and bring her somewhere—"

"I'm going, and that's final."

"You are the most stubborn—"

"Please, let's not argue anymore," Delia said, stopping and turning to face Marsh. "Let's just enjoy the time we have together."

She had often dreamed of walking the Promenade with Marsh, dreamed of having him kiss her as the sun slipped below the horizon. This wasn't exactly the way she had pictured them together—they had spent the past half hour of their walk debating the merits of who should interview Rosa Torres—but it might be as close as she was ever going to get. Her arms slid up around his neck, and she leaned into him. "Kiss me, Marsh."

She didn't have to ask twice. Marsh's mouth came down to capture hers. His arms tightened around her possessively. "God, Delia. I want you. Right now."

Delia smiled and shook her head. "The sun's going down, Marsh. We don't have time—"

"I know," he said urgently. "Time is running out. I can feel you slipping away from me."

She took his face between her hands. "I'll always love you, Marsh."

He tore himself free. "Damn it! That's not enough! I want us to have a life together. I want us to have a child of our own."

Delia's eyes widened. "You do?"

Marsh seemed stunned by what he had said. He put a hand to his temple and shook his head. "I don't know where that came from."

He met her gaze, and she recognized the longing there. "I do," she said. "I've had the same dream."

His arms slid back around her. He cupped her bottom and nestled her between his wide-spread legs. "What did you see?"

She resisted the urge to arch into him. "A son who'd grow up tall like you." Her thumb caressed his face. "With the North chin."

Marsh smiled. "Of course."

"With my black hair. And eyes that are gray like yours, but lighten when he's happy to a blue the shade of mine."

"Blue eyes," Marsh said definitely. "Because he'd always be happy."

Delia was having trouble keeping the wistfulness out of her voice. "It's too late for dreams like that, Marsh."

"Why?"

"I'm thirty-six years old."

"That's not too old."

"I like having a career."

"No one said you had to give up working. Lots of other women manage both."

"It isn't easy."

"I'd help."

She raised a skeptical brow. "With diapers? Two o'clock feedings? Sore throats and chicken pox?"

"I've changed a diaper or two in my time,"

he defended himself. "And stayed up all night with a sick child."

"I forgot you've been through this before."

His arms tightened around her, and he whispered in her ear, "Not with you. Not with a child of ours. I want that, Delia. So bad it hurts."

"I want it too."

Delia snuggled her cheek against Marsh's chest and glanced across the river at the New York skyline. Even in all its nighttime glory, it didn't hold a candle to the stars in a vast Texas sky. "We'd better go," she said. "We don't want to miss Rosa if she gets to the park early."

"Marry me, Delia."

She looked up at Marsh, saw the light from across the river reflected in his eyes. She made a wobbly attempt at a smile. "I love you, Marsh. I always have, and I always will."

It wasn't an answer. And it was.

She stepped back from his embrace, letting the distance grow between them emotionally as well as physically. "We'd better go," she repeated.

He didn't say anything else. Didn't plead, didn't argue, didn't bargain. She saw a muscle in his jaw working, knew he was grinding his teeth. Saw the tension in his back and shoulders. Saw the despair reflected in his eyes.

They didn't speak again as they walked briskly toward the park. It was a dreary, frightening place in the dark. Shadows became slinking forms. Sounds became guttural voices.

Marsh slipped an arm around her waist protectively as they walked slowly, carefully through the park, searching the faces of the women, looking for the one that matched the picture Rosa's parole officer had given them.

It was ludicrously easy to spot her. She was standing under one of the few streetlights. Her skirt was short, her jacket black leather, and she was wearing immensely high heels. Her bleached blond hair was tied in a topknot and stringy bangs fell onto her forehead and into her eyes. She wore surprisingly little makeup. Despite the stated age of eighteen on her record, she looked thirty.

"Rosa?"

The woman took one look at them and ran. Marsh grabbed her arm to stop her, and she screamed. His hand quickly covered her mouth. She stabbed at him with her high heels, and he gave a pained grunt and grabbed at her legs to immobilize her.

"Rosa, please stop fighting," Delia said. "We aren't here to hurt you. I'm Judge Carson. Do you remember me?"

The woman stopped struggling, but her chest was heaving, and her dark eyes were wild with fear.

"I'm going to take my hand from your mouth," Marsh said. "We aren't going to hurt you. We just want to talk to you. Don't scream."

Marsh slowly removed his hand. Rosa remained silent but wary, tensed to flee.

"I'm going to let you go," he said. "Don't run, or I'll come after you." Marsh stepped back a foot, ready to catch her again, if necessary.

Rosa stood trembling, but still.

"We only want to ask you some questions," Delia repeated.

"I don't have time for questions," Rosa said. "I gotta work."

Marsh reached into his pocket and pulled out a twenty. "How much time will this buy?"

"Ask your questions," Rosa said, tucking the money in her deep cleavage.

"Would you come with us somewhere we can talk privately?" Delia said.

"Where?" Rosa asked, her eyes narrowing as she looked from one to the other of them.

Delia and Marsh had scouted earlier and found a small bar not far from the park, which Delia named. "We can walk there," she said. "It'll only take a few minutes."

"I'd rather talk here," Rosa said.

Delia looked around her. The movement of shadows in the dark felt ominous. Surprising that Rosa felt safer here. Delia supposed it was all a matter of perspective. "All right," she conceded. "Let's move out of the light."

"I like it in the light," Rosa said, her chin tilting up. "You want to talk? Talk."

Delia glanced at Marsh, and he nodded.

"It's about Sam Dietrich," Delia began.

"Who?"

"The Brooklyn district attorney."

"Oh, yeah. What about him?"

"We wondered if . . . if he might have been a client of yours."

Rosa looked from Delia to Marsh and

hooted. "Shit, no. The man, he likes boys."

Delia's eyes goggled. "He's a homosexual?"
Of all the things she had imagined, that was
not one of them.

"Naw. He likes *boys*. You know, little boys.
The man is a pre-vert, you know? Lets them
suck his d—"

"We get the picture," Marsh interrupted.
"How do you know the DA likes boys?"

"Jaime Perez told me," Rosa said, snapping
her gum, comfortable now that she realized
she wasn't the focus of their questions.

"How do you know Perez?" Marsh asked.

"He's a cousin of mine," Rosa said.

"How did Perez know about Dietrich's pen-
chant for boys?" Delia asked.

"His what?" Rosa asked.

"That he liked boys," Marsh said.

"Oh. He seen him with one," Rosa said. "He
was dealin' dr—walkin'—in the same alley
where the DA was doin' it in his car. He recognized him 'cause he seen the man in court."

"Did you use that information to coerce the
DA into giving you a lighter sentence?" Delia
asked.

"Hey, lady, I ain't gotta say nothin'!" Rosa
said.

Marsh frowned at Delia, and she glared
back.

"We're not after you," Marsh said to Rosa.

"Maybe *you* ain't a problem," Rosa said to
Marsh. "But the judge here, she's got a reputation, you know?"

Delia flushed. "I don't want to make any
trouble for you."

"Yeah. Where have I heard that before?" Rosa said.

"Do you know Franklin Harris?" Marsh said.

"What if I do?" Rosa retorted.

"How do you know him?" Delia asked.

"I bought a used car from him."

"*Stolen* car," Marsh muttered.

Delia shot him a silencing look. "Did you tell Harris about the DA's . . . problem?" Delia asked.

Rosa shrugged. "Hey, a girl's gotta live. He was gonna take the car away 'cause I couldn't keep up the payments. So I told the man about the man—if you know what I mean."

Delia's gaze locked on Marsh. They had found the secret they were searching for, and enough of a connection from one party to another to piece together what had probably happened. It didn't take a genius to figure out that Sam Dietrich's secret had probably been passed from one party to another as necessary to pay off debts and then used to finagle light plea bargains. The problem was proving it.

"Would you be willing to tell someone else—the police—what you just told us?" Delia said.

"Hey, judge! I ain't gonna say nothin' to nobody 'bout nothin'. Ain't gonna put myself in jail for you or nobody. Understand?"

Delia understood perfectly. With Perez dead and Harris gone and Rosa unwilling to testify, they had nothing they could use against Dietrich. Even if they could get the other three to talk, it would only be hearsay evidence. Perez was the only one who had seen Sam committing an illegal act. And Perez wasn't available to testify. Delia began to wonder whether his death had been an accident, after all.

"Thank you, Rosa," Delia said.

"For what?" the woman asked. "I ain't gonna testify. I told you that, and I meant it."

"I know," Delia said. "I just meant thank you for your time."

Rosa reached into her bra and patted the twenty Marsh had given her. "Shit, the man paid for it." She gave Marsh a sloe-eyed look. "You got a little time left on the meter, mister. What'll it be? You want me to suck—"

Delia hooked an arm through Marsh's and dragged him away. She looked up and saw him struggling not to laugh.

"Don't you dare!" she hissed as she hurried with him to the closest subway entrance.

A guffaw burst free. "If you could have seen the look on your face when she offered—"

"This isn't funny! It's a disaster! Don't you see? We know for sure Sam was making deals, but we have absolutely no way to prove it. It would be his word against mine. And the accusations I would have to make are so awful I wouldn't dare do it without some proof."

"I could put a private investigator on him, someone to follow him around and get pictures."

"That might take weeks or months. I haven't got that much time. The attorney general's starting his investigation now. I need proof now!"

They had reached the entrance to the subway tunnel when Marsh grabbed her arm and stopped her. "I have a suggestion. I don't know whether you're going to like it."

"I'm up for anything."

"This might be dangerous."

Delia eyed Marsh skeptically. "What did you have in mind?"

"What if you confronted Dietrich personally with what you know?"

"What good would that do? It would still be my word against his."

"Not if you were wearing a wire."

Delia frowned. "A wire?"

"Look, we go to the attorney general, arrange for you to wear a wire and confront Sam Dietrich. You could get everything he says on tape."

"Who says he'll confess?"

"You don't think you could make the man talk?" Marsh asked.

Delia looked at him thoughtfully. "When would I do this?"

"What about now? Tonight?"

"The attorney general would need probable cause—"

"They can pick up Rosa and squeeze the truth out of her again, if necessary. There's always a judge available to sign court orders when they're needed in a hurry. What do you say? Are you game?"

Delia smiled grimly. "Bring on the DA. I'm ready to play."

Marsh hated like hell being stuck in the paneled truck with the police, around the corner

from Sam Dietrich's home in Brooklyn
Heights, unable to help Delia if she ran into
trouble inside. The worst part was, this had all
been his idea. He would never forgive himself
if something happened to her.

What could happen? She would confront
the man, he would either spill the beans or
not, and Delia would leave. No problem.
Quick and easy as throwing a two-day-old
calf.

Only Marsh had a bad feeling that wouldn't
go away. He listened as Delia checked the microphone before ringing the doorbell.

"All right, guys," she said. "Here goes."

He heard her take a deep breath and exhale.
Heard the elaborate door chimes. Heard the
door open.

"Well, well," Sam said. "To what do I owe
the pleasure of your company?"

From the mirrored window at the back of
the van, Marsh saw Dietrich look around to
see who might be watching them. He didn't
seem to notice the tail end of the paneled
truck, which was parked right around the corner.

"What are you looking for?" Delia asked.
"The police? Or the press?"

Marsh cringed. Lord, what did the woman
think she was doing? Dietrich was sure to suspect something now.

"Either or both would be equally unwel-
come," Dietrich said.

"I feel the same way," Delia said coolly.
"What I have to say to you—what I want to
ask—needs to be done in private."

"Very well. Come in," Dietrich said.

Marsh felt a clutch in his chest as Delia entered the elegant Tudor brick house and the door closed behind her with a solid *thunk*. There was nothing he could do now but listen.

"May I offer you a drink?" Dietrich asked.

"This isn't a social call," Delia said.

"I didn't think it was," Sam answered smoothly. "I'm having Chivas. What would you like?"

"Nothing."

"Suit yourself. Come into my library and sit down. We can be comfortable there."

Marsh knew from the floor plan of the DA's home he had perused that the study was in the back of the house farthest away from help if Delia needed it in a hurry.

"Damn," he muttered. "I had to be crazy to suggest this."

"Shh," one of the policeman said. "I can't hear."

Marsh scooted closer to him. "Is something wrong with the wire?"

"I don't think so. They ain't said nothin' for a while, but I don't want to miss nothin'."

Marsh sat on the edge of his seat, listening, waiting, knowing both Delia's future and his own were on the line.

"Come on, Delia," Marsh murmured. "You can do it."

"I presume you're here about the newspaper articles," Sam said.

"You presume correctly," Delia replied. "All I did was tell the truth."

"As you see it."

Sam didn't answer. Marsh pictured him smirking, nodding.

"You know there's nothing incompetent about my work," Delia said.

Sam didn't answer. In his mind's eye, Marsh saw him give an uncaring shrug.

"I never said there was," Sam said at last. "I only said you're inexperienced."

"You implied more," Delia spat back. "You suggested I'm inept, when we both know that's not the truth."

"Truth has very little to do with politics, my dear," Sam said.

Marsh heard the ice in Sam's glass rattle in the silence that followed.

"You're never going to be governor of New York, Sam," Delia said.

"Oh? Why is that?"

"Because I know your secret."

Marsh found the silence interminable. Why didn't Dietrich say something?

At last Sam replied, "What secret is that?"

"The one Perez found out. That you like little boys. You're the worst sort of person I can imagine, Sam. A grown-up who takes advantage of innocent children."

Marsh could hear the loathing in Delia's voice. And no wonder. She had been the victim of just such a man.

"Perez found you out, Sam, and he used that information to make a deal with you on his plea bargain," Delia said.

"Quite true," Sam admitted. "But Perez is no longer with us. Killed, I believe, in a hit-and-run accident."

"My God. *You* killed him!"

Marsh heard the shocked accusation in Delia's voice and wanted to slap a hand over her mouth. Was she crazy or what? If the man could kill once, he surely wouldn't hesitate to do it again.

"It was necessary," Dietrich replied. "The fool had big eyes and an even bigger mouth."

Marsh's jaw dropped. They had the DA cold. And not just for fixing plea bargains. For murder.

"Get her out of there, now!" Marsh snapped.

The policeman grabbed Marsh's arm to keep him from exiting the paneled truck. "Wait a minute! Listen!"

"Why did you attack me in the press?" Delia asked. "Why not keep it between us?"

"You were incorruptible, your honor," Sam conceded. "That made you a real pain in the ass. No. You have to go, Judge Carson. I can't have you making a mess of things."

"But I know your secret," Delia said. "There'll be no getting around the truth this time, Sam. I'll go to the press—"

"You aren't going anywhere."

Marsh listened to the silence. All he heard was Delia's rapid breathing.

"Put that gun away, Sam. It won't do any good to kill me now," Delia said. "I'm—"

Marsh was out of the van and running toward the house when he heard the single shot.

"Noooo!" he howled. "No!"

He hit the front door on the run with his shoulder, and wood splintered as it burst open. He sprinted for the back of the house in the direction of Sam's study. He stopped cold in the doorway and stared.

Sam Dietrich sat slumped over his desk, a .38 Smith & Wesson in his hand. Blood splattered the wall behind him. Delia stood white-faced in front of him.

"Delia!"

She remained frozen, apparently unable to move. Her body wavered as though she were a building teetering in an earthquake, threatening to crumple at any second. He saw her swallow before she said, "The blood on the wall . . . it's just like Daddy."

She made a sound like an animal in pain. A moment later he had her in his arms, clutching her close.

"Look at me, Delia," he insisted, shoving her chin up and forcing her to focus on his face. "There was nothing you could do."

"I know," she said. "Not then. And not now."

She stared at him a moment longer, long enough for him to realize that at long last, she had let go of the past.

"I thought he shot you," he said, holding her tight. "I thought you were dead."

"He was going to kill me," she said. "But I showed him the wire, and he turned the gun on himself instead."

Police surrounded them moments later, and Delia explained again what had happened. Marsh kept one arm around her waist the whole time, unwilling to let her go. He led her into the living room, away from Dietrich's corpse, so she could answer the barrage of questions the police threw at her. The attorney general had shown up after the police called him.

"Did you get it all on tape?" Delia asked as she stood with Marsh in the elegant front hall-way of Dietrich's home.

"We got it all, Judge Carson," the officer in charge said. "There are camera crews outside already, if you'd like to make a statement for the ten o'clock news."

Marsh looked at her expectantly.

"No statement," she said.

Marsh exhaled a breath he hadn't realized he'd been holding. He eyed Delia sideways. So she wasn't going to quit, after all. He could hardly blame her. Dietrich's last words completely exonerated her. She could go back to the courtroom with a clean slate. And why wouldn't she? She was a great judge. Incorruptible.

"Let's go home," she said to Marsh, grasping his hand.

He hadn't even realized he had let her go.

"To your apartment in Park Slope?" he asked.

She smiled. "No, silly. To Texas."

"But you just said—"

"I said I have nothing to say to the press tonight. I want time to organize my thoughts. I want to write my resignation out before I announce it to the public."

Marsh tensed. "You're resigning from the bench?"

"I have more important things to do with my life."

Marsh felt his insides unclenching. "Such as?"

"Such as marry the man I love and have his baby."

Marsh lifted her up and swung her in a circle, giving a Texas-size whoop of joy.

"Put me down," Delia protested with a laugh.

"No way, lady. You're not getting free of me till we see a justice of the peace."

"There's no one who can marry us right now," Delia said. "It's practically the middle of the night."

"If we can find a judge to sign a court order, we can find a judge for this," Marsh said.

"What about a license?"

"There must be a way around that," Marsh said.

"But I'm—"

"Incorruptible," Marsh said. "I know. So we'll fly to Las Vegas—"

"Las Vegas? Marsh, I don't think—"

"Don't think, sweetheart. Just say yes. I'll take care of everything else."

Delia grinned. "All right, Marsh. Yes."

He stood staring for a moment, unwilling to believe his dreams were all going to come true, that after all these years they were finally going to be married.

"Let's go," he said, gripping her hand tightly. "The world's waiting for us, Delia. I promise you—"

"No more promises," Delia said, looking earnestly up at him. "They aren't necessary. I don't think I could ever be any happier than I am right now. There's no way to see the future. We have to take one day at a time and live it to the fullest. That's the only promise we can keep."

Marsh felt his throat tighten. "All right, Delia." His grasp tightened. "One day at a time. Lived to the fullest."

"Promise?" she said with a cheeky grin.

He grinned back. "I promise."

✧ *Epilogue* ✧

"Don't worry, Sylvie. Your husband can't find you at the shelter. You'll be safe there." Delia twisted the phone cord around her finger as she paced the kitchen. She winced as the screen door slammed and Billie Jo appeared.

"Dinner ready yet?" Billie Jo mouthed.

"Soon," Delia mouthed back.

Billie Jo dropped a mound of teenage paraphernalia left over from a day spent tubing on the Frio on the beautiful oak floor Delia had discovered when she stripped off the worn linoleum in the North Ranch kitchen, and headed down the hall to her bedroom.

Delia gave her attention to the phone again. "The court order will require your husband to keep his distance from the house. Otherwise, he can be arrested. Yes, I know it's scary. But you're doing fine. How are Ricky and Steven? I'm glad to hear it. You and your sons will be home soon, Sylvie. I'll talk with you again tomorrow. Good-bye now."

Delia felt Marsh's arms surround her as she hung up the phone. She leaned back against him and moved his hands down to cover her belly, where their child was growing inside her.

"Well, counselor," he murmured in her ear. "How goes the war against the bad guys?"

"The good guys are winning," she said with a smile.

"Anything I can do to help with supper?" he asked.

"It's roast beef and baked potatoes. Fifteen minutes," she said, "and it'll be ready to come out."

"How about sitting on the porch with me and watching the sun set?"

"Sounds wonderful," Delia said.

She followed Marsh through the ranch house, which had undergone something of a transformation in the four months they had been married. The roof no longer leaked, and the Sears furnishings had been replaced with selected pieces from estate sales and antique stores they had visited together. The outside had been painted a bright yellow, and the windows framed with pristine white shutters. The porch no longer sagged, and they had replaced the rockers with a large swing they could sit on together.

Delia hadn't wanted to live at the Circle Crown. Too many unpleasant memories resided there. She had given the house over to the new ranch manager Marsh had hired to help him incorporate both parcels of land into one larger spread.

Marsh sat on the long wooden swing that hung by ropes from the porch rafters, drew Delia into his lap, and gave the swing a nudge with his boot.

"Happy?" he murmured.

"Umm. I loved your commentary in *The Chronicle*, the one comparing the difficulties of communication between parents and children with communication between countries. It made sense, Marsh."

"Billie Jo suggested it."

Delia chuckled. "I might have guessed."

She looked across North land that now had no fence line to separate it from Carson pasture. It was April, and immense fields of bluebonnets dotted with occasional patches of Indian paintbrush blanketed the earth as far as the eye could see. "We're really blessed, Marsh."

"I know." He nuzzled her throat, his fingers sending chills down her back as they slid into the hair at her nape. "Have you heard from Rachel today?"

"No. She said she'll be in touch after she gets settled. She finally found a house she likes near Trinity University in San Antonio. I'm glad she decided to go to undergraduate school somewhere close, so we can see each other more often."

"Have you told her about the baby yet?"

Delia shook her head. "I was waiting . . ."

"It's been nearly four months, Delia. The doctor said—"

"I know. If I was going to have serious trouble, I'd have had it by now." Delia heaved a giant sigh. "I'm afraid to believe it's going to be this easy," she said. "I mean, what woman my age gets pregnant so quickly. And with the son her husband asked for, no less."

Marsh chuckled. "Sexy sirens who forget to take their birth control pills and then don't let their husbands out of bed for a week."

Delia hid her face against his chest. "Don't remind me what a wanton I am."

"I'm not complaining."

Billie Jo shoved open the front door and stepped onto the porch. "Are you two at it again? Good grief."

Delia sat up straight and brushed at her messed-up hair where Marsh's fingers had been tangled in it. "We were just—"

Billie Jo grinned. "I was only teasing, Delia."

"Come here," Marsh said, scooting over so Billie Jo could sit at his side on the swing. He slipped his other arm around her and set the swing in lazy motion once more. "This is the life. It doesn't get any better than this."

"Wait till my baby brother comes," Billie Jo said. "That'll be even better."

"Maybe," Marsh said. "I'm just taking one day at a time."

Delia caught his eye and smiled. Some promises, she had discovered, were easy to keep.

*Next month, don't miss these exciting
new love stories only from
Avon Books*

Romancing the Duke by Tessa Dare
When her godfather leaves her a rundown, reportedly
haunted castle, Izzy Goodnight is shocked to learn the place
is already inhabited—by a recluse claiming to be the Duke
of Rothbury. Ransom Vane intends to find the castle's
rumored treasure—all he has to do is resist Izzy's charms, a
task that proves impossible once she becomes the prize he
craves the most.

The Cowboy of Valentine Valley by Emma Cane
Ever since the heated late-night kiss she shared with
cowboy Josh Thalberg, former Hollywood bad girl
Whitney Winslow hasn't been able to get him out of her
head. When she decides to use his leatherwork in her
upscale lingerie shop, Whitney's determined to keep
things strictly professional. But Josh has never met a
challenge he isn't up for . . . and he'll try anything to
convince her that some rules are worth breaking.

Wulfe Untamed by Pamela Palmer
The most enigmatic and tortured of the Feral Warriors,
Wulfe is haunted by the beauty of a woman who no longer
remembers him. He took Natalie Cash's memories and sent
her safely back to her human life. But now the Mage are
threatening Natalie and he will risk anything to protect her.
In order to survive in a world of intrigue and danger,
Natalie and Wulfe must trust one another . . . and surrender
to a wild, untamed love.

At Avon Books, we know your passion for romance—once you finish one of our novels, you find yourself wanting more.

May we tempt you with . . .

- **Excerpts** from our upcoming releases.

- Entertaining **extras**, including authors' personal photo albums and book lists.

- Behind-the-scenes **scoop** on your favorite characters and series.

- **Sweepstakes** for the chance to win free books, romantic getaways, and other fun prizes.

- Writing **tips** from our authors and editors.

- **Blog** with our authors and find out why they love to write romance.

- **Exclusive content** that's not contained within the pages of our novels.

Join us at
www.avonbooks.com

An Imprint of HarperCollins*Publishers*
www.avonromance.com

Available wherever books are sold or please call 1-800-331-3761 to order.

*G*ive in to your Impulses!

These unforgettable stories only take a second to buy and give you hours of reading pleasure!

Go to **www.AvonImpulse.com** and see what we have to offer.

Available wherever e-books are sold.

AVON**IMPULSE**

IMP 0811